Children of Rebecca

Children of Rebecca

VIVIEN ANNIS BAILEY

HONNO HISTORICAL FICTION

Published by Honno
'Ailsa Craig', Heol y Cawl, Dinas Powys
South Glamorgan CF6 4AH

First impression 1995
© Vivien Annis Bailey

ISBN 1-870206-17-7

**Published with the financial support of the
Arts Council of Wales**

Cover illustration by Jenny Fell
Cover design by Penni Bestic

Typeset and printed in Wales by
Dinefwr Press, Llandybïe

TO TIM

Long ago, far away:
Things like that don't happen
No more, nowadays, do they?

Bob Dylan

PREFACE

It is hard to believe it today – that over one hundred and fifty years ago, the hills and lanes of what is now Dyfed were once alight with rebellion and conspiracy of sufficient vigour to alarm the government in far-off London.

As a visitor to Wales, I saw only the superficial landscape, and knew nothing of its hidden history. It was only when a Welsh friend showed me the memorial stone at Efail-wen, marking the site of the first attack on a toll-gate by the Rebecca rioters, that I began to realise that the history of the Welsh as fighters for social and industrial reform went way back beyond the start of this century. Further research unfolded a rich story, within which rural uprisings took place alongside the growth of Chartism, and the working people of Wales emerged as pioneers in the struggle for democracy.

It has been my intention in writing this story to make this history accessible to anyone, and to demonstrate in particular the qualities possessed by the women of the past. They too were Chartists and rebels, playing their part in the politics of the time. Their legacy lives on in South Wales in their descendants, the miners' wives, who fought for their communities during the strike of 1984–5 and who continue to do so. I wanted to show how ordinary people, deprived of education and material comforts, nevertheless managed to marshall their mental and physical energies to challenge their all-powerful rulers. And yes, these things do still happen, as events in South Africa have shown.

My own ancestors, like the characters in the story, earned their living as labourers, servants and artisans. So, although I am not Welsh, I feel a kinship with those characters which goes beyond nationality. I hope my Welsh readers will accept my straying into the history of their country, and take this book in the spirit of friendship in which it is offered.

*****

Most of the main happenings in *Children of Rebecca* are based on real-life events, and I give a short historical note below as a background to the story. I am indebted to many historians, but I would particularly like to acknowledge the inspiring scholarship of David J. V. Jones, Keith Strange, Gwyn A. Williams and David Williams. The excellent museums in Merthyr Tydfil were a further valuable source of information, as were their helpful staff. Special thanks are also due to Tim Evans, from Llanelli, for his encouragement and help with the research.

All the personalities in the story are fictional, even where the names of real people have been used.

Vivien Annis Bailey
1995

PART ONE

Chapter One

Long ago, far away;
These things don't happen no more, nowadays.

MAY 1839

The road ran away from her like a pale ribbon in the twilight. The hard leather boots rasped against her feet with each step. They didn't fit her, but she hadn't wanted to go barefoot, and be mistaken for a beggar. The rainy wind chilled her flesh through the layers of coarse cloth she had hastily thrown on in her efforts to get away.

Bethan Morgan had been walking since dawn. She had come over the mountains, when the cloud-shadows sweeping over the dun flanks of the hills had momentarily lifted her spirits. Everything would be all right: she would get to Carmarthen, and she would find her brother Jack. But as the day went on, and her meagre provisions diminished, her feet no longer sought the smooth places on the earthen road, and she tramped regardless over stone and pebble. Her slender figure bent into the squally gusts, and now that the light was failing, the greys and blues of her faded costume made her a thing of no significance in the wide airy landscape.

With a sigh, the girl put down her bundle and looked around her. She had hoped to reach a cottage and ask for bread in exchange for fetching water or chopping wood, but the dusk had thickened. It was too late. She strained her eyes through the gloom, and surveyed the landscape. The road she was on was high; there was no moon, but the last rays of the setting sun faintly illuminated a sky of scudding indigo clouds. Looking back, she saw the blue mass of the Preseli mountains, and in front of her the country was spread out in a dark patchwork. Here and there a faint light gleamed. She imagined the cottagers with contented faces in the glow of the firelight, tending their well-fed children. She shuddered suddenly at her own loneliness.

What chance was there of finding shelter tonight? Now that she had stopped, hunger gnawed at her. Fears began to mob her as the night's cold settled upon the earth. The land was foreign to her and in the darkness concealed its population, amongst whom she must wander. She listened, transfixed, halfway it seemed between earth and sky. At first no noise met her ears but the bluster of the wind. Then she heard the trickle of water, and scrambling over the rough tussocks of grass and stones at the side of the road, she climbed up onto the moor to seek its source. The water looked dark in the narrow chasm it had cut in the soil and rock, but its familiar sound was comforting. She nestled into a hollow and began to drink from cupped hands. The liquid was chill with a sweet, musty, earthy taste.

Now she would rest, and gather her strength. She pulled her shawl around her head and shoulders, and tried to find a position of ease against the rocky tummock behind her. Her breathing slowed, and soon she felt herself falling into the safety of sleep.

* * * * *

In the gloom of the tiny cottage loft the dark figure of a young man moved. In stockinged feet he picked his way carefully among the sleepers who lay spread across the floor. Then, reaching the blue slit of the window, he slowly raised the lid of the old chest which stood wedged against the wall. As he did so, one of the children stirred and moaned, and the watcher froze until he was still again. Deftly, he lifted from the chest some dark draperies, and having held them up to the faint light from the window for a moment he gently closed the lid again.

Next he moved across to a low straw mattress where the slender body of a youth lay curled beneath a blanket. He grasped the boy's shoulder and shook it, whispering,

'Dewi! Dewi! It's time!'

The boy snatched his body away, but the older man shook again. 'Wake up! We'll be late for the gathering!'

Suddenly the lad sat bolt upright. Shivering, his voice thick with sleep, he blurted: 'I'm ready!'

The two men cautiously lowered themselves down the ladder into the pitch dark well of the downstairs room. Siôn, the elder of the two, stirred the embers of the fire to make a little light while Dewi dragged on his breeches and coat. Siôn picked up the garments he had found in the chest, and holding them towards the fire began to turn the folds of cloth hither and thither as if the openings were unfamiliar to him. Soon he was ready, and turned to face his brother with a grin.

'Iesu mawr!' said Dewi.

Siôn dipped his hand in the crock of water by the fireside, and threw some into the ashes at the side of the hearth. He bent down and rubbed his hands in the black mess, then swiftly turning to his brother he smeared the mixture over the boy's fair skin, and then his own.

'Let's go!' he said, and pushed the boy towards the door.

As he went he glanced down at a woman sleeping in the narrow truckle bed by the cottage wall. She lay with her head thrown back, and against her breast she clutched a child of two years, whose pearly skin was flushed at the cheeks, and whose fair curls clustered damply on his brow. A pang of pity surged through Siôn as he looked down at his mother. Mam should not have had to suffer.

He leaned over and snatched the old woollen shawl from the peg on the wall. One day, I shall buy her a silk one he promised himself as he closed the wooden door behind him.

* * * * *

It seemed only a moment later when the girl sprang into wakefulness. First she heard drumming, as of hooves and many feet; then murmuring, and laughing, and whooping, strange sounds that came out of the dark as though from a ghostly carnival. She peered over the edge of her hidey-hole and saw a dark mass moving along the road towards her. Her heart pounded as she remembered the stories she had heard as a child, of huge dogs and giants and kings on horseback, and she thought these must be their ghosts come to seek her for running away. She would make herself small in her hole and call on God to protect her.

She hid her face, and tried to stop her ears against the sound. If she could block them out, perhaps they would disappear. But the sound grew, and soon began to take on human tones: not ghosts or devils then, but ordinary men, it seemed, marched along the road. Now she was curious, and cautiously crawled towards the edge of the hollow and peeped over the rim.

4

In the light of the flickering pitch torch held by one of the outlandish band, she saw a huge figure on horseback: it held a gleaming axe by the shaft, and it laughed wildly as its followers yelled and whistled; its skin seemed to be as black as coal, and its eyes and teeth a glittering white. But strangest of all, and the thing which struck the greatest chill into the girl's soul, was that the great being was a woman, who wore dark skirts and a red shawl around her head and neck, while long glistening strands of hair escaped from their coverings and blew wildly in the fierce cold wind.

This virago on horseback was surrounded by a mob of sisters as ugly as herself, their large bodies distorting their female clothes and their great hands grasping torches, axes and clubs. From their throats issued cries as wild and coarse as any uttered by the savages in America which the missionary at the chapel had told her about. Behind this ferocious crew of women there followed a lesser crowd of youths, boys in rough clothes, who laughed and jumped behind the Amazon gang, but in whose eyes she saw a fear as well as an exhilaration.

The great mass swept by her hiding place: it was not her they sought then, but some greater wrongdoer, for their business was vengeance. She watched them as they grew smaller in the distance, their torches shrinking to the size of pinpricks, and their voices once more to a murmur. Soon there would be silence, and she could rest in peace.

A moment more, and then the night was torn by a distant cheer. The blue canopy of darkness first flickered, then blossomed as a shower of sparks flew heavenwards and a great tongue of flame shot to the sky.

Chapter Two

The woman plunged her arm down into the dank rain-barrel and scooped some water into the tin bowl. Then she poured the water into a large earthenware crock at her feet, and repeated the process over and over until the crock was full. Crouching down, she clenched her fists against the edge of the pot and began to shove against it. It barely moved. Shifting round to the other side, so that her back was towards the cottage, she embraced the vessel and, laying her cheek against it, tried to rock it from side to side whilst using her weight to drag it towards the door. The rough stones of the yard prevented its progress, and she paused again. The smell of the damp mossy walls and the soiled water she had thrown onto the earth, and the rotting vegetables laid down for the goat, invaded her nostrils and throat and she gagged. Against her cheek and bare arms she felt the icy cool of the earthenware pot and sought relief from it while the bile lay in her mouth.

With one final, huge effort she braced the crock against her chest and yanked it towards her. The cold water hit her with a fierce shock like a slap and she crashed backwards while the pot fell into shards around her knees.

Mair lay on her back on the stones, her clothes cold and sodden. She could not get up; she did not want to get up and she did not care if her last crock were broken. Her eyes gazed vaguely at the great white clouds speeding across the brilliance of the early morning sky.

Things had all been well at first. When she and Huw were first wed, they had played in the tiny house like children. They had set up home with the bidding gifts of their neighbours; she had polished the pans and sewed fine coverlets; she had patterned the earthen floor with chalk and whitened the hearthstone, after the manner of her mother.

It was when the babies started to come that things changed. Each one had hurt her worse than the last, and try as she might, she could not seem to gather her strength back in between. She loved her babies, God's gift to her, but after the birth of the twins, when Dewi and Siôn were still only seven and three, she began to avoid her husband's embraces. He was a good man and he had sought to help her. But still she had borne eight children and lost three of them.

She remembered the dead brother and sister lying side by side on a mattress, the still masks of their faces bearing no trace of the suffering which had dragged them from life; and then the tiny misshapen thing which God had killed in her womb. Huw was gone too now; why should she not go also and seek God's embrace?

Her daily work had lost its meaning since the death of her husband. Huw had been a man of few words. Out at dawn, back at dusk. She saw him, stocky, broad-shouldered, closing the latch on the heavy door against a winter's night. Little was spoken between them. But a smile in the firelight, a hand on her shoulder as she rested in the few moments' quiet before they went to their bed – these gestures had sealed the bond between them, born of hard work and hard times, and the physical connection of two people who had made children together.

She was proud of her four healthy sons, but now exhaustion was sapping even that emotion. As her

7

strength receded, so did the last remnants of her optimism. Somehow she had managed to keep that small sense of hope through all the hard years, like a bright pebble in her pocket, held tight since childhood. But what chances were there for her boys to have land and homes of their own? The elder boys would soon be gone from her, sucked into faraway towns whose temptations and terrors she could scarcely imagine, or drawn away over the vast Atlantic to a country peopled by savages and stalked by wild animals. Now that hope had gone, even the foundation of stubbornness that she shared with every woman in this harsh landscape had cracked and dissolved beneath her.

She closed her eyes and her mother appeared before her, her eyes a clouded blue in the worn face. She smiled up at Mair, her face illuminated as if she gazed towards a bright light. She seemed to lift her hand and reach out towards her daughter.

'Mam,' said Mair. 'Mam ...' There was an appeal in her voice. In her mind she strove to reach the dead woman.

Her youngest child was sleeping indoors on an old quilt by the fire, and stirred and murmured in his sleep. Mair started awake, and made to rise towards him; but then she fell back, dragged down by her terrible tiredness and the hurt, the grasping, clutching hurt in her belly. She drew up her legs convulsively and rolled onto her side. There was a new, warm moisture around her now. She closed her eyes and felt herself falling backwards with a rush.

'Are you hurt, Missis?' came a voice. When Mair opened her eyes, she was looking into the face of an angel.

* * * * *

In the clear light of morning it seemed to Bethan that

8

the grotesque figures who had disturbed her hillside resting place had been a dream, a vision brought on by hunger and her fearful thoughts. And yet the dry dust of the summer road was disturbed as if by many feet, and there was fresh horse dung, scarcely dry, at intervals along her way.

Despite her hunger, the warm sun of early morning renewed Bethan's optimism, in keeping with the golden green of the landscape, which fell away ahead of her to a still-misty horizon.

The road rounded the shoulder of hillside, and revealed a small cottage nestling against the bank: a low building of grey stone, with a battered roof of thatch like an unkempt head of hair. A few sheep and a goat, tethered to a peg set in the ground, cropped the thin grass with crisp tearing noises, as their dull flat eyes gazed timidly at the unexpected traveller. The sheep set up a reproachful braying as Bethan came closer.

When she saw the cottage with the pale gauzy smoke coming from the chimney Bethan had paused momentarily, then quickly moved back to a point in the road where she could not be seen from the dark window. Putting down her bundle, she pulled the wisps of hair snatched free by the wind back under her old felt hat, which she jammed on tight and straight so that no hint of jauntiness in her appearance should give the wrong impression. She checked the prim arrangement of the flannel shawl across her bodice, and brushed the mud and dust from her skirts as best she could with the back of her hand.

As she stepped forward onto the turf in front of the cottage, her heart pounded in anticipation of a curse or unkind word. She might be taken for a tinker or a beggar and turned away to walk for another day without food. Timidly, she tapped on the wood of the half-open shutter. After a pause she tried again, louder. She listened, but there was no sound except the faint sigh of the wind. Curious now, she peered into the dark gap, shading her eyes with her hand against the competing glare of the bright morning.

At first all she could see was the light from the open cottage door at the rear, through which the green hillside was visible; but then, as her eyes accustomed themselves to the gloom, she began to pick out the shapes of the room's simple furnishings. There was a small, roughly-made table, a chair by the fire and several low stools stacked one on top of the other. There seemed to be a washtub by the hearth and, near it, a dark bundle.

Suddenly a slight movement caught Bethan's eye, and she strained her eyes further to pierce the room's shadows. Across the threshold of the cottage lay a curled figure: it was a woman, and from time to time she moved convulsively. For a moment Bethan stared, disbelieving, then, throwing her bundle down, she ran to the back of the tiny building.

The woman lay clenched on her side in a puddle of water, and round her knees lay the broken remains of a large earthenware crock. On her skirt was a dark crimson stain which had lent a pink tinge to the water and on her waxen brow the sweat stood in beads.

Bethan peered into her face. 'Are you hurt, Missis?' she asked.

* * * * *

The woman had moaned slightly but did not object as Bethan lifted her head and shoulders and dragged her into the room. The girl had taken down the truckle bed which stood folded against the wall, and, summoning all her strength, had grasped the woman's limp body

10

and lifted her onto the low mattress. She loosened the strings at the woman's waist and dragged off the soaked skirts and petticoats. Then she scanned the small room to see what materials it might yield.

She grabbed a clean-looking cloth from one of the cords which festooned the low ceiling. Gently she pressed her fingers into the woman's slack belly, feeling across her abdomen in delicate probing movements. Having satisfied herself that there were no contractions, she folded the cloth into a thick pad and thrust it between the woman's thighs. She found some clean water in a jug on the table, and, when she had bathed her patient's face with a dampened rag, lifted her head and coaxed her to drink a little.

The woman submitted to Bethan. She lay with her eyes shut, closed to all awareness except a luxurious passivity. In her weakness she gave up the weight of her existence into someone else's hands, and trusted her unknown nurse as a child does its mother. Bethan looked at the woman's face, and saw in its sallow complexion and sunken cheeks the fine structure of a youthful face: strong-featured, with a straight Roman nose and deep-set blue eyes. The long wiry black hair was streaked with grey and the first glint of silver.

Seeking a covering for the feverish woman, Bethan bent to pick up the old quilt by the fireside. The sleeping infant concealed in its folds awoke and began to grizzle in bewilderment at seeing his Mam lying on her bed and a stranger in his house. Bethan made soothing clucking noises for the child as she put him aside and laid the still-warm quilt across his mother's thin body. The little lad tottered over to the bed and pulled at his mother's sleeve.

'Mam get up! Mam get up!' he cried, and the woman turned her head and smiled.

Bethan took the child into her arms and sought to distract him. She found a crust of bread and dipped it into some milk and he sucked noisily on the delicacy while she talked to him. Was he a good boy? Did he help his Mam? He nodded seriously in answer to these questions, solemnly gazing at Bethan with his fine blue eyes. His long fair locks were well-tended, and the faded frock he wore was carefully patched and mended. This mother would give her child everything that love and labour could give him, but she could not conjure food where there was none to be had, and the child's face was pale and his limbs delicate. Soon he trusted Bethan, and sat easily on her lap while she contemplated the scene in front of her and what she should do next.

The room displayed evidence of the woman's plans for the morning. By the now-expiring fire was a wooden washtub, in which some infant's soiled clothing lay soaking. On the table lay a few vegetables, some leeks, turnips and potatoes and a handful of dried barley. Wrapped in a piece of sacking on the shelf by the chimney was a loaf of bread. Bethan held the round loaf in her hand and looked at its rough brown crust. She would try not to steal bread, no matter how great her hunger. But the saliva poured into her mouth and she stood for a moment with her eyes closed before replacing the loaf on the shelf.

She carefully built up the fire with wood and peat from the stack outside the cottage door, and took the larger potatoes and placed them beneath the embers to bake. She washed the mud from the vegetables and chopped them with the crude knife and set them to cook in the black pot at the edge of the fire.

As she worked she talked to the curly-headed child. His name was Huw, he said. He had big brothers. They were out, but they would be home. When? Later. Bed-time. She told Huw that she had a big brother too, called Jack. What were his called? Dewi, and Siôn. Richard and Dan.

There had been children at Fishguard, two of them, Beti and Davey, and the little boy's earnest conversation brought them painfully into her mind. They had followed her like lambs as she skivvied for Mrs Roberts in the house overlooking the sea; she had attended to their wants and needs and played their games and told them stories of when she was small and had gone on a long journey. She had been both sister and mother to them in a house where children brought anger and suffering.

In her heart Bethan felt that she had betrayed these friends of her loneliness: she had crept past their bed-room door without allowing herself even a parting glance at their sleeping faces, for fear the sight should dash her desperate courage for good – and yet the sound of their innocent night-time breathing had nearly been enough to bring her back. Now they would be kicked and cursed by their father for crying for her. These thoughts bit into Bethan as she changed Huw's dirty dress for a clean one she found drying on a cord strung from the ceiling. But it was no good – she could not, would not go back after what had happened.

From time to time Bethan spoke to the sick woman on the low bed, bathing her face, and checking to see that the bleeding had stopped. Mrs Roberts was always ill – she had borne one baby after another, only to bury them. Bethan had wanted to love her, had wanted her to be her mother; but her childish efforts at nursing had met with rebuff and her small attempts at brightening the dingy home had been greeted with scorn by the man Roberts.

13

Once the cawl was gently simmering on the fire, Bethan washed the clothes in the tub and wrung them tight with her strong hands. Assisted by Huw, she carried them outside and spread them over the low gorse bushes and short-cropped turf, brushing aside the sheep's dung with her foot. This done, she stretched her back, hands on hips, and looked around her.

The morning was well advanced now, and the sun was high in a sky of deepest summer blue. The cottage lay on the side of a hill, where the land was poor and scrubby; to the south and west it gradually folded into wooded valleys promising richer soil and more sheltered farms, and here and there small clusters of smoking chimneys could be seen. The air where she stood was still and fresh, fragrant with the earthy smell of gorse and bracken. She felt the sun strong on her back and her bare arms, and heard above her the crazy trilling of the skylark.

The strong sunlight showed Bethan to be a slender girl of about seventeen years. She was tall and supple, with thin arms and fine hands, her face a pale oval touched with a rosy hue enhanced by the wind and rain of her previous day's journey. Her eyes were of a pale grey-green, and she scanned the scene around her sharply, like a finely-tinted bird. Her honey-coloured hair, now free of the oppressive hat, strove also to be free of the hairpins which clamped it at the back of her head, and wisps of a lighter, silvery colour flew around her brow like a halo.

Bethan found the familiar tasks soothing, the restoration of order, the sense of renewal, even though this was not her home. She began to allow herself to imagine that the sick woman was her mother, that the little boy was her brother; that this was a house where she was needed, and where her toil was not for nothing.

14

She observed the family's possessions with some curiosity. It was a poor home, in which most of the objects existed only by virtue of their purpose: there were a few cooking utensils – two pots, a tin bowl, and some wooden spoons. There were earthenware plates and cups, two or three knives and a cracked china dish with a blue and white pattern. Hanging on the wall was a billhook, and by the door a shepherd's crook.

Here and there were signs of attempts by the occupants to make the cottage more homely: there was the old quilt upon which the child had been sleeping, intricately decorated with loops and whorls of stitching; there was a strip of cloth tacked across the mantel-edge, and on the shelf an old china figurine depicting a courting couple, she with cherry cheeks and he with a mass of yellow curls.

In a basket by the chimney, Bethan found her first clue as to the character of one of the cottage's unseen occupants. It contained a mass of woodshavings and chippings, and, carefully wrapped in a piece of sacking, a spoon, ornately carved, the stem formed from twisting strands worked around a heart. As she carefully replaced the spoon in its hiding place she noticed a corner of coloured material emerging from beneath the woodshavings. Curiously, she pulled it out. It was a scrap of silk, embroidered brightly in red, white and blue, and it bore some letters. Whilst Bethan could make these out, she could not read them, and thought they must be in some foreign language, perhaps English: she traced them with her fingers. The words were 'Liberté, Egalité, Frat ...': the frayed edge of the silk cut across the embroidery and the threads fell like a fringe into her hand.

She returned the scrap to the woodshavings, lay the spoon on top and replaced the basket in the corner.

How was she going to face these men? They would think she was a thief, or worse; they might even call a constable and get her removed to the workhouse. Panic rose in her and she put her head in her hands as she sat on the rough chair by the fire.

The little boy placed his hand on her arm in a light touch of sympathy. 'Not to cry,' he said, gazing seriously into her face. 'Siôn home soon.' Bethan took the child's hand and pressed it to her damp cheek. Already they loved each other.

As the sun began to set, she fed the child and coaxed the woman to drink some of the liquid from the cawl. Now she allowed herself to break her fast, feeling she had earned the bread and nourishing soup. The tired boy fell asleep in her arms as she rested at last, watching the embers, and waiting. Then she too drifted into sleep.

Chapter Three

The tiny room where Bethan slept was silent now, except for the slightest stirrings of the ashes in the grate as they settled into the hearth, a homely sound of calm and comfort which lulled the women sleepers and spoke to them of the warmed nights of their childhood. Outside the darkness of the cottage, the evening sky retained the glimmer left behind by the setting sun, while the land had already gathered the shadows into its deepest folds and wooded hollows.

Across the sweeping valley and over the hill two figures could be seen trudging along the road towards the hovel. Their gait was that of seasoned walkers, a swinging step marked by the scrape of hobnailed clogs on the rocky surface of the road and lit by an occasional spark as nail hit stone. It was the automatic walk of exhaustion, where the body takes charge of its own progress.

Siôn and Dewi walked in step, the younger man keeping up despite being shorter by a head than his brother. They walked in a comradely silence, there being nothing that needed saying. But there was plenty to think about, and Siôn's mind was working as hard as his body.

He was about twenty years of age, broad-shouldered and tall. His straight, tow-coloured hair fell to his shoulders beneath a battered hat pulled low on his brow against the wind, and his collar, pulled up high, almost hid his features. As they reached the brow of the hill, he lifted his face to scan the valley and find the lonely cottage. The faint evening light was reflected in his large blue eyes; and there was irony in the downward cast of their outer lids, and the easy-smiling mobility of his mouth.

His gaze soon found the pale shape of his home nestling against the distant shadowy hillside: smoke rose from the chimney, but strangely, the dim light he was accustomed to seeing in the window was not there. His mother always burnt a rushlight for them, the symbol of her waiting and watching for their return: now he felt a stir of anxiety as he thought of her frail hold on life since the loss of her last baby, and her man, within a week of each other. He trusted that she had just fallen asleep early, but still his fear for her nagged as he made each weary step.

Siôn's weariness tonight was almost crushing. He and Dewi had been working since sunrise at Carnabwth with Twm Rees, shearing the sheep of their wealthier neighbour. Once their own family had kept a fine flock, Siôn's father Huw had told him, in the time of Huw's grandfather before the French wars; but the land had been divided between seven brothers, and soon there had been too many men in the family to start a new homestead at each wedding. Some had gone to the wars, while others set off to make new lives working the coal and iron in the east: some had even gone to England. Huw had been to the valleys, to Merthyr, along with Siôn's uncle Gwyn and their neighbour Iwan. But their dreams of a new life had been smashed and the starving man had returned to his family with his new wife. There was nothing for them.

They found the old tŷ unnos crouched against the hillside, a hovel their grandparents had helped to build fifty years before for a starving pair of newly-weds. Its poor soil would once have been scorned, but now offered the only hope of life Mair and Huw could expect. The abandoned house had fallen derelict, a makeshift shelter for ewes and their lambs, but they had taken it, and from its wreckage formed their home.

Times were hard now, so hard that there was almost nothing to lose except life itself. Even farmers like Twm, with a bit of land and his own horse and cart for taking his goods to market, felt their modest prosperity slipping away: now they had to pay for the right to go to market. The turnpike trusts which owned the roads had set up toll-gates, and were fleecing the countryfolk of their meagre, hard-earned cash.

Despite his gloomy thoughts a smile of satisfaction lit up Siôn's face, turning to a chuckle of amusement as he thought about the previous night. Dewi heard the laughter in his brother's throat.

'What is it, man? Share the joke!'

'It's Twm!' He threw back his head and gave a shout of glee. 'To see him in a woman's gown – the big man!'

'You looked a fine woman yourself,' responded the youth, dodging the expected cuff; then, more seriously, 'When's the next one?'

'Soon, soon, Dewi bach. We'll see what Twm and Rebecca have to say. After all, you know what it says in the Holy Book, don't you?' Waving his hand in a wide melodramatic gesture across the darkened landscape, he mimicked the pulpit tones of an evangelist: 'And they blessed Rebecca and said unto her, let thy seed possess the gates of them that hate thee ...'

Then he laughed, a cynical laugh which puzzled his younger brother. They had been brought up to respect the word of God as written in the Bible, and now Siôn was treating it as a joke. 'Worried, is it?' he jibed, poking Dewi in the ribs as they began the descent into the valley. Then he flung his arm across the boy's shoulders, suddenly feeling his vulnerability. They were risking all – transportation, even death; he had taken the lad with him, and Mam did not even know. It would kill her if anything happened to Dewi. And yet, if they were men, they had to stand up for their own people, and send the Saeson and their Church and their magistrates and their workhouse keepers to the Devil!

* * * * *

The twins were waiting for them at the crossroads in the valley. They had been working up at Penddôl since dawn, pulling turnips and then slicing them for cattle feed in a huge, hand-driven chopper under the sharp eye of the overman. Their meagre snap of bread and cold potato had not sustained their hungry stomachs until this hour and they were weary for want of food.

The four met without a word and joined their steps in the final march up the hill to Tŷ Gwyn, as their home had long since been christened. Siôn felt his responsibility heavily as he looked up towards the unlit cottage. A sick mother, with a delicate child to rear; two growing lads of thirteen years who could scarce cram enough food into their mouths, and a youth of sixteen who ate as much as a man; and then himself, just twenty, with nothing in the world except a strong body and a brain that would not rest. He must take on all this, and more, because now their father was dead. He must be son, and brother, and father too; and he must also take his part in this fight alongside the men of the district.

As they approached the cottage Siôn motioned to his brothers to keep quiet, and with a sense that all was not well he pushed past the two younger lads to reach the door first. He lifted the latch and shoved the door open, scanning the room's darkness for signs of his mother. He saw her lying on the low bed by the wall, and as he stepped towards her a slight rustle behind him made him turn. He started at the sight of another figure in the room, seated by the hearth with the child in its arms. Before he could speak the figure addressed him, half rising from the chair but encumbered by the sleeping child:

'Sir, I beg you – your mother is sick, and I am a weary traveller – I beg you sir, do not turn me out!'

Siôn could see now in the dim light from the embers that it was a young woman, her face a faint glimmer in the shadows, her voice a pleading whisper; the child Huw began to stir and grizzle at the agitation of his new-found guardian. Siôn seized him from the stranger and laid him at his mother's side, then took a rush taper from a pot on the mantel, and lit it at the fire. Turning, he held the light up towards Bethan.

She was an apparition to his surprised gaze, her loose, unbrushed hair glinting silver and her eyes filled with a wild fear. She was ready to flee at the slightest sign that she was not welcome there. She had offered love to a helpless child, and yet it seemed she did not hope for charity from others. Siôn cast aside suspicion.

'Calm yourself, sister,' he said. 'Many a traveller has stopped at this door, and been made welcome.' His voice trailed away as he turned towards the sick woman. 'What's wrong with my mother?' He stepped over to Mair and knelt down at the head of the bed, stroking her brow. 'Mam, what is it?'

Mair turned her head slowly and smiled. 'It's all right, son. Just a little rest,' she whispered. She nodded towards Bethan. 'She's a good girl ... just like my Megan ...'

Siôn looked back towards the stranger and recalled how she had held the sleeping child against her breast.

There was pity in the pale face, and a tremor on her lips as she sensed the son's anxiety for his mother. Yes, he could believe she was good.

He stroked his mother's cold hands and kissed them before drawing the coverlet carefully over her. Then he moved to the hearth and picked up the black pot containing the cawl, placing it at the centre of the fire.

'Let us eat,' he said to Bethan, 'and then you can tell me of your travels.'

The youths, clustered curiously in the doorway, now jostled forwards, competing for the warmth of the fire as Siôn ladled the stew into four wooden bowls. As his brothers noisily began their meal, tearing their pieces of bread and dipping them into the liquid, Siôn passed the fourth bowl to Bethan, with a large spoon to drink from.

'But ... you must eat first,' she said. 'You are hungry after your work.'

Siôn gave a shamefaced laugh. 'I can't. We only have four bowls. Someone always has to wait.'

Later that night, as Bethan settled down on a make-shift bed of sheep's fleece and sacking on the floor by the fire, she went through the evening's conversation in her mind. Siôn had wanted to know about his mother, and was so distressed at her account that he had anxiously examined the woman's face while she slept. These people had almost nothing to raise their lives above those of the animals on the hillside, and yet they would not submit to circumstance, at least while they had each other.

Tomorrow they would get Rebecca, he said; she would know what to do for the sick woman. But now, what was Bethan's story? As she pulled the rough and musty sacking around her shoulders, Bethan felt some relief that the tale she had rehearsed during her day's

22

work had sounded true when she heard herself utter-
ing the words; indeed it had felt true, and perhaps now
she could make it true within herself, and forget what
had really happened.

She was an orphan, she had said, and living with a
family at Fishguard as a servant; and this had been
true. Now she would bury the rest inside her, and it
would be as if it had never happened: she had never
been in the workhouse, never torn from her beloved
brother; never bullied and beaten; and most of all,
never, never, had that other thing happened. She
stuffed her fist into her mouth and rolled her face into
the oily animal stink of the sheepskin as she remembered. She wanted to kill the man Roberts for that.
Now she was gone away, she was safe, and she would
obliterate it from her heart.

She was defiant. It was his sin, not hers.

* * * * *

By the time Siôn and the boys left for their work in the
first rays of the morning sun it had been agreed. The
girl Bethan Morgan would stay and care for their
mother for a few days, and in return she could eat and
have food for her journey.

Siôn diverted from the road as they strode down the
valley, and struck across the open moorland to the east.
The rough tummocks of heather and grass soaked his
battered leather boots and coarse woollen trousers, the
heavy dew glinting silver in the bright glare which hit
him full in the face as he made his way towards
Rebecca's farm.

He thought about the stranger in his house. She had
said that she was going to Carmarthen to seek her
brother: and yet there was an uncertainty in her explanation, and a relief in the way she seized his offer of

23

shelter. From her rough hands, and the ease with which she had performed the early morning tasks of his household, he knew that she had worked hard for her living; from the fear she had displayed the night before, he guessed she had been ill-used. That was her business: there were so many to-ings and fro-ings these days that he didn't ask questions. With the generosity of those with nothing, he trusted her.

Bethan too was sifting through the happenings of the day before. She was moved by the gratitude which Siôn Hughes had demonstrated towards her for aiding his mother, and comforting the child. Easily, she took up the rhythm of household work she had begun the day before: she milked the goat and placed the milk in a crock under the slate shelter at the rear of the house; she searched for the eggs laid by the few scrawny fowls; she took the old wooden bucket to the stream on her shoulder and brought back the water to heat for the day's needs. The child Huw accompanied her, eager and self-important as he showed her the landmarks of his small world.

Mair awoke from time to time and watched the girl's easy actions. It seemed to her that God had granted her a daughter in her trouble, to take the place of the girl who had died, and as Bethan moved around the small room, unaware of Mair's drowsy gaze, it seemed to the sick woman that she saw her own Meg, no longer the pitiful death-white form on the straw mattress, but a grown maiden, with roses in her cheeks and bright hair.

By mid-afternoon Bethan felt free to sit on the bumpy turf outside the house. She watched Huw digging in the peaty earth with a stick, his dress tucked around his waist and his legs and buttocks bare to the sun. He chattered softly to invisible comrades and busily acted out his game. Meanwhile she examined the knitting she held in her hands – it was clear to her that Mair Hughes made stockings from the fleeces she kept in the bag hanging on a hook in the corner. The carding combs and spindle were a mystery to Bethan, but she could knit, and turning the four bone needles around in her hand, she strove to understand the point reached in the construction so far, and the method being used.

So absorbed was she that she didn't hear the scuffing of boots on the road or the rattling of loose pebbles as they were knocked aside by the determined step that made its way towards her. The boots were large, and made dark imprints in the cropped turf as they left the road and crossed the heath up to Tŷ Gwyn. It was not until a shadow fell across the work in her hands, and Huw shouted 'Becca! Becca!', that Bethan saw that she had a visitor. Startled, she dropped the stocking, and scrambled to her feet in confusion.

'Good day, Ma'am, I beg your pardon – I did not hear you.'

The woman was huge, almost a giantess, thought Bethan, who being tall herself still had to look up into the newcomer's face. Her eyes met a hard gaze, which in its sharpness expressed a determination to know and grasp what it saw, and would not be denied. The eyes were brown, set in a deep-creased face with a stolid dignity enhanced by the woman's imposing height. Her iron-grey hair was bound around her head in braids. She wore no hat, seeming to scorn the high afternoon sun, and her complexion was weathered like the bark of a tree. Her broad shoulders were covered with a red knitted shawl, pinned tight across her bulky chest and stomach, over an ancient gown of red and black checked flannel. She was a woman who could work like a man and her posture proclaimed her importance.

'Let me see her – Mistress Hughes.'

The voice was commanding. Bethan led the woman into the cottage, where she placed her bundle on the table and turned towards Mair with the appraising look of the expert midwife.

'Hot water,' she demanded, indicating the iron pot on the edge of the hearth. She felt the sick woman's brow, and holding her hands for a moment, muttered a few words to her that Bethan could not hear. Mair nodded weakly, and closed her eyes, safe in the knowledge that Rebecca was there. Now Rebecca opened her bundle to reveal a wad of clean linen, a handful of herbs and another packet, wrapped in sacking and tied with twine.

She washed her hands in the hot water and stripped the quilt off Mair. Then she examined the woman, speaking soothing words to her and skilfully inserting her hand into the woman's body. Mair gasped, threw her head back, but gave way to the probing hand. Afterwards, Rebecca bathed Mair, first her face, as gently as if she were a baby; then her thighs and woman's parts. The linen was torn into strips and given to Bethan with strict instructions that Mair was to have clean dressings twice a day.

Next, Rebecca opened the sacking parcel. It contained a great slab of pig's liver inside a bladder to keep it clean.

'Don't ask me where I got it, girl,' said the older woman with a wink. 'Cook this now – slice it thin and cook it with the water from your cawl. Chop it small and see that she eats it. And these –' she picked up the herbs – 'boil them in a little water and make her drink the infusion.'

When Mair was settled comfortably, Bethan and Rebecca went outside, out of earshot.

'She's weak,' said Rebecca. 'She lost a baby less than a month ago, and her man, all within seven days.' She turned towards Bethan. 'Siôn said you were going to stay here.' Suddenly she gripped Bethan's arm, her hands as strong and large as a man's as the fingers dug into the girl's thin flesh. She swung Bethan round to look closely into her face. 'Are you honest? Or are we going to find in a month or two that you're with child, and blaming Siôn as the father?'

Bethan stared straight into Rebecca's eyes, her gaze steady. 'I am honest,' she responded. She snatched her arm from the older woman's grasp and stepped away.

Rebecca waited, her weathered face at once ironic and guarded. She clearly expected some sort of an explanation.

Well, let her ask for one, then, thought Bethan.

The older woman noted the tilt of the girl's chin. There was more here than met the eye. Temper, perhaps. Determination, definitely. Dishonesty? – it was hard to say, but whatever the exact ingredients of the mix it was more than enough.

Siôn was promised in marriage to his cousin Marged. That was how the network of families was built and meagre properties consolidated and secured. Rebecca didn't want to see a good man wasted on a passing stranger.

'Where are you from, and who are your people?' she demanded outright.

There was an insolence in the girl's response which took Rebecca by surprise. She was used to being treated with respect.

'What is it to you? I'm a traveller, and an honest one, who works in exchange for bed and board. Isn't that enough?'

Rebecca drew herself up. Her eyes were steely.

'As you wish,' she said. 'But be warned – neither thief nor harlot will be welcomed here!' And with this she turned on her heel and strode away towards the road, without looking back.

* * * * *

27

Rebecca walked briskly on her way, not tempering for a moment her accustomed firm step. She knew the girl would be watching her, staring resentfully at her departing back. Cheeky besom. No girl born and brought up in the area would have spoken to her like that. She nurtured this thought as she struck off across the heather towards her own cottage. There was disquietude as well, the worrying thought that God – or the Devil – had deposited this young woman on Mair's doorstep. If it were God, then His purpose was to provide a helpmeet for the sick woman, and Rebecca knew she should be thankful. And if it were the Devil, then what was his purpose? The answer to that was obvious, she thought, remembering the girl's bright eyes and delicate colouring with some sourness.

Yet something in Bethan's gesture of defiance touched Rebecca, despite herself. It was uncomfortable, but she couldn't deny the memories of her own youth. She would have liked to have confirmed her anger by remembering herself as a compliant young woman. In fact she had had a tongue in her head herself at that age, and been roundly scolded for it. Grudgingly she recognised Bethan's spirit. But it would be to no avail. It would not divert Rebecca in any way from her chosen path, in pursuit of the common interest, of which she was a guardian. There were important considerations at stake here – property and obligation and family loyalty. A passing flibbertigibbet was not entitled to interfere.

Returning to her conundrum, and pitting God against the Devil, she decided upon the solution. God's purpose must be supported; and the Devil's thwarted. She would keep the situation under the closest scrutiny.

Chapter Four

Not many days after this Bethan stood at the roadside in the early morning mist, awaiting the sight and sound of a cart driven by Glyn Hughes of Tŷ Uchaf, a tiny farmstead higher up the valley. The weather-beaten old driver was one of Siôn's many cousins, and it had been arranged that the cart should stop for Bethan and take her to the market at Narberth.

Bethan's fair hair was pulled back from her face and hidden beneath a plaid shawl pinned under her chin against the penetrating droplets of moisture in the soft chill air. Despite the propriety of her attire, the reds and blues of the shawl served only to set off the clarity of her skin, while tiny beads of water lay on her pale lashes. On the ground at her feet was a poor little display of parcels that she was taking to the market on Mair's behalf: there were half-a-dozen eggs carefully packed in hay in a basket; some goat's milk cheese, made by Bethan under Mair's direction; and four knitted stockings, three made by Mair on her sickbed, and one made by Bethan, a little lumpy in places, but passable. She was to take the latter to the agent in Narberth, and explain to him that Mair Hughes had been bad, but that she was on the mend, and would soon be back to her full output of three pairs per week, and maybe more, if Bethan stayed.

She did not have to wait long before the hardy old bay pony came into view round the bend in the road, his head bobbing stolidly as he reached the brow of the hill, and his master pulling back on the reins to slow him down. The cart gathered momentum at the same time as the animal remembered that the pulling part of his journey was all over now. Pony and master had made this journey every week, winter and summer, barring snowfall, for fifteen years, and communication between them was streamlined to its bare minimum. Glyn Hughes sat hunched in the front of the cart, a nut-brown figure, whose head was sunk between his shoulders as if he were never upright between market days. His brown felt hat was pulled down fiercely against the mist, and as the conveyance approached Bethan his narrow suspicious eyes slid towards her without any disturbance to his features. The pony stopped automatically, without any bidding from his driver, because he always stopped here for passenger or parcel.

Anxious not to delay the party which silently observed her from the back of the cart, Bethan clumsily threw her parcels onto the floor at the back, and then scrambled aboard with ungainly haste. There was no footplate or seats and the passengers sat directly on the hard wooden boards. The more sedate travellers had made themselves cushions of folded rugs, and these would be used on the return journey to keep the evening chill at bay. Bethan, however, had taken no such precautions, and felt at once that she must be reckless in the eyes of her companions.

Their gaze was turned towards her with unselfconscious curiosity, as they sat like a cluster of crows: three old women in cloaks of ancient black, with shawls on their shoulders and old shiny bonnets brought out specially for market day. Their mouths were nipped tight at the sight of Bethan's fresh face, and their dark eyes were as hard and bright as beads in their lined complexions.

There were two girls seated together on the other side of the cart. The fair-skinned face of the elder, though rather stolid in its features, would not have been unpleasant had she greeted the newcomer with a smile; but she stared at Bethan with a look of frank hostility. The younger girl, a wide-faced creature with the look of an idiot, leant forward and picked up the fringed edge of Bethan's shawl.

'Siân!' snapped one of the crows; on the instant the simple girl fell back, and took to rocking the little dog she held in her arms as if it were a baby.

Scarcely had Bethan seated herself on the damp boards when the vehicle set off with a jerk, throwing her sideways against the tailboard while the other women looked on impassively. For a while the journey proceeded in silence, with only the creaking of the old cart and the trundling of the wheels to mask the discomfiture of the new passenger. Bethan was inexperienced in the technique of cart riding, and found herself tossed painfully from side to side every time the wheels rose and fell over the ruts and grooves of the rough roadway. Somehow her fellow-travellers were able to retain an impression of stability, each grasping the rail with one hand, and swaying easily while their bodies absorbed every jolt and pitch as the cart made its way crazily onwards.

Soon the unnatural silence began to weigh on the women. After all, this journey was their opportunity to catch up on all their local news before enjoying the feast of gossip and trivial information offered by the market; and having this suspect stranger captive in their midst was too good an opportunity to pass over. Old Mrs Jenkins accordingly began, addressing her two fellow-travellers in doom-laden tones:

'They say she'll not last.'

This was greeted by deep sighs and nods of agreement from Mistress Hughes and the other crone, her sister. Encouraged by this, the speaker continued.

'Ay, it's all up with her. My man spoke to Rebecca only last week, and, well now, do you know what she said?' They did indeed, having heard this several times already this morning, but they knew what Mrs Jenkins was up to, and they weren't going to spoil it.

She leant forward conspiratorially, as if her words were in danger of being snatched by the wind and broadcast to the wide hills, and spoke in a loud emphatic whisper:

'She said, that that poor widow was on her way to God, having lost all heart; and, mind, there are those' – and here she paused significantly – 'there are those who would like to help her on her way!'

The other two gossips repaid their ringleader with suitable expressions of shock, tutting and shaking their heads in pious disapproval.

'She has clasped a viper to her bosom, mark you, and her son does nothing about it!'

Now Bethan's senses were fully alert, as she comprehended this assault. She turned towards Mrs Jenkins, and saw that the older woman's heavy-lidded eyes were turned directly upon her.

'Some say that it is a Jezebel, and that Siôn Hughes won't stay a bachelor for long!'

At this the sullen-featured girl at the front of the cart could contain herself no longer.

'He walked out with me last winter! Uncle Huw wanted me for him since we was born!'

She stared angrily at Bethan. There weren't that many available young men in the district, and she wasn't about to give hers up to some chance passer-by who had taken a fancy to him. Bethan turned her gaze back along the road and up to the faint shape of Mair's cottage as it receded against the hillside.

The three older women laughed at the sulky girl. 'Well now, Marged,' said the gossip-monger, 'you'll have to get busy or he'll be gone in a whipstitch!' And the three cackled with loud malicious laughter at the discomfiture of both girls, until Glyn Hughes shouted back:

'Shut it, women, here's Jones, Special Constable!'

At once the laughter stopped, and all six heads craned in the direction indicated by Hughes with his whip. As they approached the spot, Bethan saw that there had recently been a fire: to their left were the remains of a small house at the roadside, and on the verge at the right lay a scorched, broken-down gate, its top spar half hacked through as if by ferocious blows from an axe. Standing on guard by the ruins was Special Constable Jones, who shifted nervously from one foot to the other at their approach.

As the cart crossed the point in the road once marked by the turnpike gate, Hughes addressed the officer of the law.

'Nothing to pay today, then, Constable?' There was only the merest trace of irony in the apparently obsequious tone of his voice, but the officer glowered, while the women pressed their lips tightly together and cast their eyes to the floor of the cart. After they had jolted past, and when they were nearly out of earshot, Mrs Jenkins shouted back,

'I hope Turnpike Tom's keeping warm these cold evenings!' At this, the scarcely suppressed laughter finally burst from the women in a great sarcastic shout, while Constable Jones stared helplessly after them.

They were still laughing when the cart creaked cumbrously into the muddy main street of Narberth, now busy with country folk and cattle, dogs, hens, children, farmers, parsons and gentry, all out to do business in the chilly damp morning.

* * * * *

Old Meg was used to busy market days, but today the poky front room of her tavern was crammed with men, and as she eased her bulky form this way and that amongst them to pass the slopping mugs into the crowd and grab the empty ones for refilling, she almost wished that half of them would disappear. The dogs cowering underneath the benches would periodically burst into vicious snarling quarrels or snap at her unwary ankles, their masters yanking at their collars and shouting curses and abuse. Slatternly girls, who didn't give a fig for ministers or sour-faced old women, shrieked with laughter and threw their arms around the necks of their sweethearts.

Twm Rees of Carnabwth was at the centre of a crowd of young men, all labourers or poor tenant farmers. He had bought them all a drink to celebrate their success-ful attack on the toll-gate which damaged his pocket and served as a focus for their discontent, and now they were in good cheer. The men stood in a knot around the entrance to the tavern, looking out over the market-place with mugs in their hands. As a result of Twm's largesse one or two of the younger lads were becoming unsteady on their feet, and grinned stupidly at every coarse jest or boast that flew through the beery air. Passers-by were the butt of many a loud comment.

During the afternoon a polished carriage pulled by a skittish mare drew up nearby. The coachman jumped down to open the door and helped an elderly man down into the mud and ordure of Market Street.

'Watch out lads, it's Holy Joe,' shouted Twm in the

direction of the drovers gathered around the cattle-pens. Parson Crick drew himself up and gazed imperiously towards the drinking men. Then with a swing of his ebony-topped walking stick and a defiant erectness of posture he began his regular weekly tour of the market-place.

Crick caught a glimpse of a few well-known faces in the instant before turning away. He felt a twinge of the fear that had started to grow in him of late when he walked amongst them.

'Rees,' he muttered. 'I'll see that man hanged, I'm sure of that. And Hughes. Went with the drovers two years running. Like father, like son. Villainy!' Huw Hughes had been to Merthyr, and look what a hotbed of rebellion and mob-rule that had turned into.

As the parson reached the edge of the square he had to negotiate a muddy patch of cobbles. He began to slip and slither, and to keep his balance he jerked his arms about as he teetered to and fro. This was treated as prime entertainment by the onlookers, who chorused in an insolent rise and fall to match his every waver.

'Watch out, Parson. Pride goes before a fall!'

Parson Crick cursed inwardly as he soaked his good shoes in a foul-smelling puddle, accompanied by a loud cheer from the assembled drinkers. There had been a time when an ageing parson might have expected a helping hand from the young men standing outside the Market Tavern with foaming mugs in their hands, or even from the lasses strolling by arm-in-arm in their best ribbons and shawls. But lately, he had noticed, they were always looking the other way when his stiff legs played tricks on him and he slipped and slithered. He could still feel the smirks on their ruddy faces as he tottered on into the market.

This bare-faced insolence was something new.

Things used to be different, he told himself bitterly. The parson had once been second in importance only to the Marlowes themselves. Then, the huge nave of the ancient church would have been crammed with country folk of a Sunday. There they learned the proper order of things, and paid homage to the family from the great house in their special pew set higher than the others, and with a little grate to keep the ladies warm in all weathers.

Parson Crick mused with pleasure over the riches of the church which he had come to think of as his own, although almost everything it boasted had been the gift of the Marlowe family. What grace and cultivation were represented by the fine classical sculptures on the family memorials! Mourning women in marble draperies lay weeping over engraved slabs, their slender, finely-carved hands holding willow fronds. The honours and achievements that accrued to every male Marlowe, and the beauty and charity possessed by every female, were recorded for posterity.

Now these ignorant people, with their barbaric language and crude habits, were being led by the nose into riot and disorder, and what was worse, their uncultured minds were being led from the paths of righteousness into a blasphemous irreligion. They were being taught to believe that any man could get up and talk aloud to God, as if He were their next-door neighbour, in gatherings held without so much as the parson's by-your-leave, let alone his God-granted divine practice!

* * * * *

As the day wore on the drinkers moved inside. Twm held forth for a while on the subject of religion, or more particularly Parson Crick. Twm was a tall, heavily-built man, a bare-knuckle fighter. He had won a few guineas in his last bout and his voice grew louder as the ale flowed. His black hair was cropped short and rough like the coat of a dark mountain pony, so that his strong neck and skull were clearly defined. His Roman nose and deep brow were marked by half-healed cuts and bruises, and his face was distinguished by a broad, white-toothed grin.

'Bloody old English parson,' he said, defying Meg's glowering eye. 'Thinks we're going to doff our caps, lads, and touch our forelocks, like our grandfathers did. But there'll be no more of that, eh, boys! Not now, thanks to Sister Rebecca!' He raised his mug in a toast. There were some nervous looks amongst the other men, as they raised theirs to join him.

Soon they turned their attention to the other topic of the day. Siôn Hughes was the butt of a good few cracks on account of the young woman who'd set herself up at Tŷ Gwyn.

'So how does Marged like her, then, your new lodger?' enquired Dic Jenkin, innocently. 'Best of friends, I'll be bound. Invited her to the wedding, has she?'

'I'm not marrying anyone, so shut it, will you.' Siôn's usual apparent calm was somewhat ruffled and his tone carried an edge of threat, but despite this his answer only brought more hilarity.

'Oh aye, he wants it but he doesn't want to pay for it! Still that's no problem round here, is it, girls?' yelled Dic, turning to the young women lolling on their lovers' laps by the fire, who shrieked their denials to the delight of the onlookers.

'No, don't get married, don't get married,' muttered a swaying youth at the back of the crowd. 'It's all fine at the neithior, the bidding, when they bring you all them fine presents, but just you wait and see, what trouble it all brings.' He collapsed onto a bench.

'What's up, Ianto, married life too much for you? You should get more rest in between, man,' responded Jenkin, to cheers from the crowd.

By now Meg was breathing heavily and the sweat prickled at the back of her stout neck and under her arms.

'Come on girl, we're dying of thirst!' came a bellow from the crowd by the door, and as she reached over to seize the empty jugs she felt herself gripped in a bear-hug from behind. The fiddler had struck up a victory tune, and Twm, her captor, proceeded to dance around with her in a crazy jig.

Meg's struggles were to no avail, as the crowd caught up the wild music and stamped their feet and yelled their delight at the old woman's discomfiture. It was only when Twm started to lose his balance and threatened to fall over backwards that Meg was released from his arms. Her angry mutters, punctuated by jabs of her broad elbows, only brought more laughter from her customers.

Meg was the least convivial of landladies. She seemed to regard her customers as intruders in her parlour as she laboured her way among them with her ungainly, heavy body. They were used to her unsmiling provision of what normally passed as good cheer; in fact they accepted her chidings the more readily because they knew her ale might lead them from the paths of righteousness. Somehow, Meg's sobriety made them feel they could keep on the straight and narrow. But now she retaliated for her humiliation with an attack upon Twm Rees of such ferocity that the laughter died on everyone's lips.

'You think because you're the big man that they can't get you! Well, my lad, the hangman's noose is strong enough even for your neck!'

38

At this the crowd fell silent, waiting for Twm's answer. For a moment there was a hesitation on his strong-featured face, as if a hidden fear scuttled through his skull like a mouse under the skirting. Then an unfriendly smile began to form, sardonic and threatening.

'Shut your mouth, you're a stupid old woman.'

Meg's pasty white face quivered. Suddenly she screeched, bracing one hand on her hip, and vigorously jabbing the air with the other as she bent forwards to the still-smirking group of young men.

'Old I may be, and God saw fit to make me a woman, but my brain's as good as yours any day, and perhaps better! I can see that chopping down a few toll-gates might ease your burden, but there's some who'll need more than sparks and splinters to bring a smile to their faces!' With a jerk of her thumb she indicated the figure of the unhappy bridegroom slumped in the corner of the room.

'Ian! Ianto! Speak up man, what is it?' said Siôn. At this the pale-faced youth who sat staring in front of him collapsed forwards, his thin shoulders riven with silent sobs. His filthy, calloused hands clutched against his ears and cheeks, leaving dirty trails on his skin.

His words spluttered childishly between each shuddering intake of breath.

'She said if we didn't have the cheese it would be all right! But now they've taken the plough and the chickens and grandmother's box. If we don't pay by Friday week we're done for!'

The young men and women in the crowd were stilled in their chattering, as they looked at Ianto, at whose wedding they had kicked their heels less than eighteen months before. This was their playmate of yesterday, who had run over the hills and moors with them in their childhood wildness. Now they were to see him and his

39

family thrown onto the road for lack of rent, and there was nothing to be done about it, because they had nothing either.

Ianto had begun a litany, a recital of the ingredients of the problem which had perplexed him for months:

'Wage, ten shillings. Rent, one shilling and fourpence. Eighteen pounds of barley flour at three ha'pence the pound, that's two shillings and threepence, that leaves six shillings and fivepence. Six pounds of wheaten flour, three pounds of cheese, half a pound of butter, half a pound of soap, one ounce of tea, one ounce of tobacco. That comes to ten shillings, see?' He looked round for confirmation. 'But the tenancy was just for a year, and now it's ended, and because I've worked so hard on the land and built a new byre, old Griffiths says it's worth more and the rent's to be two shillings and twopence! Who can take us in? Can you?' he turned to each of the onlookers in turn. 'Can you?' And each cast his eyes down, away from the wild stare of the weeping youth, for they knew that none of their hovels could take the destitute family.

Twm Carnabwth thrust a penny into Meg's hand.

'For God's sake give the lad a drink and shut his snivelling. Uffern dân – what does he think we can do about it?'

There was little heart left in the drinkers to continue their celebrations. Someone took round a hat to collect the few pence that had been set aside for beer out of meagre weekly budgets, and one of the girls undertook to give it to Sal, Ianto's wife. This was considered safer than giving it to Ianto, especially now that he was being comforted by Twm, who had placed his thick arm around the lad's shoulders and was encouraging him to drink the ale his tears had fallen into.

* * * * *

As Parson Crick stumbled though the cattle-market he saw the welcome figures of two gentlemen, discussing the merits of a particularly fine bull.

'Good day to you, Parson!' bellowed the older of the two men, a corpulent individual in an important waistcoat and watch-chain. Grayston was the leading corn-merchant of the district, and Parson Crick immediately felt safer in his presence, as he was the local magistrate. By now the elderly cleric was quite breathless, and as he jabbed his finger at the magistrate's stout chest his words stuck in his throat, just a hoarse rasp coming out to communicate the fact that whatever it was he was trying to say, he was in a state of some agitation about it.

Grayston caught the old man by the elbow.

'Steady on, man, out with it!' His hearty English voice jarred against the lively stream of the other language which filled the steamy, animal-scented air by the cattle pens.

'Has ... has ...' Taking a gulp, the parson managed to spit his words out in a torrent. 'Has anything been found out yet ... about that business at the Efail-wen toll-gate?'

The magistrate's manner changed as he leaned forward confidentially.

'Don't you worry, Parson,' he said reassuringly. Looking around with brash self-confidence, he added in a loud whisper, 'I've got my sources. There are some round here who know which side their bread's buttered!' And with this he gave a loud coarse laugh, which drew many eyes round the market square towards the little knot of well-dressed Englishmen. As Crick looked nervously round at the constantly-moving scene, a blur of ill-fed faces and rough-clad bodies, with skinny, rickety children running amongst them, he wondered who those sources might be.

'Don't you worry, old man,' reiterated Grayston, too loud for Crick's comfort, 'I've got my sources, indeed, and believe you me, there are some fine cavalrymen not too far away who'll be more than willing to lend a helping hand!'

Parson Crick smiled weakly. It was about time he was getting back to meet his carriage. Wishing good day to his acquaintances, he stumbled over the muddy cobblestones with as much dignity as he could muster, narrowly missing the filthy naked foot of a young labourer who, leaning against the tailboard of a wagon, chose to stretch his long legs out at just the moment of the parson's passage.

* * * * *

As Siôn turned to leave the tavern he felt sick in spirit. Twm called out to him,

'Don't forget now, Saturday week. Maes-gwyn. Pass it on.'

Siôn nodded his response. But something about the posture of the weeping youth stayed with him in his imagination as he left the tavern. Meg was right. Smashing toll-gates was not enough. There were other gates that had to be smashed: the gates of the big houses; the gates of the workhouse; the gates of the factories Gwyn had told him about, like those at Merthyr; but most of all the gates you couldn't see, the gates in your head, that had been erected when you weren't looking and which kept you back, kept you outside the beautiful gardens of the mind and spirit, kept you starved within as much as you were starved without.

Chapter Five

On a long glimmering evening in early July, Siôn and Bethan sat outside the low cottage to catch the last rays of light as they worked at their respective tasks. By now Bethan had become adept at her knitting, although she bent her head over her work with an air of deep concentration, not possessing Mair's easy style, born of a lifetime, where the fingers flew in apparent isolation from the mind of the knitter. From time to time Bethan would lift her head and drop the half-finished stocking in her lap, while her eyes scanned first the clear oyster sky with its bands of dusky pink and the bright star at the western horizon, and then the darkening landscape as it rolled away to the south, away from the now-stark mass of the Preseli Mountains.

Siôn worked a few feet away from her at his carving. Usually he worked at some tool or utensil – a new handle for a scythe or billhook – but tonight he had brought out the small basket from beside the chimney breast and began to unwrap the delicately-carved spoon which Bethan had found weeks before. He turned the piece this way and that in his hands, tracing each twisting strand in the spoon's stem and touching the flowers and hearts still incomplete at its neck. As he did so he glanced shyly at Bethan, who continued to stare into the far distance. Now he perceived her deep isolation which, while she worked about the cottage,

43

tending the child or fetching water, or hoeing the poor patch of turnips and potatoes, was imperceptible to those around her, who felt only her efficient energy. Now, as the fading light caught her brow, it seemed to uncover a vulnerability hidden during the harsher light of day as, unaware of scrutiny, she dipped into her own dreams like a cormorant darting down for sustenance invisible to other eyes.

Bethan had been with them for three weeks. In that time she and Siôn had scarcely exchanged words, beyond those necessary for the smooth running of the household. They brushed past each other in the tiny living space, each holding back as if the other were made of something dangerous, and should their fingers accidentally meet, during the passing of a bowl or cup, then they were withdrawn with haste as if they held a sting in their touch, like a nettle. Thus, while mere practicality seemed to shape the nature of their relationship, there was an unspoken dialogue between them, for which neither had words, even to speak to their own hearts.

Siôn was wary. Fornication was a sin, said the Minister at the chapel; but Siôn was more concerned about the watching eyes of the neighbourhood, who seemed to have collectively decided that his cousin Marged was a suitable bride for him, and that in the near future.

He thought with some distaste of the sulky young woman up at Tŷ Uchaf. Until now, he had scarcely given the idea much thought. She was strong, after all, and knew farm work and how to look after a family on next to nothing. Uncle Hughes had no surviving sons and that would mean that Siôn could take over the leasehold when the old man died, and that would leave Tŷ Gwyn for Dewi. But as he glanced again at the fair-haired girl next to him, now once again engrossed in her knitting, somehow Marged seemed to take on a coarse-grained aspect, and he realised that if he married her she would be nothing more than a work-horse to him.

He and Bethan had conversed only of food and firing and livestock, yet there was something about the seemingly simple young woman – the way she reflected on what he told her, the way she could be lost in thought even in the chaos and noise of a house full of boys – something that he wanted to share. He knew her mind was sharp and that even now, she was sifting and sorting the sensations of the moment, as she lived through her loneliness and tried to develop a plan for her future. He, too, was striving to direct his mind, while it still flowed with the flexibility of a mountain stream, before it became trammelled between the rigid walls of poverty and circumstance.

As Siôn shifted on his stool, a brightly-coloured scrap loosened itself from the woodshavings on his lap and fluttered to the ground. Bethan's hand moved automatically from her needles to pick up the object; her fingers met Siôn's, and lingered for the fraction of a second, as her light green eyes looked directly into his blue ones, and they found themselves unexpectedly close together. For once they felt no awkwardness, the serenity of the evening somehow having bestowed a silent intimacy on them as they worked; and with a smile Siôn relinquished the piece of silk into Bethan's grasp.

'It's beautiful,' she said, caressing the fringed edge of the torn piece of fabric. She traced the letters – 'Liberté, Egalité, Frat ...' – woven into the red, white and blue design. 'What does it say?'

'It's French. My grandad brought it from the French

wars. Dad told me it's the Frenchies' motto, from the time of their revolution. Do you know about that?'

Bethan looked slightly shamefaced. 'I haven't had any schooling – but I can write my name.' Bitterness shadowed her features for an instant. 'No one ever taught me anything for me. They only ever taught me things for them. How to make a pudding, how to clean the mistress's brass. When I was a little kid, really little, when – when I still had my brother, they used to tell me stories then. But that was mainly to make me be good.'

'Do you ever think what it would be like if there was no master and servant, mistress and maid? If everyone had a roof over his head and enough land to feed his family and put clothes on their backs? If everyone could read and write and look into the minds of the scholars and prophets in the pages of their books?' Siôn spoke eagerly, leaning forward. Now they looked directly at each other with no fear.

'But how could that be? Could we ever steal it all back from them? They would send the soldiers and constables and hang us all – wouldn't they?'

'Not if we did it right they wouldn't! Did you know that once some people rose up and cut off the king's head? And in France in the time of our grandparents the people rose up and got rid of the lords and ladies and started a new nation where everyone was going to be equal. That's what this means, look' – and he took the coloured scrap from Bethan's hands – 'Liberté, that's liberty, freedom … Egalité, that's equality, everybody being the same, no more Sir or Madam … Frat, that's the start of Fraternité, brotherhood, all standing together like one united family.'

No man had ever before entrusted her with such a conversation, but Bethan seized it with the eagerness of a child.

'So our king and lords and ladies had our men go to war against France, just in case they got any ideas about brotherhood over here?'

Siôn laughed, 'You're a quick one, ferch fach!' He hesitated a moment, realising he had uttered an endearment. Bethan's eyes darted a confused glance of pleasure and gratitude mingled with a new awareness. 'Trouble was, it didn't last, you see, in France: they ended up with a new king, more or less, name of Boneyparte.' That was a name Bethan had heard before, when she was a child, and Boney was always waiting to come and get naughty children in the dark, if they stole food, or told lies, or wet the bed.

Siôn's voice took on a confidential edge. 'Some people think we should start asking for more; they say we're treated worse than the beasts of the field. They met together in a great meeting and drew up a petition and took it to Parliament. Have you heard of them – the Chartists? They say that every man in the land, not just the rich, should be able to cast his vote to elect his Member of Parliament, and that any man should be able to stand as a Member of Parliament, and get a wage for doing it. Just think what that could mean ...'

Bethan scarcely understood his words, but she wanted to hear more of these magical ideas which seemed almost blasphemous in their disregard for the accepted order.

'But the petition didn't work. The rich nobs up there just kicked them out – why should they give up what they've got that easy? But some want to go further – like the French.'

Siôn put his carving on the ground and stood up, adopting a dramatic pose, one arm raised in a sweeping gesture as if addressing a large crowd. With relish he quoted the words of Henry Vincent:

'When the time for resistance arrives, let your cry be, "To your tents, O Israel" and then with one voice, one heart and one blow perish the privileged orders! Death to the aristocracy! Up with the people and the government they have established!'

He turned to see the responding excitement on Bethan's face, pale in the twilight. As they laughed together a voice called them from inside the cottage. From the open door the faint beams of a rushlight cast a glow into the fragrant damp shadows of the night.

'Come in you two, the dew is falling and you'll catch your deaths!'

It was Mair: there was no reproach in her voice, or fear, even though she knew Siôn was expected to marry Marged and the young people's laughter signified a growing friendship between them. Bethan had saved her life, and already Mair thought of her as Megan, come back from the grave.

* * * * *

The next morning, being Sunday, found the young people from Tŷ Gwyn striding down the lane towards Maenclochog, conscious of the need to arrive at chapel for nine o'clock sharp or face a tongue-lashing from Ebenezer Thomas on the evils of sloth. But the buttery sunshine warmed them through so thoroughly in their stuffy woollen clothes and high-necked Sunday shirts, and the breakfast treat of milky porridge lay so snugly in their stomachs that it was hard to keep up too brisk a pace.

Siôn walked well ahead with Dewi, and as Bethan strove to keep within a reasonable distance of these well-practised walkers she watched his swinging stride and animated gestures. Snatches of words and laughter flew back to her on the breeze, and as she watched Siôn rest his hand briefly on the nape of his brother's neck it was as if she had felt his palm on her own flesh.

She felt a disturbance running through her. She knew that for a woman there was no going back. She remembered a pregnant girl in the workhouse, weeping incessantly, dragging her ungainly body hither and thither. Then there was Mrs Roberts. Bethan searched her memory for times when Mrs Roberts might have shown signs of pleasure or happiness. Sometimes she had smiled when holding a baby in her arms, or when the older children had sung or read to her; but soon her face had only one expression, a kind of faded weariness, and a faint twist in the set of her mouth. Without complaint she had suffered the nagging, constant pain from which only death would free her. And still Mr Roberts had demanded his attentions from her – those attentions which led to muted cries in the night that Bethan had heard through the floorboards of her room.

Her memory shuddered away from the night when he had come to her instead of his wife. His sneering, demanding face, his threatening hands on her throat and mouth and the thrusting pain of his assault on her paralysed body. In his actions he had told her that she was no more than a slave to him, a receptacle for his lust and hatred. Bethan was not ready to be a slave: there were no shackles on her feet, and she still remembered the time when she was important to someone – to Jack – and so she would walk away from slavery, and search until she found her value again.

Now there was Siôn. Despite everything her heart and mind told her, she found herself thinking of his blue-eyed glance, and his strong nimble fingers.

'Beth! Bethan!' She hadn't heard the heavy boots of the thirteen-year-old twins, Richard – Dic for short –

and Dan, scuffing the rough surface of the road as they ran up behind her, and now she felt a thud in her back as they collided first with each other and then with her.

'Diawl! Watch it, you fool!' yelled Dic, the brawnier of the two, pushing aside his brother with impatience. He bent down and scooped up a handful of wild roses that he had dropped in the scuffle, and brushing his fair hair back from his brow with a dusty hand he presented the blooms to her. 'For the Lady Beth!' He gave a sweeping mock bow.

'Don't let Siôn hear you call her that! "Lady" – that's worse than swearing to him, man!'

Bethan looked at the white blooms as they lay in her palm – their fragile petals, almost translucent, the delicate yellow stamens with powdery tips, the tiny pointed leaves, the tangle of stems with minute thorns arranged along their length. Could she not ask for at least a moment of beauty in her life, even if it were to fade and die as quickly as these flowers?

She looked into the laughing faces of the boys, framed by the glossy green grasses and fronds which grew unchecked at the roadside. They were still young enough to be innocent of pain, giving up their strength to their daily labours without the knowledge that this was all there was, for them. Their lives would be as short and unremarked as those blades of grass and they lived with the same unconscious vigour. Bethan saw their shy smiles and realised that they admired her.

'Will you make us some oatcakes tomorrow, Beth, cariad?' Dic wheedled, grinning at his own cheekiness.

'Ay, I will, if you're good to your mother and don't quarrel.' Twisting the stems of the flowers together, Bethan went to tuck them into the band on the old straw bonnet she wore, borrowed from Mair. Then, thinking better of it, she tucked one into a buttonhole on her bodice and hid the rest in the loose pocket pinned at her waist. This was to be her first visit to the chapel, after all.

* * * * *

As they approached the chapel on the outskirts of the straggling village Bethan became self-conscious. She walked well behind all the menfolk of Tŷ Gwyn, and looked down as she approached the small crowd of young people gathering sociably at the entrance. At a whispered comment from one of their number the faces all turned in her direction, and the buzz of conversation was instantly stilled. She felt their hostility at every step, but as she reached the doorway something prompted her to look full in the face of the girl nearest to her. Marged returned her gaze, her features brimming with a spiteful resentment.

The chapel was a simple building still bearing the hallmarks of its earlier function as a barn: its walls were of stone, and the beams under the thatched roof were crusted with wisps of straw and bird droppings. Rows of benches faced a plain table, upon which lay a huge Bible, propped on a wooden stand. There was no decoration in this place of worship, except for the text painted in red high on the wall: *God is Love*.

As Bethan entered, the seated congregation turned towards her as if at a signal, scrutinising her closely, some with curiosity, others with an undisguised disapproval. She moved forward down the central gangway and sat next to Dic and Dan. Why should she sit at the back like a servant in a fine English church, when Siôn had told her that all here were equal? Turning to her right she found herself looking into the dark, penetrating stare of Rebecca. The older woman scarcely nodded, closing her eyes momentarily in the faintest acknowledgement before turning her face aside.

Soon Ebenezer Thomas stood before them. He wore no fine shoes or silk stockings, no black coat or white band at his throat like Parson Crick. The rough coat and trousers, the heavy boots and muffler proclaimed him a simple working man like themselves. But the set of his shoulders and his large head with its wiry auburn whiskers, his florid face with wide eyes and full, fleshy mouth belonged to a man who saw himself as a fighter in the everlasting struggle, pitting his strength against the might of the Devil and all his snares, powered by the word of the Lord.

He waited, his gaze scanning his small flock like a powerful beam, resting here and there to the discomfiture of the worshipper it fell upon: each felt that his hidden sin was spied out, each little lie, each tiny theft, each unclean thought or impure act, uncovered and illuminated; what was worse, any one of them could find his sin the subject of today's sermon, while he wriggled in secret misery, wondering whether everyone could indeed see that he was the sinner receiving the scourge of Ebenezer's tongue.

Ebenezer's waiting stance soon quelled his congregation – even the smallest children froze in their seats in fear of his booming voice, and the young lads and girls who sought each other out amongst the crowd dared not let their gaze wander while their minister addressed them. Once absolute silence was achieved he waited another moment for full effect; and when he spoke his voice was low, imbued with a sorrowful restraint.

'Brethren, let us first thank the Lord that He has seen fit to deliver us this day.' Scarcely had the people risen to their feet, scuffling, coughing and adjusting their clothes than Ebenezer continued, his eyes closed and his face heavenward, his voice raised to forceful effect:

'Lord, we lift our voices unto thee, and give thanks, that once again thou hast spared us. We beseech thee, give us strength, that we may engage in the battle into which thou hast called us, and not be found wanting; that wherever the Devil is found, we may cast him out, back to whence he came, and all his temptations, so that we may be pure in heart when we are called to thee. Amen.'

This formula presaged one of their minister's famous onslaughts on the more intriguing areas of human frailty, and there was a ripple of excitement through the younger members of the congregation as everyone sat down. Now Ebenezer's glittering eyes swept their ranks as he paced to and fro before them, at each turn moving with a sweeping emphasis as his gaze rested on the face of first one young girl, then another; and then on one youth, one young married man; finally coming to rest on Bethan, who suddenly knew what was to come.

'Whores.' He spoke quietly as he paced, as if speaking to himself. 'Whores and harlots. Jezebel and Delilah and Tamar. We have seen their works. We know of what they do. And yet we let them come amongst us! They have the Devil in their flesh and we must cast them aside!'

Now Siôn was galvanised by the threatening tones of the preacher and stared straight ahead of him. Bethan bent her head, twisting a fold of Mair's Sunday best gown between her fingers. The red and black check swam before her eyes. She had been a fool to think that in putting on this covering she could somehow assume the identity of a girl born and bred here, free from scorn and suspicion.

Ebenezer stood directly in front of Siôn. He lowered his voice to an appeal, soft and almost caressing: 'My son, give me thine heart, and let thine eyes observe my ways. For a whore is a deep ditch; and a strange woman is a narrow pit.' His gentle tone almost belied the implications of his words, except for the faintest hint of relish in his enunciation. 'She also lieth in wait as for a prey, and increases the transgressors among men.'

'Brethren – do not fail to heed these words from the Holy Book; for if ye do ye shall surely fall into Satan's ways, and the Kingdom of Heaven shall be lost to ye.'

Pausing for a moment to savour the silence which gripped his listeners, Ebenezer turned on his heel and stepped behind the makeshift lectern on the table. 'Here is our text for today,' he began, marking out the large text with his grimy nail, 'Proverbs, Chapter Seven.'

His voice was thrilling, theatrical, like that of an actor consumed by the passion of his role. He gazed high into the roofbeams and began his incantation.

'Say unto wisdom, Thou art my sister; and call understanding thy kinswoman:

'That they may keep thee from the strange woman, from the stranger which flattereth with her words.

'For at the window of my house I looked through my casement,

'And beheld among the simple ones, I discerned among the youths, a young man void of understanding,

'Passing through the street near her corner; and he went the way to her house,

'In the twilight, in the evening, in the black and dark night ...' Ebenezer was now almost singing, transported as he was by the power of his words.

'And, behold, there met him a woman with the attire of an harlot, and subtil of heart.

54

'She is loud and stubborn; her feet abide not in her house:

'Now is she without, now in the streets, and lieth in wait at every corner.

'So she caught him, and kissed him, and with an impudent face said unto him,

'I have peace offerings with me; this day have I payed my vows.

'Therefore came I forth to meet thee, diligently to seek thy face, and I have found thee …

'I have perfumed my bed with myrrh, aloes and cinnamon …' The declaiming voice strove to bind these words with a sternness of tone that would arm the heart against them, but there was a catch of weakness in it as he uttered the verses that followed.

'Come, let us take our fill of love until the morning: let us solace ourselves with loves …

'With her much fair speech she caused him to yield, with the flattering of her lips she forced him.

'He goeth after her straightway, as an ox goeth to the slaughter, or as a fool to the correction of the stocks;

'Till a dart strike through his liver; as a bird hasteth to the snare, and knoweth not that it is for his life.'

Recalling himself from his reverie, Ebenezer opened his eyes, to see the rapt faces of the young people and the fiercely clamped lips of their elders, burning with sympathetic disgust. Facing his congregation he addressed them directly:

'Hearken unto me now therefore, O ye children, and attend to the words of my mouth.

'Let not thine heart decline to her ways, nor go astray in her paths.

'For she cast down many wounded: yea, many strong men have been slain by her.'

Now his voice rang as he uttered the final chilling threat,

'Her house is the way to hell, going down to the chambers of death.'

Ebenezer slammed the Bible shut, resting his palm on the battered leather cover, hanging his head to regain his composure. When he stood up beads of sweat glinted on his brow and he wiped his moustache with a large handkerchief as his listeners cried 'Amen! Amen, Brother Ebenezer!'

Bethan scarcely heard the rest of the service. She was aware of other worshippers lifting their voices in personal prayers to the Lord; she stared into her lap as the seemingly endless contributions came and went. But she had cut herself off from them. She would harden her heart against this mortification, and show no emotion or pain or anger, because she had come here without love, and she could go on without love.

Her fists were clenched into a grip of fury; and as she pulled her right hand from her pocket she saw that she was clutching the spray of roses that Dic had given her. The blooms were crushed and broken, and as she opened her palm she saw that it was laced with tiny pricks of blood.

When the service ended Bethan walked out without looking to left or right, indifferent to the triumphant smile of Marged or the complicit glance between Rebecca and Ebenezer. As Siôn strode out of the building Rebecca laid her hand upon his arm.

'Don't take it too hard, lad – it's meant well.'

With a look of contempt Siôn shook the woman's hand away. He stood for a moment in front of her, his face expressing his struggle, the urge to strike out with fist or word; but he knew he was no match for her. With an angry disjointed gesture he turned and strode away, leaving the crowd at the doorway to revel in the sensations aroused by Ebenezer's words.

* * * * *

Later that night, after the boys were in bed and little Huw lay sleeping on his mother's bed, Bethan sat by the fireside with Mair and Siôn. He had been silent since his angry return from the chapel. He had spent the afternoon out alone on the moors, returning for his evening meal. Now he sat staring moodily into the fire while Mair's needles clicked busily.

Bethan was bruised and disquieted after the morning's humiliation. As the warmth from the fire began to soothe her, so it seemed to awaken and mingle with an underlying fear. The two feelings merged into a lost memory, a memory of conflicting sensations. When, what was it, she was trying to recall?

A lost image came into her mind, hazy and confused in its child's-eye view of a cosy parlour, where toys lay strewn in front of a warm fire; then, mingled as in a bad dream, came a sense of disturbance, and terror, as of a cold wind. Then she recalled being carried through a dark night, and calling for Jack, Jack.

She went over in her mind what little she knew of the facts of her separation from Jack. They had been orphaned, she thought, by the cholera; they had lived in Merthyr. A family going back home to Fishguard had taken her to live with an aunt, and Jack had been apprenticed. But the aunt had died after a year or so, and Jack's master proved cruel and he had run away. That was the last she had seen of her brother. She tried to work out how long ago that might have been. Eight, perhaps ten years ago; it was hard to be sure. There had been little to distinguish one year from another, until this one, that is.

She needed her brother. The shaming experience at the chapel brought it home to her again. She was an object of suspicion. She needed someone to stand by her, when even friendship such as she had found in this house was barbed and dangerous to her. She needed a home where she could be accepted without question.

Bethan stood up suddenly from her place by the fire and began to collect together her few belongings. As she collected her darned workaday stockings from a cord above the chimney-breast, Siôn drew his attention away from the glowing embers of the fire, and began to watch her movements.

She went to the box where Mair kept her few clothes and took out the ragged shawl she had used to tie up her bundle when she first arrived at Tŷ Gwyn: in it she laid first the rough woollen stockings, then her one spare shift. From the window-sill she took the ancient bone comb with the broken teeth that she had brought with her, and a sky-blue ribbon bought from a passing pedlar with a penny Mair gave her, when she had sold her first stockings to the agent in Narberth. Turning her back to him to obstruct his view, she brought out of the box the personal linen which he must not see and added it to the bundle, before tying the four corners of the shawl into a knot at the top.

'What are you doing?' His voice was harsh. His mother laid down her needles and stared into her lap. She knew what had happened. She had no strength to intervene against Rebecca and Ebenezer Thomas. But the thought of her home without Bethan chilled her, drained her of life, just as the water had seeped into the earth on the day Bethan had found her in the yard.

Bethan continued her preparations as if no one had spoken. She had been a fool to think that she could make this her home. She was an unprotected woman, and must pay for the sin of having no father, no brother, no husband to make her respectable.

She went to move past Siôn to reach down her working gown from the hook on the back of the door. As she did so he grabbed her wrist and pulled her towards him.

'Answer me!' She looked into his face, and instead of the threat she expected to find, she saw pain.

'You know what I'm doing. It's got to be done. What the preacher said ... that was just the warning ...'

He drew her down onto the stool beside him. 'Let them say what they will! There aren't many amongst them who can cast the first stone, even Ebenezer Thomas, I'll lay!'

She sighed and passed her hand across her brow.

'I'm in the way here. Marged ...'

'The devil take Marged!'

His mother tutted, shocked, but Siôn ignored her. Bethan continued steadily, avoiding his gaze.

'They want you to marry her. In any case ...' She was conscious of the fact that she was almost talking of marriage between them, when nothing had been mentioned. She had her pride. '... I have to find my brother.'

'I know that, but ...'

He moved his hand and laid it across hers.

She looked down and saw the long, tapering fingers, as fine at the ends as her own, despite the calloused skin and dirt ingrained around the nails. He spoke gently now, close to her ear, as if they were alone.

'Did I hurt your wrist? I wouldn't harm you any more than I would my own mother, because you saved her life. Some people see the Devil's works wherever they look. They've got the Devil in their hearts, if they can't see goodness when it shines in front of them. I want you to stay, Bethan, please say you will.'

Bethan looked down. She could not speak. She knew that her every move would be watched as she went about the market-place or to the chapel, that the women would whisper and the men snigger. Unless she left she would have to place her trust in Siôn, whatever happened. He might force her, he might ill-treat her, and still she would be the object of contempt and suspicion. And if he married her, then she would never find Jack.

He saw that she was troubled. She submitted to his hand, but gave no sign of acquiescence to his plea.

Mair suddenly started up from her chair, listening. 'What's that noise?' she gasped, her hand at her throat. Siôn and Bethan caught the sounds of a horse's hooves, first on the road, and then thudding on the softer surface of the turf in front of the cottage.

'Oh, please God, not the ceffyl pren, not yet,' cried the older woman, dropping her knitting and knocking aside her chair in her rush to get to the back of the room.

'Hush, mother, be calm. The ceffyl pren never came so quietly.' Siôn opened the shutters a little and peered through. 'It's Twm! Something's happened.'

He flung open the door and went out, seizing the sweating pony's bridle and holding it still while Twm threw himself from its back.

'What is it, man? Trouble?'

'Troops! The bastard English have sent their bloody troops!' Twm was breathless and his words came in bursts. 'I've been all over, spreading the news.'

The exhausted man entered the cottage ahead of Siôn, ducking his head as he came through the low door. He nodded at Mair, who busied herself finding him some food and drink. He scarcely glanced at Bethan as he sat heavily on the chair across the hearth from her, with his head thrown back and his eyes closed, his long legs spread wide in front of him. After a few moments he recovered, and drank the proffered milk in long draughts, noisily eating an oatcake afterwards. 'Bloody English! People can't even go to church of a Sunday without having their wits scared out of them by bloody English soldiers!'

'Come on man, out with it! Was there a fight? Was anyone taken?'

'No, man, nothing so exciting. I was at Narberth, see, minding my own business,' – and here he winked at Bethan, because it was well known he visited a woman there – 'and all the good folk were on their way to church and chapel, when suddenly, what do you think? There comes round the corner into Market Street twenty-five bloody foot soldiers, with fixed bayonets, would you believe! Well everyone rushes off, there's women screaming, kids crying, all except me and some of the lads. We just stood there, stock still, and stared at them. They forms up outside the Marlowe Arms and their officer goes in to speak to old Grayston. Then after a few hours of standing, off they goes again, and us still stood there!

'It's because we smashed the gate at Maesgwyn! We got them really scared this time – they've called the troops in from Brecon. And at the sessions on Friday, they brought in the Cavalry in case of a riot, and then no witnesses could be found to bring anyone to book! Didn't you get my message at chapel this morning?'

Siôn laughed cynically. 'No. Too much on my mind.'

Twm looked at Bethan's embarrassed face. 'So old Ebenezer's been pointing the finger, has he? I knew Rebecca was up to something in that direction, the old witch.' He leaned forward and grasped Bethan's knee. 'Don't worry, cariad, come into the Market Tavern next market day and you'll meet lots of girls who like a good time, won't she, Siôn?'

Bethan snatched herself away from Twm's hand, her face sullen.

'Oh, touchy, is it?' Twm grinned. 'Bit of spirit there, mun, by the look of it.'

Siôn gestured impatiently.

'Leave her alone, you'll not see her in the Market Tavern. Just tell me what happens next – we can't let them get away with this.'

'Wednesday week. Efail-wen. We're going to smash that gate once and for all. Thomas Bullen can go without his roast beef on Sundays if it means me paying eight shillings to bring up a cartload of lime!'

Twm and Siôn discussed in detail the plans for the next attack on the toll-gate at Efail-wen – now represented by a mere chain across the road, after two violent attacks with fire and axes, and lately, with guns shot into the air. The two men laughed as they spoke of their disguises, Twm recalling how he'd gone to Rebecca to find a gown large enough for his height and girth. Bethan knew now that he was the virago on horseback who had terrified her in her hiding place the night before she found Tŷ Gwyn, with his dark side-whiskers, hooked nose and white-toothed grin.

She looked beyond him to Mair standing in the shadows away from the fire, twisting her apron in her hands. She felt Mair's fear, which she dare not utter, but which gripped her in her belly like the hand of a torturer. Her sons might be captured, taken from her, sent to the gallows or the ends of the earth, but there was nothing she could do about it. Without this resistance they might as well lie down under the wheels of the rich man's carriage, for they would have as little to live for as a beetle on the road.

When at last Twm stood up to leave he addressed all three of his listeners.

'Don't forget, this Tuesday. Young Ianto and Sally. They're losing their place – the eviction's going through. There's nothing we can do, but we might as well get up there and give the magistrates a scare.' He reached forward and chucked Bethan under the chin. As she reared back Bethan looked into his eyes, and saw the danger there.

'Doesn't she ever smile? I like a girl who knows how to laugh, myself.'

With this he went outside with Siôn, and soon the sound of the pony's hooves could be heard cantering over the soft turf towards the road.

Chapter Six

At every downward swing of his pick Siôn felt the air escape from his lips in a grunt of effort, sucked in again cool in his mouth as the tool came up, the sweat moist on his upper lip. The clods of earth jumped as the curved prong slit the baked crust of soil, sometimes slipping easily under the surface, sometimes jarring against a hidden rocky obstruction. Siôn cursed the heat of the clammy morning, its steamy moisture held under the blanket of grey cloud.

Since that Sunday he had found it hard to cease his brooding. It wasn't just the injustice he felt in the way he had been humiliated at the chapel. It was the realisation that his people had banded together against him, in support of another of theirs – against him, for Marged. A woman of the community had a claim upon him. Therefore interlopers must be discouraged, and he must toe the line.

This infuriated him. It seemed to sum up so much of the place. On the one hand it would support you against all odds, against attack, wrongdoing, the law. On the other, it made demands of you, placed expectations on you. These simple rules had somehow turned justice inside out and branded an honest girl a whore. What was her crime, Siôn wondered, apart from not having been born in these parts? It was just that she was friendless, as if somehow a woman could only be honest if all her relationships were known and set out before everyone like an open book: whose daughter she was, whose sister, whose promised one, or whose wife.

Siôn thought with exasperation of his friends and neighbours, who worked with him and demonstrated their equality in the chapel on Sunday. Rebecca and Twm were determined to stand up to the powers that demanded more and yet more payments from them for the privilege of travelling the highway with lime for their land or produce for market. Rebecca had lived a life of unknown independence for a woman – owning her own land since the death of her husband, she had disdained all offers of marriage, preferring to be her own mistress. She was a rock amongst women, travelling wherever she was needed to tend births, deaths, sick-beds, as if by her own celibacy she had freed herself from danger and must atone for it. And yet her formidable intelligence was inward-looking. A strange girl came and she must be cast out.

Twm, Siôn reflected, lacked Rebecca's selflessness, although he shared her courage. He was a farmer first and foremost, albeit only a smallholder. Twm's workers and neighbours were supported and tolerated in relation to his view of the world, with himself at dead centre. He relished the adventure and threat of their night-time excursions as much as he relished the risks of the boxing ring. But Siôn knew that his interest went no further than the number of golden guineas Twm could store up, in the hopes of having enough to marry a wealthier farmer's daughter.

As Siôn swung his pick the weight of the curved blade lifted the tool as if to contradict gravity, then down it came. His two hands moved together, side by side, as the blow came, shuddering to his shoulders as he pulled against the clod, and the process began again. As the tool lifted against the sky, his hands slid along the wooden shaft, smoothed by his palms over the many years since he had made it.

Somehow the work was soothing in its aggression, on and on, freeing him to think, and think again. Old Meg in the Market Tavern had been right. It was no good just skirmishing with a few constables over turnpike charges, or even setting fire to the odd workhouse as had happened earlier that year at Narberth. Something more had got to be done.

Images came into his mind from his two journeys. He had taken to the roads for two summers in succession, walking with the drovers from the west to the heart of England, driving the cattle to the farms and marketplaces of Hampshire, Sussex and Kent. When his father had been alive, the future had seemed full of possibilities. These walks had been like the opening of a book to him.

The landscape had unfurled in front of him, from the airy hills of the west to the bleakness of the Black Mountains, the lush green valley of the Wye, the gorgeous farmlands of Herefordshire, the gentle woodlands of Hampshire, the chalk downs of Sussex and Kent. Sometimes they had walked on the highway, but many times they followed the ancient paths, along the sides and tops of the hills until the whole of southern Wales and England seemed to him to be linked in a continuous chain.

All along their way they passed the homes of the poor, whether of stone and slate, or cob and thatch or timber; all along their way they saw children with rickety limbs labouring in the fields, old women bent under huge bundles of furze for firing, tramps and beggars and gypsies sleeping under hedgerows. Once they met a young woman with a baby in her arms, and a toddler by her side. She had run away, she said: she was going to be removed to her parish, for the sin of having no man; she was to live in the workhouse amongst the old women and the mad, whilst her children would be sent to another chamber, and risked being put out to the homes of any strangers who would take them on payment of half-a-crown.

They had stayed at an inn where the young maid had stared at Siôn every time she walked past with bread or beer for a rowdy customer. Later that night they had kissed and grappled together in the dark, whispering wood beyond the outbuildings. It was Siôn's first freely-experienced sexual encounter, but it had ended in disarray, the girl too terrified to let him do more than touch her under her clothes. Later, in a back bedroom in the market tavern of a country town another girl had made love to him, shocking him by taking off her clothes and lying on the bed with her eyes closed while he stared at her naked body. He had never seen a woman's body before, except in an image of Eve engraved in an old family Bible shown to him by another boy many years before, but Eve had modestly covered herself with her hands and her hair.

Working now, he wondered guiltily whether he had left any children behind him in his pilgrimage to knowledge. Bethan, he knew, had something to fear from men. It would be easy to take advantage of her, make her his mistress. After all, who would help her? She was dependent on him for food and shelter, and also for protection. She had no menfolk to take charge of her. Some men would say she belonged to him already – in fact, some did.

But the thought of pressing his advantage sickened him, no matter how her physical closeness attracted him. She had rescued his mother and his brother when they were in trouble. And yet it was more than this. He wanted something honourable, clean. He didn't want to enslave someone any more than he wanted to be enslaved himself.

* * * * *

On Wednesday the seventeenth of July, Siôn returned to Tŷ Gwyn at midday. Grimly he moved around the cottage making his preparations, avoiding his mother's eyes as he unwrapped the cudgel he had made from a stout oak branch specially cut from a tree on Twm's farm in anticipation of this day.

At a signal from Siôn, Mair picked up the bundle of clothes from her chair and shook them out, holding them up for her son's inspection. The older woman said nothing, but as Bethan cleared away the remnants of their meagre meal she saw her tired resignation. She was helpless in the face of men's decisions.

Next Siôn and Dewi began to dress themselves in Mair's creased and stained old garments, rescued for this special purpose from their usual fate of transformation into shirts for little Huw or patches for bed quilts. Dewi's gown was of a faded sky-blue, so narrow at the waist that he could fasten none of the laces at the back: only Mair knew that it had been her wedding gown. The boy's gangling arms protruded from the tight cuffs, and his grinning, blackened face emerged above the grubby but still-dainty trimming at the neck, of which she had once been so proud.

Bethan watched the ritual of preparation with curiosity. She marked the contrast between the comic aspect of the men's costume, acknowledged by Dewi in his gawky embarrassment at wearing skirts, and the stone-faced determination of Siôn, whose easy humour had of late taken on a harder edge of anger. For him the old joke had turned serious.

Without a glance at his mother, Siôn nodded his readiness to Dewi, then turned his attention to the two younger boys, whose fear and excitement mingled in equal parts. They had enthusiastically blackened their faces in the hopes of being allowed to follow the mob. 'You two – at the back. If there's any trouble, troops, firearms, you clear off, get it?' With that he pushed past Mair and left the cottage.

The two women stood at the window watching the strange little party descending across the turf towards the road, Siôn and Dewi marching in front with the unaccustomed encumbrance of skirts around their legs, followed by the two boys running excitedly first to the front and then the side, shouting and laughing. As distance blurred the image they appeared to be a wild family, with strange, striding, bulky women, their garments flowing, and mad untrammelled children. Without a word, Bethan quietly stepped from her place at the window. She took her plaid shawl from the hook behind the door and went out.

Mair's anxious voice followed her. 'Beth! Bethan! You can't go! Please, come back!'

Bethan stopped, and turned back to Mair.

'Don't worry, mother. I'm not afraid of harm. And if we women don't go too, half our strength is lost, see?'

With a smile she turned, and Mair watched the young woman walking to the road, her gaze fixed on the small group of men now well on their way. When she reached the rutted surface of the turnpike Bethan turned and waved at the thin figure standing at the front of the low white building. The child clutching Mair's skirts waved his merry response, but his mother stood motionless.

Now Bethan set herself a brisk pace, pulling the shawl over her head, lower on her brow than was usual, and fixing it in place with a pin taken from her bodice. As she walked, her mind roved over the events of the last few weeks. She thought of Siôn, and how he talked to her late into the evenings. His father Huw had taught him to read, having learnt himself from a travelling teacher in a barn school. Siôn told her of the stories he knew of country folk like themselves, who had resisted the theft of their land, and of working men in the iron foundries in the east, banding together and asking for more money for their labours. He talked of his travels with the drovers, and his father's stories of the French wars and … her mind was almost over-flowing with ideas, where once it had been empty, or so it seemed, except for puzzlement and anger.

It was as if a crazy patchwork had been held up before her, and the seemingly random shapes and colours had begun to form themselves into a great picture, an image of a world in which she was no bigger than a tiny stitch in the lowliest corner: and as she looked she knew that the picture was not beautiful. It was full of distortions, whereby the most promising patterns and threads were cut and frayed. The ugliest, coarsest fabric was spread the widest; and the rest of the cloth, which should have been vibrant and full of colour, was stained with its deadening mark.

And then there was the eviction. Looking to her left she could see the roof of the hovel until recently occupied by Ianto and Sal. With the rest of the neighbourhood, Bethan had gone at dawn to stand under the dripping trees. At first they had watched in silence while the pair's last few belongings were put into the carrier's waggon to be sold. There were some filthy blankets and two rickety stools, both made by Ianto and proudly carved with the initials of himself and his bride. There were the couple's last remaining cooking utensils, an ancient black pot and spoon, the good ones they were given at their wedding having already been sold. Ianto

70

stood by the waggon holding his ten-month-old son, who smiled incongruously, while his father's face was white and streaked with grime, his shoulders sagging.

Then a commotion was set up inside the building, a woman's rasping screech, and the rough, dismissive curses of men as the bailiffs emerged through the low door, banging their heads and elbows as they carried out a large rigid object. Sal was clinging to its rim, her knuckles white, her heavy pregnant body dragging it downwards, her face a mask of rage. She screamed her despair, and a sympathetic sound stirred the crowd, first a sigh, and then a shout as they saw that the object was a cradle, clumsy in shape, carved with a heavy design of flowers, and made by the young father's own hands.

After that the bailiffs and constable had carried out their dirty work under a barrage of threats and insults. As the cart trundled off Sal sat with her few belongings at the edge of the roadway. The women knelt by her side to comfort her. They held her hand and bathed her face with a damp rag, then placed in her lap the few small offerings they could make: a loaf, a goat's milk cheese, a little coat for the baby.

The people cursed the new law, which forbade the payment of parish relief as had always been the custom, and their own poverty, which meant that however hard they tried – and they had – they could do little more than offer a few victuals. There was no money or spare produce to help their neighbours with rents and tithes and taxes.

Tears filled Bethan's eyes as she walked past the cottage where no homely fire now burned. After a few days sleeping in a barn Sal and Ianto had made their way to the workhouse. Ianto would go east to find work, Sal said; but it was clear from her face that she feared she would never see him again.

Now other wildly-clad figures were moving across the fields to join the small band in front of Bethan. By the time they reached Efail-wen they formed a strange army which grew as they marched along the straggling village street, and men and boys in disguise slipped quietly out of doorways and and from behind walls, while stout mothers stood with arms crossed over their aprons by the roadside and old people peered out of windows.

Bethan saw that they had made a topsy-turvy world in which to right their wrongs; grotesque in their costumes of grandmothers' gowns and wives' shawls, their skin blackened, they had blurred the distinctions between man and woman, day and night. The younger men laughed, embarrassed in their self-consciousness. But they were deadly serious in this signal that once again the only law that mattered was their own law, not the one that was imposed upon them. Beneath the surface order, tolerated through fear and poverty, there was an upside-down world where the weak had the power, and tollhouse-keepers and constables and magistrates had better be aware of it.

Now the crowd was fifty yards from the chain which marked the site of the toll-gate destroyed in the last attack. A small band of special constables moved across the road in front of the chain at a command from their officer, attempting to invest their movements with the same kind of manly strength that he achieved. The crowd halted at a distance and showed their derision at this display of force, the special constables being culled from the puniest, most craven men of the surrounding area, who had been half-bribed, half-bullied into the position by the local magistrates, who were desperate to improve policing in the locality.

Silently the crowd parted and a huge figure moved

to the fore: it could have been no one but Twm, and yet it was not Twm; it was a hook-nosed, black-faced wild woman with horsehair locks escaping from beneath a flannel shawl, robed in a red and black check gown which scarcely contained her broad torso. His own character was lost like that of an Indian chief under his war-paint, and he turned fiercely to his army of braves:

'My children! Twice we have destroyed this gate of those who hate me, and yet still it rises! What shall be done?'

There were shouts and laughter from the crowd. 'Level it again, Rebecca!'

Relishing the evident terror of the special constables, Twm declaimed:

'I will go before thee, and make the crooked places straight: I will break in pieces the gates of brass, and cut in sunder the bars of iron.'

'Amen, Mother Rebecca!' came the response, and at a signal from Twm the crowd surged forward. The chain was down in a moment and the constables set to their heels, pursued by roaring, yelling figures who cursed their long skirts and fell back, laughing, when their victims escaped. One special was lame and was soon caught by the side of the road; his grunts and cries could be heard while the women, children and old men at the back of the crowd laughed and danced over the spot where the chain had been, and kicked at the ruins of the tollhouse. It was going to take more than a troop of horse scaring a few church-goers to keep this toll-gate in place.

That evening the little alehouse at Efail-wen did very good business, and singing and music could be heard in many a cottage and farmhouse until late into the night.

Chapter Seven

AUGUST 1839

One warm August afternoon not long after this event, Bethan and Siôn were walking on the sun-browned turf and dried-out heather that flanked the lower slopes of the Preseli Hills, their steps leading them towards the steep dun-gold mass crowned by the stones of Carn Bica. As they walked they laughed, Siôn's animated voice snatched by the gusts which, though warm, warned of the chillier breeze they might expect as they ascended.

Bethan no longer went to chapel, but her laughter was tempered by remembered anger as Siôn gave a rendition of Ebenezer's sermon of that morning. His rhetoric had been at a pitch of fervour following Rebecca's success in felling the gates of her enemies.

The ground was rough beneath their feet, and soon their conversation lapsed as they began to ascend. Bethan had tied her shawl around her waist, and hitched her long skirts into it for ease of movement, revealing the dark knitted stockings and worn-out boots. Siôn's woollen shirt was open at the throat and the sleeves rolled to show his brown forearms with their strong wrists and sinews. Over his shoulder was slung a cloth bag containing a few oatcakes, some cheese and a leather bottle of water.

He was used to pitting his strength against the earth, and allowed his gaze to roam over the widening landscape. But Bethan had never rambled on the wild hillsides. She turned to view the scene that was being laid down behind her like a carpet, while above her, growing in fearsome detail and stature, were the hills, their sweeping contours crowned with outcrops of grey-blue stone in strange unearthly forms.

The afternoon sun beat on their shoulders and now the wind provided relief through their thick clothes. Bethan felt the sweat dampening her back and soaking her dress under the arms. Secretly she cursed the layers of clothes, the shift and bodice and petticoats, and envied Siôn when, having passed his bag to her, he pulled his shirt over his head with one movement, and climbed on, bare-chested. She saw that his skin was fine, and his smooth shoulders were the colour of the pale brown speckled eggs laid by the hens at Tŷ Gwyn.

After his return from chapel he had packed his bag for a walk on the hills. Ever since his boyhood this had been his way of finding time to himself, to think and read. But today he had asked Bethan to come with him: he had promised to show her north, south, east and west all at once, and to tell her all the tales he knew from the ancient times. They had set off, shy at first, walking well apart, and hardly speaking in the embarrassment at being completely alone. But soon the comradeship which had grown between them since the scene at Efail-wen overcame their self-consciousness, and they began to enjoy the privacy afforded them by the wide landscape, where they could each wonder at the other without the gaze of prying eyes and judgemental gossip.

Soon the hillside rose so steeply that Bethan had to use her hands to grasp the tufts of heather between the rocks to pull herself up. Siôn was more surefooted and reached the summit well before her; but seeing her distress, he scrambled down to meet her, holding out his hand and yanking her upwards in a swift movement that left them breathless and laughing after they had collided, with enough force to knock Siôn over backwards.

Now they knew they were alone: they had felt each other's touch. Bethan stepped away, and ran forward over the broad expanse of the hill's crest. She felt the sun's warmth on her body, and the cool buffeting of the breeze on her cheek. She gasped as she saw set out beneath them a panorama of green and gold and brown beneath the dense blue of the sky. Towers of white cloud sailed in front of her. Down below, slivers of water shone among the patchwork shapes of the fields. Racing shadows skimmed the land, extinguishing for an instant all glint and sparkle and dulling all in their path. But ponds of light swept behind them, reviving the land's colours into glorious summer again.

It was a lush wooded valley, bounded at the southern edge by the dun moors at the base of the hills, dotted with sheep and marked by the passage of streams which fed the rivers, the Nyfer, the Bannon, the Brynberian, the Clun-maen; here and there among the complex patterns of the valley could be spied tiny cottages, hidden hamlets, and the ribbon strips of roads. To their right, in the north-east, their eyes soon failed to distinguish the separate shapes amongst the hazy green-gold pattern; but as they gazed at the blue horizon it began to form itself into indistinct massy shapes. These, said Siôn, were the mountains of the north, so high that their tops were capped with snow even in summer, and which would make the Preselis look like the mud pies Huw made in front of Tŷ Gwyn.

Now he directed her towards the north-west, where she could see the silvery glint on a blue afternoon sea.

'That's the way to Ireland,' said Siôn. 'In the old days the saints came from Ireland. You see that mountain?'

76

He pointed to a peak set slightly apart from the main chain of hills, with a craggy, pointed summit. 'That's Carn Ingli. It's said that Saint Brynach meditated there, and could see the angels. But there's more to see. Come on!'

They ran down towards the valley, Siôn catching Bethan's hand and leading her towards the rocky out-crop of Carn Alw that rose up like a little castle lower down the hillside. They climbed the sunwarmed rocks, following the narrow pathway which seemed to have grown naturally with the grey stones. They found a seat amongst the rocks, sheltered and warm, like a throne. He told her the stones had once been a fortress, built up by the ancient people, and when they looked down they could see the rings of pointed stones thrust-ing up from the ground, set down as a trap to fell the horses of the invaders. Now they could rest and drink, passing the bottle one to the other, each aware of the moisture from the other's lips as they drank. Above them loomed the triple points of Foel Drigarn, the stones heaped up centuries before to honour the dead. The peak had become the watchtower and place of safety for a people whose marks now mingled, uninter-preted, with those of nature.

As she rested, Bethan leant back against the warm rock. She closed her eyes and let the sun warm their lids. She unpinned her bonnet and took it off, shaking her head with relief and letting her light hair slide around her face and neck.

'Beth ...'

She opened her eyes, squinting against the sun. Siôn's face was close to hers, his eyes a dusty bright blue against his tanned skin, like the cornflowers she had passed at the roadside on her journey.

'They say you must be my girl. Will you be?' He

77

caught her hand, and held it in both of his, looking down. 'We haven't got much, mind, but you know that, don't you? Mam needs you, and the boys will soon have to go to be servants, so there'll be more room, like.' He looked up to gauge her reaction, and saw her confusion.

'Tell you what,' he said, getting to his feet. 'I'll show you what to say.' He scrambled down from their rocky perch and began to run down the hillside, darting from side to side and leaping to avoid the jagged rocks. When he stopped and turned back to look at her she could see his smile before he shouted, through cupped hands: 'Will you? Will you?' And in a moment, from nowhere, came the response, 'Will you? Will you?' Then Siôn answered, 'I will if you will!' and the voice from nowhere yelled back, strong but somehow remote, 'I will if you will!'

Laughing at the trick, Bethan clambered down to meet him at the bottom of the outcrop.

'Well you answered me, cariad, didn't you, so that's agreed,' he said, pulling her to him and kissing her gently on the lips.

They rested against each other, sleepy in the sun's rays. She could feel the smooth skin of his chest as she lay against it, feel its warmth and the vibrant tremor of his heartbeat. Gently she wound her arms around his waist as he kissed her hair. But as he began to stroke her body, pressing her against him, she broke away.

'Don't! I can't! And I don't know what to do!'

She expected anger from him, but instead she saw his intelligent sharp gaze as he stood against the green mass of the hill, his eyes screwed against the light and his long brown hair whipped around his face by the wind.

'I know someone hurt you,' he said. 'It's all right, I can wait.' He turned away for a moment, scuffing the rocks with his boots. But then he looked up, and he was smiling. 'Come on, let's go to the highest peak of all, and you shall see even further.' And with this he took her hand, and they set off in a westerly direction towards Foel Cwmcerwyn.

As they walked Siôn set a fast pace, and although his eyes were fixed on their goal, the smoothly-capped peak to the south-west, Bethan knew that he was pre-occupied with thoughts of the problems that had been laid in store for them by other people, and the simple circumstance of having nothing. But soon the effort of the walk, and his interest in sharing his knowledge of the scene around them, brought him back to his enjoyment in their few hours of freedom. Now the sun had moved well to the west and cast long shadows behind them as they walked along the spine of the hills: looking back, they laughed to see the two giants striding along behind them, and somehow it was easy to fancy they heard the pounding of mighty footsteps in the wind whenever they turned their backs to their silent, long-limbed companions.

Down on the lower slopes to their right they could see a shepherd herding his sheep, the shrill whistles flying on the wind in snatches, and the slinking black and white dog creeping on its belly or running with the speed of a panther. Sometimes they saw ponies, grey, white and brown, but the shy creatures would rear skittishly and canter away as they approached. There was no lark song now although on their ascent the wild trilling had accompanied them for a good way; but there were buzzards, wheeling high above them, or hovering, having spied a tiny terrified creature in the heather: then one would drop, like a stone down a well, extinguishing in a single deadly swoop its victim's universe of feeling and pain.

When finally they reached the tip of Foel Cwmcerwyn the sun was slipping towards the horizon in the west: the sea was a splash of burnished silver and Ramsey Island lay like an unknown land of hope and promise in the ocean.

'That's the way to America,' said Siôn, shielding his eyes against the direct rays of the setting sun. 'Many a starving pilgrim has set out in that direction. We could try that, I suppose. And this way ...' and now he turned Bethan to face the long line of hills behind them. 'That's the way to the ironworks and the factories and the coal mines. Exhaustion, and slow starvation, and bosses. Should we do that, do you think?'

Lastly they turned to look at the moors and wooded lands where their own dwelling lay, and which descended south to another pale line of sea.

'Can you see the dragon?' He pointed to the south-east, and Bethan saw a strange snaking headland resting on the horizon. 'That's Worm's Head, fifty miles away at least, way past Carmarthen.'

'Carmarthen!' she responded, shielding her eyes and trying to read the darkening landscape. 'That's where Jack is ...' She turned to Siôn. 'I must find him.'

Siôn put his hand on her shoulder in a gesture that was deliberately brotherly, rather than the caress of a lover:

'I'll take you there. We'll find him, one day.'

* * * * *

Already as they descended in the shadow of Foel Cwm-cerwyn the hillside had begun to settle into evening. Ahead of them the landscape still bathed in the warmth of the declining sun, but Bethan shivered and drew her shawl more tightly around her. As the sun slipped away behind the hills, the mellow light which had fixed the land in stillness was replaced by a gathering blue. The three-quarters moon rose silvery-pink against the evening sky, its mouth an ever-open O and its brow drawn in a furrow of anguish.

They followed the course of the Wern, striking off across the rough moor towards Gors Fawr. There was no need for words but they held hands, Bethan sensing at last the soothing power of a trusting, open love where they could walk together, like children.

'Here it is,' said Siôn, indicating some dark shapes ahead of them in the dusk. Going closer, Bethan saw that the shapes were large stones, irregularly placed, and made to form a circle about forty feet across. Standing in the centre, she slowly turned and followed the formation with her eyes, while Siôn walked around the outside, a dark blur in the twilight, dipping to caress each stone as he passed, weaving in and out amongst them, in a solemn version of the games of tag he had played there as a child.

'What is it?' she asked.

'It's an ancient place,' he answered, his voice disembodied in the darkness. 'It's where the men of old came to worship their gods. They say that if you listen hard you can hear the cries of the people they put to death, right where you're standing.' Half-joking, he had expected her to shriek, but she stood silent, straining her ears to the quiet night.

He too stopped, resting against the chill surface of a stone: and the wind blustered against their faces, redolent of the damp perfumes of heather and marsh. It bore no sounds, and yet they heard its message, of the constancy of the hills and the blue-black sapphire sky. People lived and died, and the landscape rolled with the earth, and the sky wheeled with the stars. Nothing remained but turf, heather and stones. Suffering was as nothing, as if it had never been.

Siôn came towards her, a slight figure in the centre of the circle. He took her face in his hands, and saw her pale skin glimmer in the moonlight, while her eyes glittered its reflection.

'Arianrhod – silver disc. That should be your name.' He kissed her gently on the mouth, then on her cool cheeks and brow. 'Come on, Mam will be wondering where we are.' Hand in hand, they set off towards the road.

Chapter Eight

SEPTEMBER 1839

Siôn stood up to straighten his back, wiping the sweat from his brow with his bare arm. The wall he was repairing at the back of Twm's cottage was proving awkward and his empty stomach told him it was time for his snap, although the two cold potatoes would not go far. He heard a step on the dusty yard behind him, and turned to see a stocky wizened man, white-haired, who eyed him quizzically, pausing, before throwing his arms wide with a laugh.

'It is you – it must be, Huw's boy, though you were no higher than a two-month lamb when I last saw you.' And the man stepped forward to greet Siôn, his alert blue eyes and wry smile startling in their boyishness, despite the leathery texture of his complexion. 'You know me, now, don't you, fachgen – I'm Gwyn, your father's brother!'

Siôn dropped the chisel and took the man's hand, shocked by this apparition whose features and warm voice so resembled those of his father, dead these three months.

'Father's gone.' He looked down at the man's eager face and watched the mouth drop. 'He wasted to nothing, and Mam lost him and her baby in the one week.'

Together the two men sat among the heap of stones Siôn had prepared for his work, and Siôn told him of the troubles of his family. Gwyn, in turn, told how he had left Merthyr. He had been laid off from his work in an iron foundry and had turned to the west and walked, home to the hills of his youth, not knowing what he would find there.

Gwyn was no stranger to death. His first wife, a Merthyr girl, had died in childbirth at the age of twenty, the baby surviving her by only a few days. His second wife, an Englishwoman widowed when her first husband died of the cholera, brought with her three children; only one survived, scarlet fever having claimed the first two. She had borne seven children to Gwyn and later succumbed to consumption, aged thirty.

He told his troubles sadly, and expected no special sympathy.

'Live like animals, die like animals,' was his comment. 'We'll never see the streets of Merthyr full of well-fed mothers and healthy children while we're tied to Crawshay and the rest for our livelihood, and no voice to make ourselves heard as loud as they do.'

Siôn's response was eager. 'Tell me, man, what's happening? Are the men combining? Will anything get started?'

'Easy, easy, now,' said Gwyn. He was satisfied to see that the boy shared the anger which moved him, too. He could see Siôn's potential, knew it would go to waste if left to stultify here. 'I'll tell you everything tonight. Get me fixed up with somewhere to sleep, and we'll have the finest talk you've had in these parts for many a year.'

* * * * *

That night the one room of Rebecca's cottage was crowded with neighbours and friends. Lit only by the fire and a lantern, the figures were shadowy, their faces intent as they listened to the traveller's tales. Gwyn was a gifted talker, and his talent was respected. He seemed to be their voice, able to grasp the loose strands of life, to make the listeners see the tangle the strands were in, and how gracefully woven they should be. For his part, Gwyn was comfortable with these people. They could not offer the fiery argument of the Chartist lodge in Merthyr. But he was at home with their quiet country ways, and he was prepared to give good entertainment tonight.

As they gathered round him, the peaty smoke of the fire mingled with the odour of their clothes and bodies, while the ale which warmed in a cauldron on the grate gave off its seductive, yeasty perfume. As he looked at the faces of the young ones seated at his knee in the lantern light, he could catch the look of friends and cousins, brothers and sisters long dead – even the faces of his own children were reflected there. In the faces of his contemporaries he now saw the etched lines of time, and the memories of grandparents flitted in front of his eyes. They were good faces, family faces, and they belonged to the people of this land, who had been here for generations. But how much longer could they stay here, where they belonged?

Latecomers squeezed through the door and found a space for themselves as best they could, Gwyn nodding affably in mid-sentence or calling his greetings to each new arrival. When Siôn came in, Gwyn called out:

'Make a space here at my feet for my brother's boy, neighbours, if you will ...' He faltered a moment at the sight of Bethan, hesitating on the brink of the gathering, 'and for his young woman too, welcome that she is.' Seeing the frown on Rebecca's brow, Gwyn nudged her none too gently.

'Come now, old friend, you were young once too, or don't you remember?' Even Rebecca smiled grudgingly as room was made for Bethan to move forward and sit by the fireside.

The steaming drink was ladled into the assortment of pots and bowls brought especially for the occasion by each visitor. Gwyn tamped up his pipe and, having lit it with a burning spill, sucked and pulled on it noisily until the reek of tobacco was added to the room's aroma. Then he settled down to telling the tale of his last eighteen years in Merthyr,

'That stinking hole,' he called it, 'where the streets run with our own filth so the stench is worse than your old byre on a summer's day. You people here, stay where you are, all the while you can eat, because at least you have pure air, and clean water, and your children aren't taken from you by the dozen, like ours are. By the dozen!' Gwyn's voice was taut, and his listeners looked down. They knew that every one of Gwyn's seven children had died. Scarlet fever, measles and diarrhoea were the scourge of the young and tender in that pit of disease.

Gwyn sighed and looked into the fire, his eyes moist. He passed his hand across his brow and pinched the bridge of his nose, seeming to shake new life into himself.

'We were living down by China. That's a place in Merthyr, you know,' he added as an aside to the children. 'Down by Pontystorehouse. We were really down on our luck. That's when Susan was still alive. We had to move into a cellar with the three little ones because we got so bad in debt that we thought the bailiffs would come to our rooms in William Street. Some people down there were so poor they just rented a bed; when they got out someone else got in. The joke was that the bed never got cold.'

Dan and Dic were impatient with the narrative. They wanted some action.

'Did you have the Scotch Cattle by there, Uncle?' asked Dic, his eyes round in the dim light.

Gwyn laughed ruefully. 'No, lad. The Scotch Cattle were in the coalfields further down the valley. Rough boys, they were, mun, I can tell you. When there was a strike or a lockout, blacklegs had to look out, and the bosses too. They'd come down from the mountains in the night, faces black, rattling chains like the dead come to life.' His audience stirred and laughed conspiratorially.

'Oh aye, I know all about what you lads have been up to. But believe me, this went further. If a man heard those chains he knew he was for it, his door smashed down, his bits of furniture and clothes on the fire, and himself given a pasting. It was a different game, you see – life and death. Some poor bastard would cave in at the sound of his whining kids and go and work for less than his neighbours. That way no one's kids were better off. It was a nasty business.' Gwyn paused for a moment and drew on his pipe with its long curved stem. 'But no, lad, we didn't have them at Merthyr, although, believe me, there were times when I wished we did,' he added bitterly.

'I was working for Crawshay – the biggest boss in the place. We were luckier than some, he kept on making iron while the other bosses threw men out of work. But at the beginning of 1831 our wages were cut and 84 puddlers were sacked.

'The kids were going hungry, our wives were at their wits' end trying to manage, getting bits of credit from shopkeepers, pawning everything, even the bedcovers. Then we got in debt, borrowing from here and there. The people next door to us, the man borrowed five shillings from the moneylender to get a physician because his wife was so sick. The physician cheated him by giving her bottles of coloured sugar and water, then when she died the bailiffs came round and took his table and chairs, and the body not yet cold.

'We wanted work, a fair wage, food in our kids' bellies. We wanted an end to the bullying by bailiffs. When they took our stuff they'd sell it off to anyone who'd buy it cheap. You wouldn't think anyone would buy such tainted goods, would you?' He appealed to his listeners. 'But believe me, there are always some who will tread on their neighbours to better themselves.'

Gwyn paused for a moment as he remembered. By the spring of 1831 he had thought that he and Susan could not stand much more. He wanted to take her to Pennsylvania to find a new life, but her nerves had been so weakened by childbirth he didn't think she would last the journey.

Merthyr had been seething with people drawn there from all over Britain, bringing their ideas with them in their strange languages and strange accents. Men from Newcastle spoke powerfully of the need to combine into trade unions. If they all refused to work, they said, the bosses would see their gold trickling from their fingers. If they all stood together, that was the way to get better wages.

Gwyn resumed his tale. 'Things began to get very hot, there. Hotter than the furnaces that sent their fiery beams up into the night sky!'

He addressed the children again, their faces turned expectantly towards him. 'If you look into that fire there, stare into the red-hot caverns – then picture that made big as a church – that's what a furnace is like. And at night, the iron foundry is like the very gateway to hell, so hot and bright it is, with the workers scurrying to feed the monsters' gaping mouths like poor souls captured there in eternal torment ...' Gwyn smiled as the children's eyes grew rounder at his description.

'But I'm losing my thread. When I say things got hot, I mean we began to fight back.'

Gangs of lads had roamed the streets, looking for things bought from the bailiffs – clocks, watches, furniture, Bibles, everything. They had asked people nicely first to give them back, then if they wouldn't, they just went in and took them. Then they had terrorised the worst bailiffs. Messengers were sent to all four ironworks to stop the furnaces and bring out the workers. Then the gangs had got hold of the account books where the people's debts were written and torn them to shreds and thrown them to the winds. There had been a huge crowd in the town the next morning, and at the front, a red flag, blood-red for revolution, with a loaf of bread stuck on the top of the pole.

Gwyn shuddered as he remembered the arrival of the Highlanders. 'Then the soldiers came from Brecon. They were lined up in front of the Castle Inn to protect the ironmasters and the magistrates. Some of our men went in to try to negotiate. Lewis the Huntsman was one, and of course Dic Penderyn.'

Gwyn's listeners stirred sympathetically at the mention of the familiar name. 'But the bosses wouldn't give anything. The place erupted. The soldiers were surrounded, they were squashed so tight by the crowd that they couldn't raise their muskets. I was there, we were pushing forward, forward, challenging those bastards as if we could drown them with our numbers.'

Gwyn sighed, and paused for a moment. 'Then it happened. Lewis the Huntsman shouted "Boys, take their guns away, off with their guns!" The crowd went for it then. Some of us managed to get guns off the soldiers, but others were stabbed and cut in the process by the bayonets. There were men falling dead, others groaning and crying out. Time after time we rushed the passage-way of the inn, time after time we were pushed back by the soldiers inside. Then a voice rang out, 'Fire!' Soldiers appeared at an upstairs window and began firing on us. For a moment we didn't believe it, then we panicked.

'Some started to run, and as they ran the balls flew at them, people were shot in the back. But some of us stayed.' Gwyn snatched the air with his fist. 'The moment had come and we weren't letting go of it.' His eyes glinted in the lamplight with the spark of the battle of long ago.

'We fought with the muskets snatched from the soldiers, we fought with sticks, we fought with fists. We were forced off the streets, but Lewis the Huntsman wouldn't give up, he led charge after charge through the stable yard at the back of the inn.'

Gwyn paused now, seemingly exhausted by the telling. His mouth trembled, he closed his eyes as the memory swept over him.

'At the end of that day sixteen of us were dead – twelve men, three women and a boy. The injured crept away to hide, and some of them died too, over the next few days.' He rolled up his sleeve and showed a long white scar down the back of his forearm. 'I got off easy – just a scratch. We weren't beaten yet though. Not quite.

'We managed to keep it going for a couple more days. But it was no good. In the end they got the better of us with their superior might – yet how could that be? Think of us in our hundreds, our thousands, and them in their few score! But with their guns, and their officers, and their planning, and their confidence, and their horses, and their messengers, and their food, and their threat of imprisonment, and transportation, and hanging! Why, they had the strength of God himself!

'As for us, we didn't know which way to turn, we were squabbling amongst ourselves. We had no real plan, see?' He appealed to his listeners, his voice emphatic. 'This is what you must learn from this. We had no plan. And so, we were weak. When it happens again, we must stand together, but we mustn't be taken by surprise. We must plan it as well as an army plans its battle campaign. But things haven't stood still, mind. After this was all over, the anger was bubbling, we channelled it like an underground stream, and man after man through the iron towns and across the coal-field swore their secret oaths and joined the union. But I haven't finished my story ...

'The soldiers took twenty-eight prisoners but only six were found guilty – the others were released. Four people were sentenced to transportation. Think of that, children. All the way to the ends of the earth, torn from their loved ones, to a life of penury and hard labour.' Gwyn shook his head, lost in thought for a moment, while the children clustered closer together.

'You may think that was bad, but worse was to come. Lewis the Huntsman and Dic Penderyn were to be hanged. They said that Lewis had ordered the crowd to take the soldiers' guns outside the Castle Inn, and that Dic had stabbed a soldier in the leg.

'Everyone knew that Lewis had been a leader in the rising. We weren't surprised that he was to have the rope. But with Dic it was different. He hadn't been a leader at all. Then the news came that Lewis was to be reprieved, and transported instead. But we weren't to get off scot-free. Someone had to die, so that the scent of death would fill our nostrils, so that we would be warned. "Learn the order of things: defiance is death." That's what they were telling us, when the message came from London that there was to be no reprieve. Dic Penderyn was to die.'

Gwyn had sunk back small into his chair, his arms slack. The lines on his face seemed more deeply etched as weariness seized him. Gently, Siôn clutched his hand, and the old man smiled ruefully at his nephew before he continued. His voice was scarcely more than a whisper now.

'It was a Saturday, mid-August, hot. We walked to Cardiff in our hundreds, setting off in the early hours. Our hearts were full of lead, that at the end of our journey we should have to stand by helplessly and watch one of our own murdered in his prime.

'He was only twenty-three, not much more than a lad.'

There had been no way out. The scaffold had been surrounded by soldiers facing the crowd with muskets at the ready. He was to die for them, for all their sins. But now he faced the last struggle of a prisoner in front of the executioner. Would he go with dignity, defying their might? Or would terror take him, as he awaited the torture that would jerk him through the doors of death and into the unknown?

The old man stared into the fire. The gentle stirrings of red-hot peat as it settled into the hearth were the only sounds now as every listener shared the scene in his imagination. One child lay his head on his knee in anticipation of worse to come.

'Dic was brave. As they led him to the noose, he shouted to us that he was not a murderer, that he had done no worse than hundreds of others. He cried out in a voice of anguish I shall never forget until my dying day. "Oh Lord, what injustice!"

'His young wife was with us, Mair was her name. She had walked all the way, though she was big with child. When the hangman pulled on his legs to hasten his end, she fell down in a faint. She lost the baby of course. So they killed her man, and her baby.'

He looked at the faces of the young women amongst his listeners, fresh-complexioned and innocent, troubled by his tale. Then he saw the young men, their good, strong bodies as yet unbowed by their labours, their brows knit with sadness and fear. They deserved better. How many more of the young were to be sacrificed?

'The next day we took him in a farm cart all the way to Aberafon. They wouldn't let us bury him in Merthyr for fear that we might mete out some justice of our own. So we took him to his birthplace, and buried him at the churchyard gate. He was denied the sanctity of the churchyard, and his wife and mother were sorely grieved. But we told them that, as he was innocent, they could be sure that his soul was at rest. And as we spoke, a white bird settled on the coffin.'

Gwyn turned away from the faces of his young listeners. At this moment their hope was too much to bear.

Chapter Nine

At the cattle fair there were enough eyes on them to make Siôn uneasy. Unlike the other young couples they didn't wander arm-in-arm, proudly displaying their attachment. Bethan went with Mair and Huw to inspect the pedlars' trays of ribbons, pins and laces, the stalls of cloth and produce, while Siôn was left to drink with the men after the ritual of the auctions. Under cover of the noise and confusion he was seeking his uncle's advice.

'Take no notice, mun.'

Gwyn's tone was dismissive. He and Siôn stood at the edge of the crowd of drinkers, gazing out over the milling crowds.

'They won't do nothing. I'll see to that,' Gwyn continued. 'It's all talk, lad, all talk.'

Siôn was unconvinced, and his face showed it. There was nothing some people enjoyed more than a chance to wreak entertaining humiliation upon a sinner. There were powerful interests at stake too – matters of property and marriage.

'That is, of course, unless there's something in it?' Gwyn raised an eyebrow ironically in Siôn's direction, and paused for effect. 'Fornication, I mean ...'

'No there damn well isn't,' Siôn snapped. He turned aside angrily, and as he lifted his jug of ale the brown liquid slopped over and he danced backwards, cursing the splashes down his clothes and over his boots.

Gwyn wasn't a moralist. He had seen too much. In Merthyr a widowed woman with a clutch of whining infants needed a man, fast, and wasn't too bothered about a wife in some far-off village. Starving girls prostituted themselves under the bridges of the Taff, and lonely boys far from home paid their last three-pence for an embrace. Yet he knew what was right.

'You know what to do about it, lad, I think,' he said. 'They won't like it, of course. But once the deed is done – well, "let no man put asunder" ...'

Siôn looked down into his beer. His uncle was talk-ing sense. Suddenly he was clear in his own mind what he should do. He would have to broach marriage with Bethan. She seemed to have her eyes still set on the horizon, down towards the blue line of the sea to the south-west, as if she were only passing through. But he would do it.

'Uncle ... will you ... will you talk to them, to Rebecca I mean, and get her to tell Rees to put the word out that ...?'

His uncle smiled, and clapped him across the shoul-ders.

'Course I will, lad. And duw, will you take that wor-ried look off your face? You'll make the ale go sour.'

Every now and then he would glimpse her weaving amongst the crowd, her fair hair shining in the sun-light. She loved the little boy, Siôn could see that, as she bent to show him a calf or wipe the toffee from his mouth. And yet he had nearly lost her that day after Ebenezer's sermon. There was a loneliness inside her that was hard to touch.

The mood of the fair began to heighten as twilight fell. The Irish fiddler scraped out a jig, his eyes closed, tapping his foot in ragged stockings, while a beggar shuffled his feet in a step-dance beside him. There were acrobats and tricksters of all kinds, the crowds open-mouthed around them and always a fool ready to lose a shilling trying to win a sixpence. There was a travelling preacher who pointed skyward and begged God's forgiveness for the sinners around him.

In the dusk the green smell of the crushed grass penetrated the chilly air and excitement began to grow around the area roped off for the boxing match. Pitch torches were set in the ground around the circle, ready to be set alight for the main bout, between Twm Carnabwth and Dai the Fist. The betting was fast by now and a collection would be taken before the match as a purse for the winner.

Meanwhile, the Strong Man who travelled with the acrobats took on all comers. Dressed in an embroidered vest and drawers, his arms tattooed with roses, his moustache thick and curled, he strutted the arena while his accomplice announced his prowess to the crowd. Sturdy labourers, usually a head shorter than the Strong Man, came forward, fired with drink and the cheers of their mates, but after a few wild swings were swiftly despatched by their opponent. Once or twice a knuckle reached the Strong Man's jaw, whereupon a glint came into his eye and he pummelled the upstart, his bare fists ringing on the unprepared chin, until the victim fell, dazed and bloody, and his girl sobbed from the sidelines.

Bethan still wandered among the crowds. She had left Mair and Huw sitting around the bonfire with Rebecca and the older women, and she warmed her hands on a baked potato just out of the fire, its ashy skin smelling of charcoal. She was happy. She had enjoyed a day of freedom from work, she had bought a ribbon for herself which Mair had fixed around the crown of her borrowed hat and tied in a bow at the side. She had been able to buy a ha'pence worth of toffee for Huw and a nosegay for Mair, all from the proceeds of her knitting. Later there was to be singing, music, and dancing, a thing she had never experienced. As she moved amongst the people some now acknowledged her, but still the young women cold-shouldered her and some of the boys sniggered as she went by.

Twm was always at the centre of a crowd, and had raised his jug of ale to her, sometimes with a wink and a laugh echoed by his companions, sometimes with an almost gallant bow; somehow he never missed her and wherever she went his eyes seemed to be upon her. Once, as she pushed through the crowd around a puppet show, she had come up against Twm, and he had brushed against her.

'I'll see you later, love, when I've a few guineas in my pocket,' he had said in a rush of beery breath, pinching her breast as he passed by. Now as she watched the posturings of the Strong Man, she felt someone close behind her, and smelt that breath again on her neck.

'You know it's only me holding them back, don't you?' he whispered. Bethan went to move forward but felt a hard grip on her upper arm. Looking down she saw the fingers, calloused and scarred, and the glossy black hair curling on the back of the hand. 'Come on, cariad, don't pretend you don't know what I'm talking about. The rough music, the ceffyl pren. Some of the lads would love to see you sitting astride that, back to back with your lover – they can see you like a rough ride.' With this he made an obscene gesture against her body with his other hand.

Bethan turned partway towards him, her face taut with anger, conscious of his body pressing against hers.

'Get your hands off me,' she hissed.

But he whispered closer against her ear, his breath hot and moist.

'Look, love, it'll be more than just my hands if the

boys get hold of you. It's simple, see? Be nice to me and I'll keep them off. Meet me after the third dance, behind the barn.' With this Twm thrust her forward, twisting the flesh of her arm and clasping her buttocks through her dress.

Bethan stood trembling, looking down at the trampled earth, one hand pressed to her mouth, the other clenching and unclenching. She felt the vomit rise in her throat and swallowed it back, and struggled to control her anger. She remembered the grip of Mr Roberts's hands at her throat, and suddenly pushed her way through the crowd. Running forward, she saw Siôn deep in conversation with Gwyn on the edge of a crowd of drinkers. Without pausing, she diverged from her path.

* * * * *

Siôn did not see Bethan as she ran from the crowd. Gwyn was talking to him now about the events of the last year. The older man had been living in the thick of political turmoil among the pubs, streets and workplaces of Merthyr. He told Siôn of the Chartist clubs where people argued and sang, recited poems and read from tattered copies of the *Northern Star* to rooms full of impassioned comrades. He told of the drinking Chartists and those who thought drink would be their undoing, of those who went to chapel in special blue uniforms and viewed Jesus Christ as 'the greatest reformer of his time', while others abhorred religion. They were united in one thing though, in their hatred of the English church.

Now Siôn learnt that there were people who openly spoke their hatred and suspicion of all religion, even the chapel. They were expressing what he had only felt, its crushing of the human spirit that it claimed to free; the way it spoke of humility to those who needed pride, and peddled joy in something no one could see, touch or eat while denouncing those joys that were to hand.

Siôn knew that Henry Vincent was in prison 'for violent and seditious language' and he knew that the Charter had been turned down in May. Now Gwyn told him of John Frost's speeches up and down Britain. He had spoken before huge crowds, who had cheered his words ecstatically. He had said that some of the leading men in the country should be taken hostage if any more Chartist leaders were imprisoned – maybe the hostages should be kept in a coalmine! Gwyn spoke more quietly now, drawing Siôn behind the wagon against which they were leaning.

'It's got be physical force now, see? There's no way they're going to give up their power by us just talking, is there? We've tried that. It makes sense, when you think about it – there's thousands of us, and only a few of them, so, if we're together, with our own men and men from other iron and coal towns, it must be possible, mustn't it?

'Listen close, now boy. There's going to be an uprising, sometime this autumn. They're starting to prepare it now, collecting weapons, pikes, muskets, anything anyone can lay a hand on. People are hiding the stuff, in barns, in attics, caves, anywhere. This time we've got to act together, attack all the big towns at the same time, maybe not just Wales, but Yorkshire, Lancashire too. We'll have to stop troops getting to Wales from England – blow up the bridges on the Usk, sink ships in Newport harbour.'

Siôn was fired by Gwyn's words. At last, the action he had dreamt of seemed possible.

'When, Gwyn, when? And where shall I go – which town?'

'I knew you'd come. You're my brother's son all

right.' Gwyn embraced his nephew. 'I'm not just here for a visit. I'm touring the area to spread the word. I'll give you the name of a contact in Merthyr who'll put you up and see you're all right. Don't expect to see me for a while, but when the time comes for us to show our mettle, don't worry, I'll be there.'

Siôn knew straight away that he would have to go. He would ask Bethan to marry him. She would have to stay and help Mair until his return. He would ask Twm to help them out with money, until he could get work in a mine or foundry and send something back to them somehow.

It was settled in his mind. He would ask Bethan tonight, after the dance.

* * * * *

The flaring torches cast a lurid light over the faces around the ring. In the shelter of the crowd Siôn ventured his arm round Bethan's waist and moved her to the front row against the boundary rope. She complied but seemed distant, stiff, and Siôn put this down to her nervousness at their being seen together in public.

The crowd was well-fuelled now, men and women, laughing and shouting at friends across the other side of the ring, singing snatches of song and calling for Twm, the local hero. Dai the Fist had brought his followers, too, who shouted their protagonist's powers by way of challenge.

Twm and Dai stepped into the ring on opposite sides, to cheers and whistles from the onlookers. Stripped to the waist and barefooted, both wore thick, brass-buckled belts over cloth knee breeches. They strutted round the ring, displaying their strong torsos to the crowd – Twm's skin surprisingly white with glossy black hair covering his chest and belly, while Dai Fist was a mass

100

of freckles against a red skin. At a signal from the referee the two men took their positions opposite each other, feet apart, arms akimbo, eyes locked. Another signal, and they were clamped together in a tight grip, their faces contorted, while the crowd's cheers rose to a frenzy.

At last Twm threw Dai to the ground, and as the red-haired man sprang nimbly to his feet Twm threw a bare-knuckle punch that caught him full on the jaw. Dai staggered back, but recovered, and launched himself forward with a ferocious onslaught of blows against his opponent's head and face.

The two were well-matched for physique and anger and for several rounds no one in the crowd could tell which man would win, although the pence, shillings and guineas to be won in the betting fired them on to a pitch of excitement. Between rounds the fighters swigged from leather water bottles and spat jets of water into the earth in defiance at their enemy, before strutting forward again.

Gradually signs of tiredness began to show. Each man's face was a mass of cuts and bruises, and their knuckles bled profusely. Bethan began to sicken at the sight and the sound of bone smashing bone, but was fascinated by the spectacle, not knowing whether she wanted Twm to win or lose. The fighters started to stagger, taking on the looks of wounded animals, their eyes growing wild and vacant as their movements lost co-ordination. With one huge final effort, Twm threw his fist at Dai and the man crumpled to the ground, unconscious.

The crowd went wild. Dai's followers were mad with anger at their lost guineas, as well as their fallen hero, and a few scuffles broke out on the edge of the crowd, as water was poured over Dai's head to revive him. Twm stood triumphant, the purse of money held aloft, while his friends surged around him, congratulating themselves on their good fortune. Bethan found herself propelled forward by Siôn. Twm looked straight into her eyes as he shook the bag of money.

* * * * *

The dancing was wild, in keeping with the fighting. The musicians fiddled and bowed with abandon, and for the first time in her life Bethan danced. Galloping, twirling, laughing and crashing, the drunken dancers forgot their elders' admonitions and gave themselves up to their youth and vigour.

After the third dance, breathless, Siôn and Bethan left their eight. Siôn slipped away to relieve himself, leaving Bethan to drink from his mug of ale, tapping her feet and humming to the Irish jig. A moment later her arm was yanked backwards, sending the mug and ale flying to the ground. Bethan was propelled round by Twm's vicious grip and found herself running and stumbling across the grass to the darkness behind the barn.

Twm slammed her against the stone wall.

'Stupid bitch! I told you after the third dance!' She could see his face in the flickering glow from the torches back at the ring. It was livid with bruises, the blood congealing around his mouth and nose, his eyes bloodshot. He pushed his face up close to hers. 'This is quite simple, sweetheart. Give me a bit, or you and your man are going to get the full treatment.' He held up a half-crown, which glinted in the dim light. 'See this, well take it, you stupid whore, and there's more where that came from.' He prised open her clenched fingers and tried to force the coin in, closing her fingers around it with his.

When he relaxed his grip, Bethan loosened hers, and the half-crown fell into the mud. 'Proud, eh? Have it your own way,' he sneered, forcing her backwards against the wall and thrusting his hand between her legs.

Bethan gasped out, pressing against his weight. Her voice was harsh, sarcastic.

'You think I'm easy meat, don't you – you and your evil friends!'

Twm drew back slightly, and she caught the glint of a far-off torch in his eye as he started to laugh. She was going to put up a fight. He enjoyed a bit of a struggle.

'Well, I'm not!'

With all the force she could muster Bethan brought the heel of her hand up under Twm's bruised and bloody nose. He gasped and staggered back, sobbing with pain, whilst she fled.

Running round the front of the barn, Bethan darted into its shadowy interior. She shinned over the front of an empty stall and threw herself into the hay, pulling it over her. Then she waited, silently, watchfully, like an animal, until all was quiet, and the grey light of dawn filtered into the gaps in the thatched roof. She would have to leave. It was time to continue her journey. She brushed the hay from her clothes and climbed out of the stall.

Peering round the side of the barn she started in the direction of the road. As she passed the spot where Twm had held her, she spotted something shining in the mud. It was the half-crown. She wanted to crush it into the ground with her foot. She was not to be bought. She made to go forward, but checked herself, looking back at the coin. Then she stooped, and prised it from the mud with her nail, brushing the dirt from it. She slipped it into the pocket at the waist of her skirt.

Twm watched from the back of the wagon where he had slumped after his skirmish. He smiled to himself. Women were all the same.

PART TWO

Chapter Ten

SEPTEMBER 1839

It was early September. Siôn tramped eastwards into the rising sun. On his shoulder he carried a bundle containing his few possessions, a knit shirt his mother had made him, a knife and a horn spoon and cup, all wrapped in a coarse blanket. Although the dew was still on the ground, his thick cloth breeches and woollen jacket made him sweat and from time to time he paused to wipe his brow and the inside of his battered hat with the kerchief he wore round his neck, his brow showing incongruously pale against his tanned face.

As he followed his meandering, hilly route towards the magnet that attracted him – the iron and coal centres of the east – his clear blue eyes failed to see the landscape around him, and the villagers and passers-by who saw him on his way received no greeting, no nod or touch of his hat to match the natural courtesies of the country. He seemed a man touched by a deep sadness, and they turned away to continue their pursuits, their threshing, milking and fruit-picking, as the mist rising from the moist fields and riverbeds disappeared into the warming autumn air.

As he walked Siôn allowed his mind to run back yet again over the thoughts that troubled him. Why had she gone? How could she leave them so suddenly, leaving Mair ill and confused, and the little boy who loved her without his companion? And why had she walked out on him when he had pledged to wait until she was ready?

He remembered his bitter anger when he realised she was not going to come back. The last thing he had done that night was to throw his carving into the fire. The flowers and twisted stems that made up the handle of the spoon had been as fanciful as his love for Bethan, the moonstruck fancies of a boy. The fire had consumed the carving as surely as his rage had consumed his love, and now there was nothing but ashes.

Of course the talk was that she had tired of hard work, that she really was the Jezebel they had made her out to be from the start. Some had even said they'd seen her with a man at the fair, and that she'd gone off with a pedlar for the price of a few ribbons.

This Siôn did not believe. They had not talked deeply about their feelings, nor had he asked her about her past with men. Yet her reluctance to respond to more than an embrace set her apart from the other girls of the district who were eager to secure a husband. He sensed the pain that held her back and now began to wonder. Was there something in her past that she feared to tell him? The questions revolved around his mind, returning each time more lurid, each time more mocking and impenetrable. Her departure had brought about the final downfall of his family.

He recalled his frantic searching at the dance as he moved in and out of the jostling drunks looking for Bethan. He had concluded that she had gone home in the wagon with Mair and Huw and the older women, although he could not think why. And then Mair's puzzlement when he arrived home without her, and his searching the next morning and losing a day's pay. Mair's health went into an immediate decline, aggravated by the child's endless questions. Where was Bethan? When would she come home? asked Huw. She does still like us, doesn't she? On and on, and every day Mair becoming more tired and wasted, unable to cope with the task of stretching the meagre food to match the appetites of the family of young men, unable to keep up with the washing and the tending of their chickens, goats and garden as the clawing pain in her belly returned.

Within a month Mair was dead. It was as if she could not stand the loss of another daughter. The twins had been taken on as farm servants near Narberth. He had gone with them to see that they had good places, and Twm undertook to see that they were well treated. The thing that had pained Siôn most, after the burying of his mother, was leaving Huw. He was in good hands: Rebecca had taken him, promising to bring him up as her own grandchild. And yet Siôn's heart pained him every time he recalled that day, when he had walked with the solemn little boy to Rebecca's cottage.

The child had clutched a doll made for him by Bethan, out of rags stuffed with sheep's wool, its eyes, nose and mouth stitched on with threads pulled from any scrap of fabric she could find. His small hand lay trustingly in Siôn's as they negotiated the grassy hillocks in the moorland between their home and Rebecca's. Siôn had told him that now his Mam had gone to heaven to be with the Lord, he must be a brave little man and go to stay with Rebecca.

The child was trustful, and went willingly into Rebecca's arms. Yet, as Siôn went to leave, Huw turned his blue eyes towards him and his face crumpled with terror. Siôn strode through the door and away down the hill towards the road without looking back. The terrible pathos of childhood afflicted him: the child's helplessness in the face of events, his total reliance on others, his inability to speak his pain. Now Huw joined the ranks of those making their painful journeys alone.

As he marched Siôn thought of Tŷ Gwyn, looking out over the valley, the dark mass of the mountains behind it, but empty, and the grate cold.

* * * * *

Bethan crouched in a doorway down a filthy alley that stank of urine and dog turds. She had managed to keep going at first without thieving, especially as she moved across country and told her tale to those who gave her a meal in exchange for a day's work. She was a poor servant girl, she said, whose mistress had died and now she was going home to her mother. After all, soon she would be in Carmarthen, and she would find Jack, and he would help her.

But now she was here, and wherever she went she had asked, 'Do you know Jack Morgan?' The answer was always the same: no one knew of him, or where he might be found. As the weeks went by, she lost her look of blooming health; her hair, skin and clothes were ingrained with dirt, and hopes of finding respectable work became fainter with every day. In fact, she had begun to get a reputation in the public houses as being slightly touched. She slept anywhere, in barns, doorways and cellars, and men approached her, offering her threepence if she would go with them. She vowed to herself to hold out against this, but she knew that it would not be much longer before she would have to succumb.

Watching fom her doorway, Bethan had seen a neat maidservant come out of a gateway into the yard. The girl was clean and looked well-fed, her dark hair drawn up under a white cap, and a clean apron over her grey stuff dress. On her feet were polished black boots, and she carried a basket over her arm. Bethan watched with envy as the maid closed the gate behind her and turned to go towards the market-place on her errand.

'Please, miss, can I do an errand for you?' she begged in an obsequious tone, rising from the doorstep and moving towards the girl. Bethan was a full head taller than she, and obviously an intimidating sight.

'Clear off, the mistress won't have tramps nor beggars at the door! And if you don't, I'll call the constable!' The maid's sharp features were matched with a tone of unmistakable superiority. 'Clear off, I say, and stand back!'.

Bethan felt a sudden rage.

'Who the hell do you think you're talking to?'

The maid's eyes opened wide with astonishment. She turned on her heel and walked away down the alley, at first primly, then breaking into a run. Bethan bent down and picked up a stone, and lobbed it after her.

As soon as she was out of sight Bethan slowly lifted the latch of the large green-painted gate, and peered into the yard on the other side. As it was wash-day, there were tubs and implements standing on the flag-stones, and the scullery door stood open, but the washerwoman was taking a break for a gossip and a glass of beer with the stablehand while the prissy maid was out of the way.

Bethan crept closer and closer, attracted by the comfortable murmur of conversation and the occasional burst of laughter audible from the interior of the house. The high kitchen window was open, and the smell of a meat stew wafted into the yard. Standing on an overturned tub, Bethan drew herself up to look over the window-sill. There was the washerwoman, relaxed in a large oak chair by the black iron stove, the stablehand leaning forward from his stool as his tale reached its climax.

On the table in front of the window was a display of fine china and silver, freshly washed and polished from the grand dinner of the night before. When the maid came back she would be replacing those in their cabinets for safekeeping, but Mrs Richards had promised to keep an eye on them for now.

Bethan's thin hand slipped through the open window and snatched a silver serving spoon like a heron seizing a fish. She leapt from her vantage point and sprinted down the yard and through the gate, knocking aside the returning maidservant. She could hear the screams of rage from the kitchen as Mrs Richards met the returning Nancy.

Bethan thrust the spoon inside her bodice and felt its cold weight banging against her heart as she raced hither and thither, through the network of alleys, across the dung-covered roads, darting between the horses, carts and pedestrians, down towards the maze of shacks and hovels on the river's edge. Falling into a doorway she drew breath, her heart pounding.

She must be safe now. She drew out the spoon and admired the pinkish sheen of the silver. She cupped the bowl in her hand to feel its weight; she even tried it in her mouth, imagining it full of soup, then she rubbed it against her cheek and felt its silken smoothness. On its slender stem the spoon bore a tangle of graceful engraved initials. She traced them with her finger and tried to read them.

Suddenly the sound of running feet and yelling reached her ears. She threw herself from the doorway down a steep flight of steps until she reached the quayside, where the fishing boats were moored and the rigging slapped in the wind. She paused, not knowing which way to turn, and the sounds of pursuit again broke from the mass of tumbled cottages and tenements behind her. Bethan snatched the spoon from its hiding place in her bodice and dropped it into the water.

She saw it sparkle for an instant as it went down, just as the dishevelled figure of a young girl ran at full tilt round the corner. Without a glance at Bethan she clambered into a boat moored at the quay, and pulled a pile of canvas sails over herself. The pounding footsteps were coming nearer, and Bethan followed the girl with the wild panic of an animal.

When the pursuers had passed by, the two girls cautiously emerged from their hiding place and looked at each other with suspicion. Bethan saw that the other girl was a scrawny-looking thing, with a sharp, cunning little face and brown hair hanging loose and unkempt around her thin shoulders. With a smile she drew a loaf of fresh bread from under her tattered shawl and broke it in half.

'Hello,' she said. 'My name's Clemmy. Short for Clementina. Me Da named me after a Spanish lady he used to know when he was a sailor.' She gave Bethan a roguish wink. 'Are you down on your luck ? I'll help you out. Two can do better than one.'

The two girls hung over the side of the boat to look for the silver spoon but it had vanished into the murky waters.

Chapter Eleven

Clemmie was just fourteen years old, but she was versed in the ways of the underside of the town's sprawling, bickering life, in the language and the smells and the rules of the filthy alleys and fish-stained quaysides by the river's edge. She worked as a pot-girl and prostitute in the drinking-houses which served the fishermen, the sailors, the strangers and wayfarers who washed up the River Towy amongst the coracles and tarry smacks that smelt of the sea. She was an amateur in that she went with any boy she liked the look of, but only if he paid, and she wasn't interested in the drunks with thickened features who filled the public houses from noon till night, never mind if they had their six months' wages with them from their last trip to New York or any of the other fine places she knew nothing about.

She was a scrawny child, straight-hipped and flat as a boy herself, wan with lack of nourishment, but the spark in her hazel eyes lit the oval face in its nest of ill-brushed brown hair. Her filthy third-hand dress, cut down from someone much larger than herself, did her no justice but around her shoulders lay a jaunty yellow print shawl of a paisley design, only a little torn and stained, a gift from a sailor lad who had brought it home for his mother. She slipped in and out of the man's world she inhabited with the agility of an eel, doing their bidding in the public house, but picking and choosing her next boy. In between times she occasionally picked a pocket or lifted a handkerchief from a market stall, with a tiny flick of her wrist no eye could detect.

After the scare of their pursuit, Clemmie had taken Bethan back to her home, linking her arm companionably through that of the older girl, and swaggering cheerfully along, 'To throw them off the scent, the old dogs,' she laughed. She led Bethan up the rickety staircase of a tumbledown wooden house with crazy floors and a pervading smell of mould, then from the first landing they climbed a ladder into a dark stifling loft. The only light came from a hole in the slate roof, a piercing ray with motes dancing in the flat slab of yellow it brought to the grey-stained walls and floor.

'Mam! Mam, wake up, I'm back.' Clemmie moved into the darkness under the eaves. Bethan's eyes strained to see a woman lying on the floor on a bundle of rags made up as a bed. 'Mam, this is Bethan, she's going to stay with us. Two of us'll pay the rent quicker than one, and she's good, and pretty too, she'll get lots of tips just for smiling.'

The woman on the floor lifted her hand towards Bethan. Gently the girl took it, and, feeling its chill, cradled it with her other hand and rubbed it.

'Where are you from, girl? Where are your people?' Clemmie's mother spoke in a clear voice, despite her prostrate body. 'No, don't tell me, I have no need to know. I was a beauty like you, and not that many years ago neither, but now I just lie here like a living corpse. Some say the thing that's eating me is my punishment for sins, but it didn't seem like sin.' She laughed, a dry rasping laugh with no humour in it. 'It always seemed to me, that if you're a good woman, you die from having your man's kids and scrubbing his floors and eating the scraps left over, so I thought, why not be merry, and to hell with sainthood!'

112

So the two girls became as close as sisters, living in the tiny garret, carrying their water up the ladder and their slops down, and eating stale bread, bloaters and potatoes cooked by street vendors, rarely having a fire of their own. Bethan went with Clemmie to the Lamb and Flag, where she started work cleaning the beer-swilled floors and rinsing out the pots in the back courtyard. Shyly she went into the smoke-filled rooms packed with laughing, shouting men, whilst Clemmie pushed and jostled amongst them, her sharp tongue firing back abuse and wisecracks every bit as quick as theirs, and sometimes quicker. Clemmie would give one young man the eye, brushing against him, leaning over him, filling his pot a little fuller than landlord Jones would like. Sometimes after work she would disappear, leaving Bethan to find her way through the lanes alone, weaving between the drunks and beggars pulling at her skirts.

What Clemmie was doing would have shocked Bethan once. Now she accepted the other girl's way of life without judgement. The girl was strong, she had her time of pleasure, she cared for her mother. Priests and ministers, what did they know? And fine people, and the ones who called themselves God-fearing? Clemmie was staying alive, not just in her body; she took something back, instead of having everything taken from her.

Night after night, Clemmie lay down next to her, and their bodies grew together like those of two animals in a nest. Night after night they turned this way and that in the same pattern and drew warmth from each other as the autumn turned to winter, and their breath froze in clouds in the icy air of their rooftop home.

* * * * *

Between them the two girls pitted their wits against the problem of making the sick woman comfortable. Clemmie showed Bethan all her tricks for finding scraps of food, clothing or odds and ends for pawning, while Bethan in return used her skills to make a broth from a ha'pence worth of bones and a few crushed vegetables picked up from the ground after the market. She knew how to mend and sew, and, thanks to Mair, how to knit, and soon got herself some outwork from a woman further down the tenement, although Clemmie would have none of this.

'You can keep it, sitting with my eyes down, going blind, to make things for rich folks' kids! I'd rather go under the bridge with a blind tinker, it's a quicker way to make thruppence!'

The woman who gave Bethan the outwork kept a shilling per dozen of the babies' dresses she made, then the agent she took them to kept his cut, so Bethan made about half-a-crown for two weeks' work, without the cost of the candle and thread. All the work was done after her day in the Lamb and Flag, or early in the morning when there was enough light. Taking the work to Mrs Evans's room of an evening, she would find the other woman sitting amongst a pile of cut-out cloth, stitching relentlessly, while her own children lay in the rickety bedstead under a heap of bedclothes.

'Keeps 'em warm, see. Saves on fire. Then I can get on with my work.'

Dozens of women came to Mrs Evans for work; she knew all their names, the names of their children, their problems with husbands, rent and moneylenders. She could neither read nor write, but kept accounts in her head, so that she knew exactly how much the agent should give her, and exactly how much each woman should get, and what her own cut should be. If she liked a woman, and knew that she had problems with her man or a sick child, she would give her an easier job, or even throw in one or two of her own bits of work to make up her numbers. But if she thought a woman was a cheat, or cruel to her children, she would pick at her work and throw it back at her.

Anne Evans was a wiry woman in her thirties, her face pared of superfluous flesh, her mouth set in a shrewd but not humourless line. Sometimes when Bethan called on her she would find a woman seated by Anne's fireplace, abject, eyes turned aside or head in hands.

'Wait a moment, cariad,' she would call to Bethan through the half-open door. 'I'm just seeing to Mrs Rees.' A few whispered words, and the other woman would come out, brushing past Bethan and hurrying down the staircase.

'If you have a problem, my love – you know, with men – you can always come to me,' Anne said on one of these occasions. 'I don't judge and I know as much about it as anyone,' she added, nodding towards the three children sleeping in the bedstead. 'My man went to sea three years past. I had one letter, which Jones of the Flag read to me. "My dear wife", he says, "do not grieve for me. I am staying in the New World, and goodbye to the old. Kiss my children for me, and marry another man. Tell the minister I am dead, for he'll be none the wiser, and God will forgive you." God will forgive me, and his the sin!'

Anne sat down in her wooden chair at this, and taking the blackened kettle off the fire offered Bethan some tea. Bethan had rarely drunk tea and relished the aromatic black fluid, cradling the thick mug in her hands. The older woman sewed all the while she spoke, her hands small, strong and sinewy, the sides and tips of the fingers calloused from the rubbing of the thread and cloth.

'What about you, my dear? A pretty young thing like you – you must have had a young man?'

'Oh no, not really … no one to speak of …'

Anne knew there was more, but sensed the girl's bad experience. There was something about the way she sat hunched over her tea, her eyes fixed on the fire. There was a sadness there, a need.

'You can tell me, you know. Nothing I haven't heard, you can be sure of that.'

Bethan hesitated. 'Something bad happened to me once. The master in the house where I was working.'

Anne's face softened as the girl spoke, her voice husky and ashamed. She could hardly get the words out. Anne waited.

'So I ran away from there. Then I met a good man, but I was afraid … and he was promised to someone else. The people there didn't want me. Then it happened again, another man tried to hurt me. Is it my fault, do you think?' She turned her wide eyes to her listener.

Anne sighed, and grasped Bethan's hand. Her voice was firm, authoritative.

'No, love, it isn't, and you must never think so. That's the way men are, my dear, and there seems little to be done about it.'

She feared for the girl, alone and without protection in this rough town. The chances of her finding her brother seemed slim.

'Look, sweetheart. Be careful here. Clemmie, she can cope, but she'll get caught one day. Either it'll be the clap, like her poor mam … Yes, my dear, that's what ails poor Clara. What the ministers call the wages of loose living and fornication. Or it'll be a sickly babe that she doesn't want, that'll die in her womb or out of it, and be found washed up on the banks of the Towy.'

116

She looked at Bethan as she sat in the firelight, her fair skin reflecting its glow and light wisps of hair moving slightly in the draught from the door. She stared into the flames with clear, fine-drawn green eyes, her cheeks smooth and unsullied in the pale oval of her face. Anne felt a deep sense of sadness looking at this girl's beauty. What was there for young women like her?

In her youth Anne had worked in a great house as a nursemaid, making clothes for the children of the house, her skills at fine embroidery prized in the making of christening dresses and the like. She had seen girls then, well fed, cossetted, dressed in fine clothes, girls who could read and write, play the piano and sing, protected by minders and servants and parents as if they were made of the finest china. And in the same house, sleeping under the eaves, were girls far from home, unprotected, at risk from the depredations of male servants and drunken sons of the house, and crying for their mothers in the dark.

Seeing Bethan, Anne saw herself twenty years before.

* * * * *

Clemmie decided to undertake responsibility for the search for Jack. She put the word out amongst the loiterers, the bar-room lingerers and the beggars, to let her know if Jack Morgan showed in Carmarthen, and to keep their ears open for any whisper of such a name on their travels from west to east, north to south. One-eyed Jem, Cardiff Billy and Limping Sal swore to Clemmie that she'd be the first to know should hide or hair of Jack turn up anywhere in Wales or the west of England, and in return Clemmie smuggled out a quart of dregs from the slop tray under the beer-barrel. This was strictly forbidden by Henry Jones the publican, who wasn't going to be taken for a soft touch by turnpike tramps, despite his radical politics.

To Bethan these acquaintances of Clemmie's seemed like so much flotsam and jetsam, washed up like the floating refuse that landed on the shingly beach at Fishguard where she had wandered with the Roberts children. That rubbish had been bits of cork, planks of wood from ships wrecked against the rocks of Strumble Head not far to the west, some of it carved or painted, and then there had been fruits and vegetables and once even a bale of cloth which she had washed and made into dresses for herself and the children. The rubbish came from far-off places, by accident, and although scarred by the grinding of the salty waters, it still had traces of its former life about it, the wood warm and fragrant, the fruits richly coloured, the cloth faintly patterned with an exotic print.

So too were Clemmie's friends, battered and unappealing for the most part, but each one bringing something of a former self, and finding a way of going on as life demanded, and even finding something new that could make existence tolerable. For what other explanation could there be for these people still being alive, instead of having thrown themselves into the Towy, or hanged themselves from one of the stunted oak trees that bent in the wind on the craggy hills?

The two young women could leave their work in the early evening for a short time, and having ensured the comfort of the sick woman they would sometimes wander down to the quayside to buy a fish for their supper and to see what news could be had. Here Clemmie might pass off a trinket or a handkerchief she had stolen or which a lover had given her, and as they wove their way amongst the nets and ropes and fish kegs the younger girl would call out to the suntanned

118

men seated cross-legged on deck, smoking their long clay pipes or mending a canvas sail.

One warm October evening Bethan and Clemmie approached a forlorn figure seated on the smooth, stained stones of the quay.

'There's Black Sam,' said Clemmie, and the two girls drew to a halt in front of the man, whose head lolled forward with closed eyes. Sam was clothed in ill-fitting rags, sailors' cast-offs, and his broad, flattened feet were bare. Bethan stared with unconcealed curiosity at the dark, tightly-curled hair and the shining brown skin, the large hands with pale palms turned up loosely to the sky. Clemmie laughed at Bethan's look and went up to Sam, and leaning over she shook his shoulder.

'Wake up, you old fool, sing us one of your songs and you can have some beer!' She shook the stone bottle of Jones's dregs so that a few drops landed on the dusty brown feet.

Sam lifted his head. Bethan saw a strong-featured face, the nose flat but straight, the jaw and full mouth protruding, the cheeks scarred with tribal marks. His large, brimming brown eyes rolled in his head until they focused on the pitiless girl. Automatically Sam set up a high-wailing rhythmic song, nodding his head, his eyes closed, his mouth smiling a lost, far-away smile. Clemmie laughed, tapping her feet, then when Sam's song faded and his head rolled back against the wall, she poured some ale onto his cracked lips until they parted wider. Bethan watched in horror as the red mouth opened and Clemmie poured in more beer, until it over-flowed down the sinewy neck. She caught Clemmie's arm and pulled it roughly back.

Clemmie snatched her arm away petulantly and started to walk away from her victim.

'It's only what everyone does,' she said, with a brittle

laugh, but any further protests faded as she saw Bethan's face. Clemmie was not going to risk losing Bethan, for despite her seeming toughness, the older girl's skills and sense had made her life a lot easier. They continued to walk as Clemmie explained how Sam had come to be there.

'He came to Swansea on a sailing ship. The captain brought him from the West Indies as his servant when he was just a little lad. He stuck faithful to him, and the captain was good to him, or so they say. Anyway, the captain died, and Sam was sent here to Carmarthen with all the captain's possessions, to his wife. She said he was a devil and cast him out of her house. Now he just sits there when he can get some drink. Some say he has a broken heart.'

Bethan looked back and saw the dark figure slumped back against the wall, his song forgotten. Another chance for food or pleasure might come his way. A song or word from his native tongue would touch his consciousness, a flash of colour from a long-forgotten flower, the scent of a dark woman's skin as he leant against the wall in the last warmth of this northern autumn day. Or else his next moment would bring a kick or a curse, cold, sickness, hunger. His only awareness as the two women walked away was of their murmuring, but however he might give himself up to the warm sunlight, the only certainty was that further misfortune was massing for him like storm-clouds on the horizon.

Chapter Twelve

OCTOBER 1839

The Lamb and Flag was a place of great talk, a place where men came to argue and debate as well as to sup landlord Jones's ale. As Bethan retrieved the empty drinking mugs and carried plates of food, she observed the rituals of male conversation, and listened without giving any sign that she was doing so.

From the front the drinking house appeared like any other cottage in the area, stone-built and slate-roofed. Upon entering, the patrons stepped down into the low-ceilinged main room, furnished with rough stools and benches and always warmed with a smoking fire, whatever the weather. Beer was served from jugs on a long table, and these were replenished from barrels in the scullery outside. From the flagged yard at the back a stone staircase led to an upstairs room where Henry Jones held his radical meetings.

One evening in October the discussions in the Flag grew animated.

It hadn't taken Bethan long to realise that the conversation buzzing excitedly in the Flag over the few weeks since she started work there was the same sort of talk she had heard from Siôn. It was all of the Six Points of the Charter and the Petition and the Rights of Man. Dai Richards, a self-taught scholar and poet, and Bryn Taylor, a farrier known as 'Iron Hand', were engaged in a vigorous debate with two respectable-looking men as

121

they sat around a table, oblivious to Bethan's presence as she worked nearby.

Dai's voice was loud and edged with sarcasm as he confronted his listeners.

'Are you seriously telling us there is any other way, man? Look, you can go to church and chapel till you sprout angels' wings, you can dress up fine in your collar and linen at your throat, you can collect signatures for all you're worth, but they'll still do the same – kick it back at us, and not even bother to hear the petition.' Dai was a large man, with strong expressive features; deep-set blue eyes under dark brows which curled fiercely upwards, his nose a strong Roman curve, his mouth sardonic.

Now, as he jabbed the table to make his point, the elder of the two strangers waved an elegant hand in dismissal of his argument. John Healey's eyes were both acute and humorous as he quietly resisted Dai's assertions. He was a man of about fifty years of age, dressed in a good coat of dark brown cloth with a linen stock at his throat, and his voice was that of the educated Dubliner, a light-controlled brogue that seemed to mock at Dai's more vigorous expression.

'My good friend – really now, your irony is a heavy hammer indeed! You talk of the working man as if you and only you have his welfare at heart. But there are many like myself, if I may say with all modesty, professional and gentlefolk, who are only too aware of the injustices which are bearing down upon the poor and the hard-working men of the manufactories and mines and foundries. But intimidation cannot be the way –'

Dai's impatience could not be restrained. 'Intimidation be damn'd! It's action – doing what needs to be done, instead of grovelling at our masters' feet waiting for the crumbs from the table ...'

'But do you not see, friend, that a rising up of working men, a confrontation with the military, would not only risk the lives of those you hold dear, but also jeopardise the support you have from the educated classes? Men who could bring their influence to bear while you muster your arguments in the most persuasive way possible, encouraging all spheres of society to ...'

'Damn your professional and gentlefolk!' Dai was not prepared to listen any more, but his companion Bryn Taylor cut across him. His quiet, persuasive manner seemed at odds with the compact stocky body and sinewy arms which qualified him for the craft of the smithy. He spread his broad hands on the table in front of him, the fingers stubby and scarred, and looked directly into the eyes of his more educated listeners.

'There are working men all over Britain, desperate to feed and clothe their families, to get a decent living for a decent week's work. We have more in common with them than with shopkeepers and the like! Their philosophical sentiments may be all very fine, but their loyalties are to their own kind.' Bryn's voice was patient, its tone light and neutral.

'The only answer is to join forces with other working men like ourselves – we make the wealth that the shopkeepers and ironmasters and coalowners revel in, and then they taunt us with poverty and ignorance!'

Bryn lowered his voice even further. 'Believe me, in the next week or two you will see the truth of our words. There's going to be a fight that'll have the wealthy classes running scared! It's not enough to talk of exclusive dealing with sympathetic shopkeepers and withdrawing savings from savings banks – most people haven't got enough to live on from day to day, let alone save, and exclusive dealing can't be more than a local irritation. The national holiday idea won't work because people can't afford to go without a month's wages, and even the three-day strike in the manufacturing districts didn't work because people knew it was just a token.'

Healey's companion was listening intently. A fresh-faced man with fair hair and large, greenish eyes, he leaned forward with his elbows on his knees as if enthralled as Bryn continued.

'You must have heard about the meeting at Blaina, at the Royal Oak, Zephaniah Williams's place? There were five hundred there, shouting for action. John Frost of course told them to wait patiently for orders from him, because the rest of Britain wasn't ready.' Bryn's tone was edged with sarcasm as he added, 'He wasn't ready, more like.

'Look at the situation now. All our leaders are either in prison or on bail awaiting trial – Vincent, O'Brien, Lovett, Collins and O'Connor. Frost is charged with seditious speech and criminal libel. Our petition was rejected, they wouldn't even receive it. Our people are oppressed by the 'Starvation Law' that punishes them for poverty and tears man from wife, parent from child and forces working people to take the meanest wages, throwing others out of work. Physical force is the only way, man – you must see that?'

The fair-haired man turned to Healey with an ironic smile.

'You have to admit it, Uncle, their arguments and their passion make a fine combination. And they can count on me – I've had enough of fine words and high morals!'

At this moment the men noticed Bethan. She had paused in her work, and stared as if entranced at the conversation. Now that she was not living in Siôn's house, the exercise of her mind was confined to finding the wherewithal for the next day's food and kindling.

124

'Will you look at the girl!' laughed Healey. 'Is she simple, or has she fallen in love with you, Patrick, my friend?'

Patrick O'Bryan laughed at Bethan's confusion as she quickly moved away and resumed her work.

'Perhaps she wants to start a female radical association,' he said in his warm voice, whose tones were aimed at her, if the content to the men. As the others greeted this suggestion with mirth, Patrick gallantly raised his mug of ale. 'And why not? To the lovely radical ladies!' and the men drank a toast, amid general laughter.

Later that evening the house began to fill with men, all eager to talk over the latest rumours and reports, passing from hand to hand tattered copies of the *Northern Star* and Chartist pamphlets brought especially to Bryn by a travelling speaker from a blacksmith's forge in Merthyr. Bethan was sent upstairs with jugs of ale before the meeting, and paused in front of the green banner fixed to the wall behind the speaker's table. She stared at the white lettering, unable to read its meaning.

Suddenly she felt a hand on her shoulder. Startled, she turned, expecting a shove from Mrs Jones for dawdling about her work. Instead she saw the fair-haired Irishman, who smiled and turned her around by the shoulders to face the banner again.

'Let me help you,' he said gently. 'At the top it says, "United Trades Working Men's Association". Then underneath it says, "A Vote for Every Man". A fine motto, is it not?'

'Yes indeed, thank you, sir,' said Bethan, rapidly setting out the mugs from her tray on the side table as she had been instructed. She was conscious of the man watching her, and glanced up to see a friendly, somehow intimate smile on his attractive face. He seemed really to see her, rather than just be faintly aware of her as most of the men seemed to be as she worked around them while they took their leisure.

He moved confidently towards her, hand outstretched, and in a surprisingly comradely fashion shook Bethan's hand, wet and dirty though it was.

'Patrick O'Bryan at your service, ma'am.' Bethan muttered her own name in response as she bobbed a curtsey and wiped her hands on her apron. She was astonished that what seemed to her such a fine man should even notice her.

'Perhaps you should like to read a newspaper yourself?' O'Bryan enquired pleasantly, as if Bethan's illiteracy were not an obvious fact. 'Allow me the honour of reading to you one afternoon. There is much fine correspondence for ladies in the *Northern Star*, I can assure you!'

As she washed pots in the back scullery later that evening, Bethan could hear the muffled voices of the men in the upstairs room. The declaiming voice of Dai Richards, the subtler tones of Bryn Taylor, the booming of Henry Jones as chairman, and in between the softer, richer tones of Patrick O'Bryan seemed to reach her through the cool air of the yard. With surprise she reflected that she had agreed to meet Patrick for a walk along the river bank the following day.

* * * * *

Clemmie had taken to frequenting a drinking den down on the quayside, the Half-moon. She would go there late at night after finishing at the Lamb and Flag, not returning until the early hours or just before dawn, her eyes hectic, her cheeks and lips smudged with livid red paint, bought from a pedlar. She would fall into bed beside Bethan and instantly drop into the deepest of sleeps, her breath perfumed with gin, her limbs heavy against the other girl and unresponsive to attempts to move her over to a more convenient position.

Then she announced that she was giving up the job at the Flag. 'They're taking me on at the Half-moon, a shilling a day plus all meals found, and half a pint of gin for good measure, because Ben Finney says he likes my pretty face. So you can tell old Jones that I said you could have my place. I'd rather be watching the fun down at the Moon than listening to all that talk, talk, talk, at the Flag, so you're welcome!'

At least this meant that Bethan's status was enhanced at the Lamb and Flag. Now she took on more of the serving work at Clemmie's old wage, and a twelve-year old girl was engaged to wash the pots and mop the floor for less than Bethan had earned, so Henry Jones wasn't out of pocket, and even made a few pence on the transaction.

Soon Clemmie stopped returning late at night to sleep in the garret with Bethan and her mother Clara. Sometimes she appeared in the morning, her eyes smudged with shadows, her face blowsy with sleep. The old ragged grey dress and yellow shawl had been replaced by more gaudy finery, a stained taffeta dress of a deep cherry red. Her hair was caught up in a tortoiseshell comb but was still matted in an unbrushed mess at the back. On her head she wore a flirtatious bonnet of fine straw, trimmed with tattered artificial daisies and forget-me-nots.

Clemmie's get-up was a parody of the outfits she saw on the backs of the fashionable young ladies of the town, walking through the streets with their mammas on Sunday mornings on their way to church. She had the look of a porcelain doll with tarnished clothes, thrown aside by a rich child. Her round bright eyes and flushed cheeks bore the same look of shabby innocence as she picked her way through the filthy lanes in the too-long gown.

One evening when Bethan returned she found Clara out of bed. She had begun to fret about her daughter. Whilst the child had been sleeping under the same roof she had been able to turn a blind eye to her comings and goings, but now she was afraid.

Clara was leaning against the wall in her frayed night-gown, one thin hand against her mouth, the other clutching the flimsy garment around herself against the cold night air. Her long hair, once a bonny brown, hung in a heavy iron-grey plait to her waist. In the dimly-lit room Bethan could see the echoes of her faded beauty, the now-dull brown eyes wild against the translucent parchment skin.

'Where are you going, Clara?' asked Bethan gently, taking the woman's arm and trying to lead her back to her mattress.

'Clemmie … I've got to find Clemmie.' Clara pulled her wrist away and began to shuffle towards the door.

'You can't go out there – you're half-naked.' Bethan put her arms round her and lifted her bodily back towards her bed. Now the sick woman began to cry, and lay down obediently. Bethan soothed her and stroked her brow until she seemed calm; but suddenly Clara seized Bethan's wrist and pulled her close.

'Save my girl – I beg you. There's nothing you can do for me now – but save her.' Her face was lucid, her eyes focused and the intensity of her voice chilled Bethan. She must be close to death.

Bethan released her wrist from Clara's painful grasp and gently laid the exhausted woman down on her mattress.

'Don't worry, my dear,' she whispered. 'I'll go for her now. I'll see she comes to no harm.'

The Half-moon was nothing more than a stone-built storeroom underneath a warehouse on the quayside. A yellow half-moon was daubed on a board fixed over the door. As Bethan approached she saw the door was casually guarded by two young men who leant against the door-frame and blocked the entrance of everyone who approached, until a few murmured words had established right of entry. Bethan hesitated a few yards from the door, but then boldly approached as if she expected to be let in. One youth's leg swiftly barred her way as he grinned down at her from a grimy, stubbled face.

'Not so fast, lovely. Who do you want, and what do you call yourself, now?'

'Let me pass, I'm Bethan Morgan, and I've come for Clemmie Williams.'

'Well, we're always pleased to see a friend of Clemmie's, aren't we, Jem? Especially pretty ones who like to do a favour for a good turn.' He stood aside to let Bethan through, but as she passed the two men closed together so that her body had to brush against theirs. She entered the room to the sound of their guffaws.

The room was windowless, lit by a few guttering candles and a smoking lantern. It was crammed with people, some sitting on benches and upturned half-barrels, others leaning against the walls and each other. The air was thick with the smoke of tobacco pipes, and a faint smell of fish mingled with the smell of ale and the sickly stench of unwashed clothes and bodies.

Bethan heard a babble of conversation, a mixture of Welsh, English and Irish as she recognised fishermen from the quay, standing shoulder to shoulder with Irish labourers and travellers and English sailors, a volatile mix policed by Ben Finney and his supporters. She pushed her way through the crowd as she searched for Clemmie, brushing past jackets of thick fustian, smocks of black calico and knit frocks of dark blue and undyed brown. The flash of a red neckerchief, a gold earring, laughing mouths, uneven teeth, brown and fair hair curling round collars beneath battered hats and caps, all swam before her. A slovenly misshapen woman lolled, hanging on one man's arm, her bodice open, rolling her head in a brazen laugh while another man whispered in her ear. Young girls moved between the men with mugs of beer and tumblers of gin, calling out fresh orders to each other as they passed, and wisecracking to the men who tried to catch them as they went.

In the corner furthest from the door a large group was gathered, laughing and tapping their feet to the shrill melody of an Irish whistle. The musician was standing on an upturned keg, his eyes closed, his billycock hat askew, his face at once tense with effort and transported by the ceaseless, winding variations of his tune, while an old sailor with grizzled locks shuffled a rusty hornpipe by his side. Bethan shoved her way through to the edge of the crowd, and there was Clemmie.

She was seated on the lap of a man much older than herself, a swarthy, stocky man, with large dark eyes and thick black curling hair, streaked with grey. Clemmie had her arm about the man's neck with a proprietorial air, while his large stubby fingers lay comfortably along her thigh. Her eyes were bright against her painted cheeks and rouged lips, and in her hand she held a tot of gin. It was a few moments before Clemmie noticed Bethan and in those moments the older girl realised that she had never seen Clemmie so happy. She was a child in the arms of a loving father.

When at last Clemmie's eyes turned towards Bethan

she gave a shriek and leapt forward and grabbed the other girl to her in a hug.

'Beth! You've come at last! We'll show you how to enjoy yourself, won't we Ben?' she called to the swarthy man.

'He's going to marry me, he says I'm the best girl here. Isn't that right, Ben?' and as Clemmie threw her arms around the man's neck Bethan heard his hearty laugh, and saw the knowing smirk of the blowsy woman passing behind the lovers. Tonight Clemmie was queen of her little kingdom. She was the darling of the man with money, the hub of this shabby circle of outlaws and ruffians, caressed and petted. At last, the world had righted itself, and Clemmie was the focus of love and attention from someone who knew what to do.

'Clemmie, come home. Your mother's sick, she's worried about you.'

The drunken girl grimaced, and took another swig.

'Oh, not now, Beth, please, not now. Ben wants me here tonight. Tell her, I'll be back by morning, and not to worry, I'm getting good money here,' and she rolled her head back and kissed Ben full on the mouth. 'Tell her, I'm with Ben Finney, and he's going to see we're looked after.' At this a fiddler struck up in tune with the tin whistle and Clemmie jumped to her feet. She grabbed Bethan by the waist and went to whirl her round, but the elder girl broke away angrily and pushed through the crowd to the doorway.

Once outside she leant against the wall, breathing the cool night air that smelt of the river. Angrily she jerked herself away from the wall and strode along the cobbled quayside. In the dark doorways and down the alleys the outlines of couples were visible, their whisperings and muffled giggles faint on the wind.

As she went past a dark entrance Bethan saw one couple locked in a tight embrace. She heard the girl gasping, sensed a tension and a controlled struggle, and realised the girl was an unwilling partner in an act that was more than a lovers' embrace. The man's back was hunched, the cloth of his coat a fine dark green, and his boots shone black. Bethan started to run, and was well on her way towards the tenement when the man loosened his grip on the shuddering girl and adjusted his clothing. He thrust a shilling into her hand and walked briskly away. It was Patrick O'Bryan.

* * * * *

When Bethan met Patrick at the appointed time for their first walk together she had been almost speechless with shyness. His clothes were both well-made and cared for, his neat hands and fair hair clean and washed, and his boots of a fine, shining leather. As they walked along the river path he talked freely, gallantly, with an assumption that she, too, was at ease, his speech laced with a light wit, until she realised with surprise that she was at ease, and laughing at the character portraits he made of travellers he had encountered on his journeys.

Watching the currents and eddies of the river, he described to her his home in Dublin, comparing the methods of the fisherfolk with those of the Liffey, and praising the beauty and elegance of his home town with a note of nostalgia in his voice. Patrick was by trade a printer, he explained; he had been apprenticed for seven years to his uncle, John Healey, in Cardigan, where he had learned Welsh from the other lads at the printing press. He had been to the Chartist convention in London, but was now helping Healey to set up a new modern press in Carmarthen.

132

He spoke fluently to Bethan in her own tongue, with a gentle Irish lilt which was at once strange and wonderful to her ears. He asked about herself and her family, and how she came to be in Carmarthen. He listened gravely to her tale as she explained that she was an orphan who had lost her place after her mistress had died, and that she had come to Carmarthen to look for her brother Jack. She made no mention of the cruelties of the Fishguard house, nor of Siôn, nor did she describe her home with Clara and Clemmie.

By now they had walked some way from the town. The trees hung over the pathway, forming a shadowy tunnel, as brown autumn leaves fluttered gently to the ground to form a thick rustling carpet. Patrick laughed and kicked up the dead leaves in cascades, talking of his boyhood games in the great parks of Dublin, until a layer of dust dulled the sheen of his boots. When a large chestnut leaf spiralled down in front of them, he snatched it from the air and examined it, tracing its five points with his fingers. Then, holding it delicately by the stalk he presented it to Bethan like a bouquet, with a smart bow and a slight military click of the heels.

'Perhaps, my dear Bethan, you would agree to keep me company during my stay here?' Taking her hand, he stood in front of her on the narrow path, so that she could not go forward, nor sideways into the nettles and brambles; then he lifted her chin so that she was looking into his green eyes, fringed with long fair lashes. She felt the caressing in his voice, which he used with as much skill as his words themselves: 'Dear Bethan, forgive me my haste. But your beauty shines in its drab surroundings like a rose in a thorn brake, and to see you so alone and unprotected, I cannot hold back from offering myself as a friend to take a special interest in you!'

At this Patrick lifted her thin, roughened fingers to his lips, then clasped her to him, his mouth on hers in a passionate, sexual kiss. The breath seemed to leave her body as she swayed against him, and his arms wound tightly around her slender back. When the kiss ended, she lay her face against his chest, feeling the fine wool under her cheek and conscious of a masculine smell of tobacco and ale.

After a moment she stood back from him. There was a confusion in her expression, but at the same time she seemed to be looking at him sharply.

'Bethan, what is it? Please forgive me if I have offended you – it is my ardour for you that swept me along.'

She hesitated for an instant.

He put his hand on her shoulder, a generous, encouraging gesture.

'Come, speak.'

'It's very kind of you, sir …'

'Patrick, my dear girl, Patrick.'

'Well then, Patrick, it's very kind of you to take an interest in me, I'm sure, but … why?'

The smile on his pleasant face faltered momentarily.

'What do you mean, why?'

'Well, you could have the pick of any of the young ladies of the town … I …'

She was looking at him again with that shrewd expression. He realised that she was intelligent, and felt an unaccustomed sense of disadvantage. No servant girl had ever questioned his motives before. Surely it was understood?

'Bethan, to me you are the pick of the young ladies of the town. Now come here, like the good wee girl y'are.'

He held her round the waist and twisted a lock of her hair in his fingers, smiling a little as he examined its gold strands, bright in the chilly waterside air. Then as he held her a smattering of rain began, and he brushed the droplets from her face with his fingers.

'It puts me in mind of the words of the poet of old –

> "Our life is short: and our days run
> As fast away as does the sun:
> And as a vapour, or a drop of rain,
> Once lost, can ne'er be found again."

'True words, indeed, are they not?' Seeing her puzzlement at the English lines, he smiled, and translated them for her.

She shuddered, and looked out across the wetlands and the shining snake of the river. He kissed her lips again, lightly this time, and she abandoned her trouble.

Siôn was far away, and Jack was a phantom from the past. Patrick was real. His face and body were vibrant with life and desire for her, and she had responded to him, not just with her body, but with her heart, lost as she was without a friend. She would not be able to turn down his offer.

After this they met daily. Patrick came to the Lamb and Flag and spoke to Bethan as she worked, and often walked back with her to the end of the lane where she lived after her work was over, although she never allowed him to know exactly where her home was. When she had free time he would talk to her of the Charter and the Six Points, and read to her short extracts from the *Northern Star*. He began to help her trace the sounds of words through the mass of hieroglyphics she saw when she looked at the printed page, and then suggested to her that she join the Chartist school that met on Sunday mornings in a chapel.

When he realised that her reluctance to go was founded on her shame at her shabby clothes, he gave her a crown to spend on a new gown and boots. Bethan went straight to a pawnshop and bought the best she could for two and sixpence. Then she went to the apothecary's and bought a bottle of laudanum for Clara, and from the butcher's she got a piece of beef to make their first meat meal for months. That left six-pence for emergencies.

* * * * *

Patrick seemed to revel in presiding over Bethan's development. Onlookers were surprised to see a man of his apparent quality taking an interest in the shabby serving-girl. There were knowing winks enough between the customers at the Flag, and yet he did not pursue his advantage with her in their physical relationship, though his kisses were as fervent as the first.

He began to talk to her about the female radicals he had met in other parts of the country, and how he knew of other women in Carmarthen who were going to set up a society, suggesting that soon she might be ready to participate. Bethan was secretly terrified at this suggestion, wondering how she could manage the social niceties of meeting even with artisans' wives, let alone some of the schoolmasters' and ministers' wives and daughters Patrick referred to. Then he began to question her about Jack, asking what she had learned through her enquiries in the town.

'There's a chance – a slim one, mind – that I might be able to help. I can't say how. Just leave it to me.' His manner was hesitant, almost furtive, as he made this offer. Bethan's surprised but gratified look was greeted with a stammered response. 'Just don't ask me about it. If I've got anything to tell you I'll tell you.'

Under Patrick's tutelage Bethan felt her confidence

beginning to grow. Looking in a broken mirror she saw herself clearly for the first time. She began to pin her hair in a neat braid at the back of her head, and altered the pawnshop dress to fit more closely. At the Sunday morning classes she began to hear her own voice speaking aloud, at first hesitant, then more strongly, as the skill of reading came to her.

Bethan thought little of the future, and shied away from questions in her own mind about Patrick and his motives towards her. It was not worth entertaining any idea that he might marry her, and yet neither was she willing to face the obvious conclusion that might therefore be drawn as to his reasons for befriending her.

When she could, Bethan still did home work for Anne Evans, although her output had dropped considerably with the combined demands of the Lamb and Flag and Patrick. Taking in a bundle of handkerchiefs which she had hemmed and embroidered, she was surprised at the older woman's ironic smile as she took the work, and, having counted the pieces and checked the quality, placed it with the bundle she was preparing for the agent.

'And how's the young gentleman, cariad? Come now, it's the talk of the yard, how the fine Irishman has taken up with the maid from the Flag. Of course, they say he's after the one thing, but I said, Beth Morgan's not another Clemmie Williams, and with the example of poor Clara in front of her, she's not likely to be.'

Bethan refused the offer of a seat by the fire, not wanting the conversation that she knew would follow. She didn't want to think about it. There was something sweet and colourful in her drab world, a man who treated her as if she were worth something. She would take the risk.

As Bethan went to leave with a new bundle of work Anne caught her by the elbow. Reluctantly Bethan looked into the other woman's face. It was worn, tired, but the direct gaze expressed a compassion and knowledge which made it clear that she knew and understood Bethan's reactions. As Bethan diverted her eyes Anne's grip tightened almost imperceptibly. Her voice was urgent, authoritative, quiet.

'It won't be any different for you, you know. He might make his fine speeches and treat you like a lady. But he'll play by their rules in the end, they all do, whether they're potboys or princes.'

Bethan snatched her arm away. 'It's all right, Anne, I know what I'm doing.'

'Do you?' came Anne's response. 'That's what Clara used to say. Now look at her.'

Bethan opened the door and ran down the rickety staircase of the tenement building, the sounds of crying infants and screeching mothers ringing in her ears through the thin walls. The yard was festooned with washing hung on ropes between the buildings, and gossiping women eyed her with interest as she rushed past. Knowing glances passed between them as they concluded that if Bethan wasn't yet one of Anne's customers, she soon would be.

* * * * *

One evening a small boy came to the Lamb and Flag with a message for Bethan. Clemmie wanted her to go to the Half-moon that night to pick up some food and a bottle of brandy she had got for Clara. It seemed that Clemmie's presents for her mother were increasing in proportion to the reduction of her visits, and with a sigh Bethan agreed to call in, despatching the boy with her reply.

Patrick hadn't been to the Flag for a night or two. There had been no explanation, and just as he frequently turned up unexpectedly at different times, so too did he sometimes not appear at all, without warning. On these occasions Bethan worked doggedly but with a sense of disappointment, that somehow the day had lost its lustre. Even the smoky rooms of the tavern had acquired a glamour in her mind since Patrick's arrival, so that going to work had become something to look forward to after her early morning chores.

She was known at the Half-moon now. The grinning doorkeepers would stand aside to let her through, on Ben's orders. On this night as she approached the warehouse along the quayside she saw that the crowd of customers had spilt out onto the cobbles, and the wild sound of an Irish jig, underscored by the rhythmic pounding of the bodhrán, escaped through the door and filled the night air along with the whoops of the dancers.

Pushing through the crowd, she looked for Clemmie and saw her in the midst of the throng as she danced with a muscular sailor. As she whirled round and around in the lamplight, Clemmie's head swung back, her eyes closed, and her white throat glinted against the ruby glow of the taffeta gown, all stains erased by the soft illumination. The sailor's eyes were fixed on the girl, his body alive to the music as he swung her round, acting as an anchor to her lighter weight, while her feet scarcely touched the ground.

The onlookers stamped and clapped in time to the beat of the relentless drum, while Ben Finney sat enthroned on a stool set on the platform alongside the musicians. As he smoked his long curving pipe, his eyes were narrow as they fixed on the whirling dancers at the centre of the throng. Behind Ben, high on the wall, a tiny chattering monkey ran to and fro along a ledge. It wore a red felt jacket on its shivering torso, its grinning face a mask of terror with round, owl-like eyes, its long bony fingers picking and scratching nervously as it paused at the furthest points of its lateral journey.

No sooner had she stopped to take in the scene than Bethan felt herself caught from behind, and turned round into the arms of a bearded man who urged her on in a strange language, his reeking breath hitting her full in the face as he jerked her hither and thither to make her dance. She was seized from his arms by another man, then another and another, until the infectious laughter of the other girls at her crazy plight made her laugh too, while her prim bonnet slipped sideways over her ear and her shawl came off her shoulders and flew out behind her. A drink was thrust in her hand and she took a mouthful of the cool perfumed liquor, then another. Soon she was drifting in a dream of colours, aware of the men's attention on her like a beam of light in which she had at last become brilliantly, recklessly alive.

Now she was in the arms of a different man, whose movements were those of a tutored dancer, lighter, more graceful, who buried his face in her loosened hair and kissed her ears and neck until she shuddered against him.

'Bethan,' he whispered, 'why are you here? Like me, you must have come here for love. Better to have it from me, with kindness, than from a stranger.' As the dance ended, and the exhausted couples fell back laughing, their arms around each other's necks, Patrick moved Bethan against the wall in the shadows of the corner, and kissed her on the mouth, his body pressed against hers and her head thrust back. 'Let's drink, my love. Life is short, youth is shorter.' He held the cup of gin to her lips, and Bethan drank, and when the liquor ran down her chin and neck Patrick kissed it away.

Some hours later the crowd spilled out onto the quayside. Women shrieked and laughed as they fell against their lovers of the night, songs were sung in strange languages, and men pissed into the river and slumped against walls. Couples headed for any spot where they could snatch some privacy, a doorway or an alley, fish-stinking, damp and dark. Their breath misted in the cold night air and for many the pains of daytime were lost in the love of a moment.

Patrick took Bethan into the darkness at the side of the warehouse. Stooping, he protected the back of her head with his hand and pushed her into a low entrance. Inside, the store smelt of musty, tarred rope, and he pulled her down beside him onto a bundle of fishing nets. They embraced and she lay encompassed in his arms with the blissful trust of a child, freed by the drink into a consciousness without inhibition. He began to kiss and caress her, whispering her name and calling her his darling, his love, his true wife. She did not flinch from his hands as they moved over her body and loosened her clothing, nor did she resist as he stroked her naked thighs above her stockings gartered over the knee. Patrick made love to her gently, finely, and she responded to him with a sweetness that took his breath away. At last, they slept.

Bethan awoke feeling chilled as the sky began to lighten to an inky blue and an opaque mist penetrated the alleyways and the low shed where she lay. As she struggled into consciousness she heard a soft whisper close to her ear – 'I must go now my love, God be with you!' – but when she turned she was alone. Sitting up slowly on the pile of nets she was momentarily disorientated, her head and eyes aching, her body cold. Drawing her knees to her chest, she hugged herself, rocking slowly, thinking about what had happened. Carefully, stiffly, she rolled off the nets and stooped under the low doorway into the damp chilly morning.

She walked slowly through the lanes and alleyways, and reaching the tenement yard, went boldly through, impervious to the curious looks of the early risers already at the pump, about their household business.

Chapter Thirteen

OCTOBER 1839

Siôn sighed wearily as he struggled to pull off his stiff, soaked leather clogs. Around him several other men moved restlessly on their straw mattresses, one of them muttering complaints about the light of the smoking candle-end, while downstairs a baby screamed. There was a metallic clang as the man in the downstairs front kicked the cooking pot across the room. His wife's loud objections ended in muffled thuds and curses.

After extinguishing the candle Siôn lay back on the thin straw mattress, still in his woollen shirt that was rancid with the sweat of many days' work. He pulled the ragged blanket around his shoulders and sought vainly for the childlike comfort of warmth and rest. He lay first on his side, hoping his exhaustion would turn instantly to sleep. But his head was too full and he rolled onto his back, trying to ease the stiffness from his muscles and straighten the clenched vertebrae.

Now he ached with loneliness, and the image of Bethan tormented him. He saw her with her halo of yellow hair, moving around outside the cottage in the morning sun. He longed to hold her in his arms, but all he had was nothing, an emptiness. He cursed his own slowness, that he had not seized his chance earlier. It was his own fault. He had been cowardly: he had feared the spying eyes and whispering tongues. Yes, he was to blame.

His first anger, bitter and destructive, had turned to sadness. Someone had made her afraid of love and she had fled. He thought of her as alone in the wilderness, as one who had been found, and then lost. Tears pricked behind his eyes, and he brushed them fiercely away. He too was in a wilderness, a Babylon of fume and fire, a place where life was short. It was past.

The sights and sounds of Merthyr Tydfil rolled over Siôn, attacking his senses with the crashing violence of an unstoppable cataract. Even as he lay in his bed he could hear the roaring of the mighty furnaces at Cyfarthfa, the shouts of the men and the clanging of the trucks on the tramway.

As he made his way back to his lodgings from the ironstone mine where he worked as a haulier he walked through the centre of the great works, a scene which outstripped even Ebenezer Thomas's wilder descriptions of hell, and where thousands of light-and-shade figures toiled in their endless labours. The night sky over the massive furnaces was obliterated by a violent red glow, whilst great beams were sent into the heavens from the triple circular holes in the walls of the casting houses. Sometimes as Siôn passed he saw the seal at the base of a furnace broken open and felt the heat sear his eyeballs as the white-hot river of molten iron poured into the moulds on the tight-packed sand. As the white turned to red, stick-figure children darted between the sow and the pigs to remove obstructions to the flow. One slip and a foot could be lost, the fragile flesh and bones melted by the corrosive heat.

He stared at the open beams of the roof in the low-ceilinged loft, where each man had hung his few belongings from a hook or scrap of rope. In the glimmer of reddish light which seeped into the narrow window from the works below the coats and trousers took on new forms, their dark shapes hanging limply like the victims of some dreadful execution, seeming to shudder and move as the light flickered. Siôn felt a cold terror in his stomach as the illusion took hold of his mind. Even as he forced the image to change back into a harmless pattern of drapes and folds, so it reverted to the ghastly motif.

Although Siôn refused to submit to the superstitious dread that had started to rise up in his mind, he had to acknowledge that he was afraid. The fight they were planning to take on went further than any of them could imagine. It was like the stories he had heard as a child, sitting round the fire wide-eyed in the glowing heart of a pitch-black mountain night. His grandmother would tell of the hero who must fight the raging monster to achieve his heart's desire. Then his dread at the thought of the ordeal to come was outstripped only by the horror of the description of the monster itself; he was overwhelmed by the knowledge that failure and death seemed inevitable, yet success was imperative; and somehow, because the hero was good, and honest, and true, the monster was slain and peace and beauty were achieved in the land.

But this monster must surely be the greatest any man had ever tried to slay. It did not take the form of a ravening beast, although it made its slaves run around eternally to feed its furnaces with iron ore and coke and limestone. Its form was more subtle, and took a myriad shapes: judges, priests and ministers, bailiffs and toll-gate-keepers, constables, gaolers and executioners, and behind these, the army. These monstrous agents all seemed to know what they were doing, and who they were doing it for. Somehow they all conspired, to keep themselves comfortable, to protect those who were even more comfortable. Even the heart of the beast was not a single entity. It seemed to consist of the wealthy law-makers who made the poor into criminals – the land-owners, the aristocracy, the ironmasters, all seated on the cushion of the gentry. And the rest of humanity could go hang.

In his heart Siôn knew that only a miraculous coming-together of forces would overcome this beast with its myriad powers. But somehow the fight would have to proceed, as inevitably as the confrontations in the old stories.

* * * * *

The whole place was an assault upon Siôn's senses, tuned as they were to the slow pace of country ways, the unblemished skies and fresh breezes of the far-off west. People had swarmed to Merthyr like ants to a honeypot and now scurried about their daily business with the same frantic, miscellaneous purpose. The great central swathe of the valley was overtaken by chimneys, furnaces, puddling houses, tramways, the road, the canal, the two confluencing streams flowing into the River Taff. High on the hill to the north-east, the vast works at Dowlais sent up its black fingers of chimneys, which pointed their fumes into the pall of dull cloud that constantly hung over the town. The glare, the smoke, the noise continued night and day, the tide of humanity pouring in and out of the great buildings at the appointed times, the ceaseless demands of labour drawing them forth from the hovels and houses that had washed up among the works and now rose up the valley walls like a scum.

The sheer quantity of people massed together in one place overwhelmed Siôn: in the early morning, as he stumbled stiffly and sleepily down the rough tracks and cobbled lanes he found himself amongst a streaming population, grim-faced in the grey light: strong-backed artisans with their tool bags on their shoulders; gnarled and shrivelled Irishmen in ragged coats; pinch-faced women with shawls tight across their shoulders; pale, malnourished children, their faces full of an old weariness, their eyes still wide and wondering. Used as he was to labour and hunger, he was still shocked by these early-morning spectres.

Gangs of young girls and women passed him by, many knitting as they walked, their wooden-soled clogs sounding a clatter on the cobbles. Silent in the morning chill, they walked to spend their days breaking lime-stone, or to load the kilns from the top with a mix of coke, lime and ironstone. Others worked on the slag, their job to clear the drams of burning cinders; and at the ironstone mine girls of eight and women of eighty wash-ed the earth from the ore in the icy mountain streams.

Returning from their labours the women attended to their families, cooking a meagre meal if firing could be found, washing clothes and looking after babies left in the half-hearted care of women too old to do anything else. Their bodily needs went unattended as they took a lesser share of food than their men and children, and their menstruation, pregnancies and menopause took their toll, each woman's private miseries, with scarcely a vocabulary to describe them, and the old support of village, farm and family lost to them.

Many of these women were tough and pugnacious. Their rough work amongst a constantly shifting popu-lation of men – no longer kept in check by the watchful eyes of village gossips – demanded of them an ability to stand up for themselves. The very labour, where the woman was young and healthy, developed a wiry physical hardness that made her a match for many a man. The myriad chapels of the town sought to preserve the moral character of the young girls by impressing upon them the dangers lurking amidst the brightly-lit gin shops. Many responded, anxiously seeking to preserve their characters so that they could aspire to a more comfortable life, marry a respectable artisan perhaps, and quit the intolerable labour before their strength and looks were spoiled by the harsh combination of cold, wind and fumes.

Down in the centre of the valley, in the teeming warren of slums known as China, other young girls sought a kind of terrible freedom. Untouched by the demands of parents and ministers, and out of the reach of gossiping tongues, they ganged up with their lovers – their 'bullies' – and set about a different kind of life. Working as prostitutes in pairs they fleeced their customers, or lured them to a beating at the hands of their pimps if they didn't hand over their earnings on a Saturday night when, too drunk to read the signs, some out-of-town booby fell for the oldest trick in the book.

Siôn's uncle Gwyn had given him an introduction to a society of Chartists who met weekly in a public house, and it was through this that Siôn had found his work and lodgings. Every Saturday evening he made his way to the Vulcan, eager to hear a lecture on the Six Points and to hear the latest news from around the country, read aloud in declamatory tones from the *Northern Star* by the association secretary.

One evening in October Siôn was surprised to find the passageway in the Vulcan, which led to the back staircase up to the meeting room, clogged with men, craning their heads forward to look into the open doorway of the downstairs back parlour. Their laughter and murmuring was stifled by a loud 'Shhhhh!' from inside and a slightly tremulous female voice could be heard within the room.

'I know it is said that we women should bide at home – that politics should be of no interest to us. I know it is said that if women go to meetings, they must be neglecting their husbands and children ...'

Siôn pushed his way to the front of the crowd of men blocking the passageway.

'What is it ?' he asked the man next to him.

'It's those daft women who want to call themselves radicals. They need a good hiding if you ask me, especially the loud-mouth.'

The woman's voice continued, growing in confidence and pitched towards the men in the doorway as much as to her female audience.

'What those critics should know is that we do not step out of our sphere of home and hearth out of a spirit of rebellion. We step forward to take our place in support of our menfolk, as they strive against the injustices of a class legislation.' At this there was a ripple of applause from the women.

'Have we not seen our mothers, sisters, neighbours, struggle to maintain their homes in comfort, such as our hearts told us should greet our menfolk after their fatiguing labours?'

'Yes, indeed, sister!' came the reply.

'Year after year has passed away, and even now our wishes have no prospect of being realised, our fathers, brothers and husbands are overwrought, our houses half-furnished, our families ill-fed and our children uneducated.'

'It's true!' murmured the women, and Siôn, peering forward, saw their eager faces as they turned to each other, and some turned towards the men in the doorway, both affirming and seeking affirmation, in the habit of a lifetime.

Edging forward, he saw the slim young woman

standing on the makeshift platform, leaning forward towards her audience, the male onlookers forgotten. His impression was of a sharp face, large bright eyes, and a burning passion as she forgot her nerves and warmed to her subject. The words began to flow in a torrent now.

'You have seen our menfolk ground down to the strength of ghosts, or shadows, by the reduction of wages, or the laying off of workers. How can you stand by when the Bible says you should be a helpmeet to your husbands? You have seen your children in rags, no boots on their feet, and nothing warm in their stomachs, because of lay-offs and the fall in the price of iron. And yet the rich roll by in their carriages, and their lady wives tell us to be more thrifty!'

This was greeted with an outburst of applause, and even Siôn's cynical neighbour was listening.

'We know, who have to eke out our meagre budgets, that even with the most rigid economy we are unable to provide for the actual necessities of life.

'As women, we share in the indignities wrought upon our men. We share when they come home exhausted, worn out with toil, with no time to rest. We share it when we go to work ourselves, if we are not fortunate enough to be able to keep to our homes. We share it when we seek to comfort a crying child whose hunger cannot be assuaged, or an ageing parent who cannot have medicines because the household has no money. Women! Do not say we should not join this struggle!

'As women and mothers we have a special part to play. Let us instruct and encourage each other, that our children shall be brought up in education, that they shall know their rights as citizens, and continue the fight that we have started!' Cheers, now, encouraged the orator.

'We must boldly declare our conviction that nothing less than the adoption of the principles of the People's Charter can remove the existing distress, or secure the safety of the working classes.'

As a final flourish the speaker turned to the green and white banner propped against the wall behind her. With deliberate drama she declaimed the embroidered words: 'Why grind ye the faces of the poor saith the Lord. Freedom's cause cannot be lost, it is sacred before the Lord of Hosts.'

'Amen!' came the cry from around the room, as the women burst into rapturous applause. The woman nearest the door rose and, with a satisfied smile, closed the door in the faces of the men peering in from the corridor.

* * * * *

Siôn was both confounded and thrilled by this spectacle. He had never heard of such a thing – women taking it upon themselves to meet in a public house, discussing questions of morality and politics without recourse to menfolk, addressing questions of national importance and reading from newspapers! The most shocking thing of all was to see a woman standing up in public, while men were watching, capturing the attention of dozens of people, without shame, owning and asserting a viewpoint as if that were a right for women as for men. The young woman's commanding, vigorous tone, her face flushed with anger and indignation, pity and determination by turns, had captured him completely. He wanted to know who she was.

'Annie Taylor,' answered the man he asked in the front bar of the Vulcan. 'What do you think of her, then? She wants to set up one of them radical female societies. Been allowed to read too many books. Can't see how she'll ever get a husband, myself, for all her talk about menfolk. She'd talk him to death.' With this Siôn's companion directed a beery smile in his direction, pleased with his joke.

Siôn found by dint of persistent questioning of his drunken friend that Annie was the daughter of Elishah Taylor, who was a member of the Chartist Lodge at the Three Horseshoes. Elishah was a skilled man, a puddler, so the family were better off than most, although like everyone they had had their share of hard times. Annie had learned to read through classes at Shiloh Chapel where her father was a preacher, and now it was said that she had read more books than any other woman in Merthyr.

'Not difficult,' snorted Siôn's informant.

Walking back to his lodgings that night Siôn followed his usual, safe, route; but passing by a shadowy cobbled lane, lit only by the dim rays of a distant lamp and the reflected glow from the sky over the ironworks, he paused, tempted to enter the realms of China where he knew thieves and pickpockets lurked in waiting for young men like himself. He could hear laughter, and the distant strains of a barrel-organ. After a moment's hesitation he diverted his step down the dark lane, past the shadowy couples sniggering and whispering against the mossy stone-walled buildings, past the gin houses where the human wreckage lay strewn on the pavings.

Out of the darkness, a tiny waif stepped forward, hand outstretched, pointing backwards at a bundle of rags which stirred and separated into the figure of a mother and her child. Round the corner a young girl appeared, her face in the dim light turned up to him in a pale oval, beseeching even as her voice wheedled her

152

practised invitation. She was no more than thirteen years old.

A gang of youths ran, shouting and laughing, down the narrow lane, dragging sticks along the walls and banging on doors. They thrust Siôn aside and knocked down an old beggar who was shuffling painfully along the refuse-strewn pathway. A bold-faced woman with black hair and reddened lips and cheeks stepped out of the darkness and put her arms directly round Siôn's neck.

'Come on, now, lovey, what would you like then?' came her husky voice, her chest thrust suggestively against his. Siôn knew that this was what he had come for. Despite the risks, the temptations of this place intoxicated him after the measured courtships of home, the furtive embraces, the watchful eyes.

He allowed the dark-haired woman, whom he sensed was not as young as she seemed, to lead him through a doorway into a back entry and to the foot of a steep narrow staircase. As he groped for her in the darkness he heard a scuffling noise behind him. A fierce blow struck the back of his neck, while his eyes were blinded with flashing lights. When he hit the floor kicks lashed into his ribs, back and head. Unseen hands rummaged through his clothing and he was propelled at a high speed back out through the entry until he landed in the muck and filth of the lane.

Chapter Fourteen

After the meeting Annie Taylor sped home, her plaid shawl held tightly round her shoulders and the notes for her speech folded up small in the pocket at her waist. Her companions, Sarah, Esther and Mags, chattered excitedly about the meeting, but Annie's mind was too busy as it raced ahead to what she might meet at home. Pulling her arm away from Esther's, Annie began to run.

'Can't stop, girls! I've got to get back before Da.' With this she ran along the muddy lane, across the tramway with scarcely a look to right and left, scrambled up onto a raised walkway and disappeared into the alley beyond.

'She's going to catch it sooner or later,' observed Esther. 'There's no way she can keep this quiet – it'll be all over Georgetown by morning.'

The girls continued their stroll, arms linked, steps matched, each thinking about her own bit of explaining. Mags laughed suddenly.

'No need to worry about Annie. She's got more talk than an Irish tinker. She'll get round Elishah before you've got your boots off.'

Reaching the doorway of the cottage Annie paused for breath. Lifting the latch she entered quietly as if returning from a prayer meeting. Seeing that the neat parlour was empty, with the fire carefully banked up for the night and the children's clothes ranged along the rail to air for the morning, she entered briskly and

sank back into the fireside chair with a smile of satisfaction. The smooth wooden chair, with its tall shaped
back, the slats moulded by steam, and its round-ended
arms so comforting to the hands, was the most imposing feature of the room. In fact it was the only real piece
of furniture other than the rickety, rough planked table
and a few stools. Her mother often complained about
the chair, dragging it hither and thither over the rough
flags with one hand as she scrubbed the floor, part of
her daily ritual of cleanliness and respectability.

The scrubbing sometimes seemed to take her mother
over. Every day the step outside had to be scrubbed
and whitened. That was the most important part,
because the other women were out there doing theirs.
During the last part of mother's confinements, Annie
had had to take this over, rubbing the scrap of lye soap
into the coarse-bristled brush, jarring her knees on the
flags as she heaved her body to and fro with straight
arms. She lacked her mother's speed, skill and strength
at the task.

How she had hated slopping the filthy rag over the
floor and up the stairs to mop up the water. How she
hated old Ma Jenkins from number four, who had
cackled at her ham-fistedness and said 'That'll bring
you down a peg!' Most humiliating of all was when the
boy Jenkins, all sixteen years of him, had swaggered by
on his way back from an early-morning poaching trip
with two rabbits over his shoulder, and shouted out that
that was how he liked to see women, on their knees.

The annoying, comforting, obstructive chair was of
course her father's. Here he sat after his day's toil,
reading his Bible by the light of the fire and a single
candle, turning the pages with his stubby, roughened
fingers, their nails rimmed with dirt. Annie thought of
the way he would hold the thick book up to the candle

flame and peer at the words, running his finger along the lines. His worn beaked face would be intent, the fine lines around his eyes thrown into relief by the reflected glow from the book's pages. Sometimes he would take down a pot of ink from the mantel, and a worn quill. Patiently he would shape the nib with his pocket knife, the precision and care reflecting the significance of his undertaking. Drawing the corner of the table in front of him he would begin to write with great deliberation. That was how his sermons took shape.

Annie's eyes fell upon the neat row of boots lined up along the wall by the door. Scraped free of mud by her mother, and greased to keep out the wet, were the patched and mended clogs of Nellie, Siân and little Betty. Then there was a space, and then her mother's boots stood with their toes almost touching the wall, but not quite, for fear of marking the whitewash. With a start Annie realised that her father's boots weren't there. Quickly she unfastened her wooden-soled clogs and placed them in the gap next to her mother's. She lifted the latch of the door in the corner of the room and crept up the ladder-like stairs.

When Elishah eventually came home he sat down heavily in his chair and closed his eyes. Essentially a gentle man, he was no hell-fire ranter. He scorned the kind of sensationalism that drew crowds who wanted to shudder in terror, be told how bad they were. As if that made some sense of the dirt and squalor around them, the diseases that took their babies and children away from them! As if even the innocent were subject to the wrath of God.

No, he wasn't going to point the finger at his own people. He could see quite clearly where the Devil's work lay – in the doings of ironmasters, mill-owners, landowners, judges, the whole tribe of Lucifer got up in fine coats and white linen. They scorned the poor for their dirt, their ignorance and their rough manners and yet in their souls they harboured cruelty, greed and hypocrisy, which no amount of washing could launder away.

For this reason he had embraced the Charter. At least this offered a practical opportunity for people to better their lot – using the gifts God had given them, gifts of minds and tongues and brotherhood. His was an active, not a passive religion, not waiting for miracles, but looking to God to work through Man.

It was clear to Elishah that his task as a godly man who could read and had been blessed with a thinking mind – a mind that had never let up, since his earliest childhood days, its ceaseless dialogue and questions – that his task was to help his brothers and sisters in God to understand that they too had a part to play in the forward march of humanity. He encouraged singing, loud, joyful singing. One voice was weak, but many were strong. A surge of strength came to the singers as they made their natural music and wove their net of harmony, and lifted them to a sense that they too had beauty and power. These were gifts that were the right of all human beings, and Elishah was determined that everyone in his flock should know that those gifts were within their grasp, if only for a few, fleeting moments on a Sunday.

The other gift Elishah wanted for his people was the gift of knowledge. His own learning to read had poured a shaft of light into his life as shocking as a Damascan conversion. The moment when the beetle-tracks of printed ink on the pages of an old Bible had suddenly adjusted into meaningful symbols had surely been an act of divine revelation. All the questions and unending torrents of thought that had almost maddened him in his early boyhood now channelled into the wide river of human knowledge and philosophy.

Elishah had wanted this gift for his children, not thinking, as a young man, that his children would be all girls. Even a little reading was unusual amongst girls of his class. But as the eldest, Annie, began to grow, he saw in her bright curiosity and constant questions the child he had once been himself. Despite his wife's constant admonitions to Annie to 'hold her tongue', he found himself treating her more and more as an intellectual companion and pupil. His wife, Nan, fretted that Annie's booklearning would unwoman her and make it hard for her to get a husband. In fact in his heart Elishah suspected that she was jealous of the girl and the special treatment she seemed to get.

Now Annie was in his eyes both beautiful and bold too, not in an unseemly way but in her intellectual confidence. He was scared at what he had done. Now Elishah saw the fresh, wet mud on Annie's boots as they stood neatly between Nan's and Betty's. So she had not long been in. She must have been to the meeting at the Vulcan. Leaning back heavily in his chair, Elishah sighed. He would speak to her in the morning.

* * * * *

Nan's tone was sour, with an edge of sarcasm.

'Politics, is it, now? You can't cook a decent pudding without burning it, you can't sew straight, it takes you an hour to scrub a floor, but you've got something to say about everything!'

She turned towards Elishah, her voice rising in the gloom of the early morning parlour. Her face was red from making up the fire and heaving the huge iron kettle into place. Now it reddened more and her brown eyes fixed him accusingly.

'This is your doing. Whoever heard the like? Getting up in a public house and making a spectacle of herself! Drawing attention to herself in front of men and talking politics!' Nan was almost spitting with rage. Ma Jenkins had been round as soon as she heard Nan riddling the ashes, saying that her Annie was the talk of the town and the laughing-stock of all the boys.

'It wasn't in front of men! It ...' Annie was stopped by a vicious blow across her face from Nan. She stepped back in shock, gasping, with her hand over her mouth as her eyes filled with tears.

Elishah's chair scraped on the flags as he leapt up, pushing Nan roughly aside.

'Leave her be, woman.' He went to Annie and put his arms around her to comfort her. The pain of his crying child was as fresh in his heart as it had been when she toddled barefoot amongst the grassy stones of the yard. 'Tell me, Annie. I know you're not a liar. But your mother is worried for you.'

'I want to do something, Da.' The girl's voice was muffled with tears. 'All the lads, the young men, their hearts are high, they know that soon they'll be called upon ... to act'. She adjusted her words, gauging Elishah's reaction. A moral force Chartist, he shunned violence, but knew that many of the young men particularly relished the idea of a fight, and were collecting arms and drilling all down the valleys from Brecon to Newport.

'But we women ... what are we to do?' Annie continued. 'Sit and sew?' – ignoring her mother's snort of derision – 'It's not just girls, you know, there were mothers, and wives, and grandmothers – Jemima Lewis, and Esther and Mags ... and Rachel Jenkins ...' A glance at Nan confirmed that the last piece of information had struck home and would be stored for future use, young Rachel being Ma Jenkins's grand-daughter, and the apple of her eye.

'Mrs Price was at the first meeting and she said that it was Woman's Duty as Man's Helpmeet to support the Six Points and not to shrink back and discourage the men as some women were doing for fear. She said that politics is a type of morals for women, because it is to do with our duty to our fathers and husbands and neighbours – she gives us religious texts ...'

Annie's words were galloping now, to check her mother's intervention. 'She quotes us from the Bible, and proves to us it would be wrong to stand idle. "Whoso stoppeth his ears at the cry of the poor he shall also cry himself, but shall not be heard" – "Why grind ye the faces of the poor?"... she had many texts and read us uplifting words from the *Northern Star* ...'

Nan cut through this breathless monologue.

'Perhaps Mrs Booklearning Price should read her Bible more closely: "A foolish woman is clamorous: she is simple and knoweth nothing" – "It is better to dwell in the wilderness, than with a contentious and angry woman."'

'But mother – women must learn from each other, must teach themselves to understand the ideas the men are fighting for in the Six Points ... then we can pass this on to our children and their morals will be of a higher order ...' her voice trailed away at Nan's contemptuous expression '... when at last they gain their rights as citizens.'

'See what you've done!' hissed Nan at Elishah, who held Annie's hand tightly as she spoke. 'You've made her useless! I wash my hands of it, and when she's called up by the magistrate for causing disorder, you can go and plead for her! I can't waste any more time, I've got work to do – and so has she.'

With this Nan threw open the staircase door and scolded the barefoot children who were perched there listening.

'Get up there and get your clothes on! Nellie, Siân, you'll be late – Betty, you're to help Mrs Williams Corner House with her Bobby today ...'

The thuds of the girls' preparations clamoured above them as Elishah sighed and stroked Annie's cheek with his hand. Was his bright bird to have nothing but toil and labour in her life, like Nan – to end up shrill and bitter and (he admitted to himself) constrained in her mind through worry, worry, worry?

It terrified him to think of the pain that lay in store for his girl and how the smooth, downy cheek would soon hollow, how the easy-smiling mouth would tighten like Nan's, even if she found a trusty, God-fearing man. These thoughts were a kind of sacrilege – Annie was a woman, and here he was trying to imagine another way for her. But he had made up his mind. He would not stand in her way. Her gifts came to her from God, through him. He wanted to throw the fetters off humanity. And if the old did not free their own young, what hope was there for the future?

As he walked briskly to his workplace amongst the shabby, ragged and hungry, he found that Nan's Biblical texts had brought another Proverb to his mind: 'The father of the righteous shall greatly rejoice: and he that begetteth a wise child shall have joy of him.'

* * * * *

Annie was apprenticed to a dressmaker. Her mother had besieged the little coterie of milliners and dressmakers in the town who served the wives and daughters of the wealthy shopkeepers and solicitors. Through sheer persistence she had ground down Miss Falk,

161

Purveyor of Mantles and Fine Gowns. Triumphant, Nan had borne home the news to the astonished ears of Tramway Terrace – Annie Taylor had an apprenticeship! Not for her the icy morning hillside, or the grimy heat of the furnaces.

Annie had some problems with the other girls in the terrace after the news broke.

'She'll be too good for us down Tramway, will she now, Nan?' asked the other mothers, as Annie's grim-faced mother yanked the girl's bodice hither and thither to get it just so, and tucked an errant dark curl back under the brim of her new bonnet, in readiness for her first day.

That had been four years ago, when Annie was fourteen. Her career since then had not been an unqualified success. When Nan said that Annie couldn't sew straight, she was not exaggerating by much. She could cut out, pin and mould the garment, she could tack and baste and dart, she could sew the seams in tiny backstitches, but she found it hard and worked slowly. Meg Brown, who was still only fifteen, could sew at twice the pace, and was being given fancy work to do, embroidery, appliqué, bead and feather work. Miss Falk treated Meg 'like a little princess' (as her mother boasted), because the quality of her handiwork was becoming famed among the ladies of the neighbourhood, and this boded well for business. Annie meanwhile got the plain work.

Miss Falk never ceased to inform Annie of her shortcomings as the three women worked in the cramped, shabby workroom above the shop. 'If it wasn't for me, young lady, your hands wouldn't be so soft! You'd be shovelling the dirt like the rest of them. I only keep you here because your mother's a good woman, and respectable, and your father's a man of God.'

The only light in the workroom was from the small leaded window overlooking the busy main street, and from the pitiful fire which burned in the grate only on the coldest days – and then only when Miss Falk was present. On the important days when she, and latterly Meg, visited the wealthiest customers in their homes, Annie was left blowing on her fingers in the dank chill.

The room was a chaos of bales of fabric, draped figurines, and half-finished garments. The floor was littered with scraps of material of every kind, jewel-bright silks, dull sensible woollens and rustling taffeta. There was scarcely time to pause from the production of garments to clear this froth that could have immolated them in a few seconds were a spark to jump from the fire or a coal roll to the floor. Once Nan had prompted Annie to ask for scraps to take home to make into a patchwork quilt. Miss Falk allowed the girl to pick up the bits of fabric after work, but made her sort the silks from the plain. Annie found herself walking home with a bundle of the dullest wool, with sad dreams of a bright silk bedspread or cushion for Elishah's chair. Nan was delighted: 'No warmth in silk,' she said briskly, tipping the bundle onto the table to get a better look.

Every stitch in every garment they made was placed there by hand. Every skirt was built of elaborate shaped gores, every bodice moulded to a dainty tight-waisted form, each sleeve constructed with pleats and gathers. Each part was perfectly complete, so that the garment could be deconstructed for cleaning by the lady's maid. Decoration flourished on every collar, cuff and band. They made linen shifts, taffeta petticoats: nothing was too fine or dainty for the wealthy matrons of Merthyr, nothing too tiresome to make, nothing too good for the ladies.

One of the perks of the job was that each year Miss

Falk allowed her apprentices to make themselves one plain gown of good stuff, so that they might look respectable and not disgrace her establishment. She, on the other hand, boasted a wardrobe nearly as fine as her customers', except that she confined herself to modest, fine-woven wool when visiting her ladies. The girls knew about the wine-coloured silk she kept for best, however, because she had let Meg embroider the mauve and white forget-me-nots around the edge of the cuffs.

Annie was out of breath when she reached the shop. She tapped at the door and Meg opened it quickly, whispering dramatically: 'You're for it!'

Without pausing Annie ran up the narrow staircase and into the work-room.

'I'm sorry I'm late, Ma'am, but little Betty took sick in the night and ...'

'Save your breath, girl! Do you think I can afford to have a trollop like you blackening my name? Radical Women's Association indeed!'

Miss Falk still wore her loose dressing-gown and morning-cap, from which her thin faded hair fell in a frizzy plait. Her watery eyes stared in outrage at Annie who stood in the doorway, panting from her energetic walk to work, with cheeks glowing and youth and health shining from her.

'Consorting with the lowest riff-raff of workmen in public houses! Conspiring to bring down the government and cut off the Queen's head! What can your father be thinking of – what of your poor mother?'

At last Annie found some words. 'It's not what you think – we're respectable women ... it's just ...'

Miss Falk was screaming now. 'Respectable! Respectable! How dare you lecture me on what's respectable? I took you in and saved you from the filth out there –

gave you a chance. Why, you could have become a lady's maid if you'd played your cards right. There are more wealthy men than ever coming here, and all their wives are vying to outdo each other to see who can be more of a Lady Muck! But you can forget that now. How could I ever give you a character? You might murder them all in their beds for all I know!'

Annie's tears, her beseeching for the sake of her mother, her little sisters, were to no avail. Half-an-hour later she was walking home, carrying a small bundle containing her own scissors and pincushion, an end-of-roll of worsted given by Miss Falk in a sop to her conscience, and a paper packet containing one shilling, in lieu of a day's wages.

* * * * *

Once the house was empty Nan sank down into Elishah's chair. A great tiredness came over her after the flurry of early morning activity. The row with Annie had left her agitated, both anxious and angry. Elishah had been a fool to the girl, and now his overweening ideas were going to land them all in trouble.

She thought back to her own girlhood. Her mother having died when she was thirteen, Nan had taken on the role of housekeeper and cook to the family of seven brothers and sisters and her father. No time for her to read books, she thought grimly. Her learning had been all of the practical kind. She had tried to bring her daughter up well, to make her into a God-fearing woman; but she feared that the girl had inherited her father's stubbornness and sense of mission. All she could do now was let events take their course, because she knew that Elishah would do nothing to curb Annie's reckless progress. But God only knew where she would find a man foolish enough to take her on.

Nan's children were growing now, the smallest being seven years old; at thirty-eight Nan felt herself withering as Betty's babyhood receded. She and Elishah had an unspoken pact that there would be no more babies. She thanked God that she had been spared through eight pregnancies, although twice she had miscarried and twice given birth to stillborn infants. All her energy, skills and talents had been poured into the making of these surviving children, as if she had taken the tiny, slippery, squalling things that struggled from her womb, and had moulded them patiently day by day; as if all her labours had been the labours of a sculptor, building up layers of pliant clay, patiently, painstakingly, until the form took shape before her eyes. All her ingenuity had been poured into finding and making food for them from Elishah's meagre wages; all her talents focused on making clothes from odd ends of cloth or cut down from adults' clothes, turning, patching, darning; all her bodily strength had gone into nursing them, washing for them, begging and borrowing for them when times were hard, and struggling to keep the filth of Merthyr at bay from her door.

Now it seemed as if the children were almost made, and times were a little easier with the girls' wages coming in. But how hard it was when the child she had striven for turned from her, as if the statue should turn from the sculptor and walk away.

The sound of the kettle coming to the boil brought her back to her senses. She couldn't afford to sit here all day: she hadn't even scrubbed the step yet. Perhaps she should take in some sewing, now that the children were no longer under her feet. She would get Annie to ask Miss Falk if she could bring home some plain work for her to do.

As she lifted the great iron kettle to pour some boiling water into the wooden keg she used as a bucket, she heard the sound of heavy clogs running along the cobbled yard. Annie burst through the door and stood with tears pouring down her cheeks. 'Oh Mam! Miss Falk won't have me in the shop!' And with that she threw the bundle of cloth on the floor, and the shilling, and ran up the stairs.

Chapter Fifteen

The women laboured on the hill above the iron-smelting works in the level gold sunlight of the October morning, their breath hanging in the air for a moment as a presage of winter. The hems of their rough skirts, and the soles of their wooden clogs, were caked in the pungent mud that churned up around the banks of the stream as they set about their task of washing the soil from the iron ore. All wore sacking aprons and shawls pinned tightly across their shoulders, but while the older women wore battered caps and old felt hats salvaged from their husbands, the young women wore straw bonnets decorated with feathers or tattered artificial flowers and bits of fur. Against their pale, hunger-sharpened features these emblems of youthful vanity blazed even brighter.

As they worked, their intercourse took on its familiar daily pattern. At first, as they started in the grim chill of the pre-dawn, scarcely a word was spoken after their greetings, while the overseer stalked up and down the line behind them to check who was there and to catch latecomers. Then, at a signal from the chargewoman, they paused briefly to break their fast, the lucky ones drinking tea that was still lukewarm from tin billycans. It was after this, as morning broke over the landscape of swarming human activity in the valley below them, that their spirits seemed to lift for a while, and conversation began.

The focus of interest this bright morning was Annie

Taylor. The damp air had brought a frizz of curls from under her bonnet, which was noticeably sleeker and less battered than those around her. Her cheeks glowed pink from the unaccustomed exposure to the wind and drizzle of the last few days, but the shadows under her bright, speckled green eyes told of her daytime exhaustion and sleepless nights.

Jen Fisher, a stocky woman with a gap-toothed grin and a ready laugh, was the first to speak.

'Your hands not so soft, now, girl? Never you mind, sweetheart, you don't want to be a dancin' round some fat-arsed bailiff's wife, with a mouth full of pins, do you now?' Annie laughed, despite herself, while the others joined in the banter.

'You won't meet no men, neither, my love, picking round with that old hen what wouldn't know what to do if she met a cock in a dark alley,' chipped in Old Meg as the girls began to shriek with laughter. Meg had been a whore in her young days, and when she got going she could leave the other women speechless with her shocking tales.

'Can't see the disgrace in it, myself,' added Betty Angel. She was called Angel because she had grown up in a pot-house of that name, but no one knew where she came from or what her real name was, as she was a foundling. 'All you done was stand up and tell a few home-truths, 'twasn't like you'd been shagging, now, was it?'

'Ssh, Betty – don't mind her, she don't know no better,' said Jen hastily. The women were aware that Annie was unused to their talk, but, kindly in their way, they had chosen to protect her.

'Tell you what, lovey,' continued Meg, warming to her theme, 'what you need is a young man. Then you can tell your Mam and Da to stuff themselves, and get him to buy you everything you want, fine and dandy. You're wasted here, with that bonny face. If I were in your shoes, I'd be off to Cardiff or Bristol in a trice, and find me a sea-captain or an officer.' Annie's cheeks had now deepened to red in their embarrassment, which Meg misinterpreted as modesty. 'Well, if you're stubborn, and won't take advantage of what God gave you, why then, you'll have to make the best of it here. A miner or a puddler, that'll have to do. They've money enough, and big strong boys they are too, and I should know!' she cackled.

As the morning wore on, the talk subsided, and the women began to sing: strong, stark hymns, or old songs remembered from far-off villages, passed on by tired mothers to grizzling babies. And as they sang, Annie's mind dwelt on her situation.

She had suffered a serious jolt when Miss Falk dismissed her. All the order of her life had collapsed like the backdrop in a tawdry theatre. Now she was plunged into the chaos behind the scenes, where a whole gamut of shabby characters jostled in the mêlée.

People had tried to make her ashamed. She was ashamed that she had brought distress to her mother, so that Nan felt herself to be the focus of ridicule of all the gossips in the neighbourhood. She was ashamed that Elishah had wept to see her set off before dawn in a sacking apron, to toil that would break her health and damage her beauty. But somehow deep down she was not ashamed. It was, after all, as Betty Angel had said.

More than that – working in the earth with the women, watching the miners entering and leaving the dark holes in the ground; then contrasting these sights with the pictures in her mind of the wives of the mine-owners and the land-agents and the solicitors and the bailiffs as they called at Miss Falk's showroom in their carriages: it was all becoming clearer. How was all this dirt translated into all that cleanliness and glitter and graciousness? Why, by the labour of all these hands, hearts, brains and bodies, all set to the service of people who would turn their eyes away if you stepped in their path with the mud of the hillside upon your clothes.

And so she was not ashamed. A determination grew in her, that she would somehow still read, although this labour was designed to crush her. She would still think and she would still attend the meetings of the Radical Women's Association.

* * * * *

Siôn had noticed the dark-haired girl on several occasions now as he joined the throng of workpeople leaving the iron mine at the end of the shift. Taller than the other girls, and somehow preoccupied, she accepted their linking arms but did not swing her walk as they did, nor did she join in their cat-calling at the young men, and their cackles of laughter were met in her only with faint smiles. Soon he located her on the hillside as she worked. Moving back and forth to load the trams of washed ironstone and transport it to the giant furnaces, he was able to look up from time to time and distinguish her from the other women. There was something familiar about her – where could he have seen her before?

He seized his chance one evening in mid-October as he saw her walking alone at the end of her shift, having become separated from her workmates by the crowd streaming its way through the gates of the yard leading from the mine. Emboldened by his superior position in the caste-system of the mine – and, no doubt, by the absence of her fearsome friends – Siôn fell into step

171

beside Annie, who stared straight ahead after a sideways glance revealed her new companion to be a stranger.

'I beg your pardon, friend, for addressing you thus – but can you be the young lady who speaks for the Six Points?' He spoke gently, almost deferentially, in Welsh and his accent revealed him as one who was new to the neighbourhood.

Annie turned in surprise. This was not what she had been expecting. The usual approach was bold and swaggering. She looked into the man's face to judge whether there had not been a hint of sarcasm, a forerunner perhaps to an assumption that a woman who spoke up in a public house was easy meat.

But there was no trace of disingenuousness in his large blue eyes. Admiration, tentativeness and a certain awe were evident in his shy smile.

As she looked away Annie registered the lank towcoloured hair falling straight to his shoulders beneath the battered black hat, the tall physique and the swinging easy walk, despite the twelve-hour shift of labouring just completed.

'And what if I am?'

Siôn persisted. 'I saw you speaking at the Vulcan – to persuade the women of their part in the struggle for the Charter ...'

'Laugh, why don't you?' flashed Annie's sharp reply. 'All the boys have had a good laugh, 'specially now I'm down here. Think it's brought me down a peg, don't you!'

'Steady now, girl, it's not that at all. I'm in the Lodge now myself, but until I heard what you said I'd never thought ... never realised ... what women could do for the Charter ...' Siôn's voice tailed off, but Annie's pace slowed imperceptibly.

172

'I'm carrying on with it, you know,' she said. 'The best women in Merthyr, they are, in our Association, no matter what some people say. And they need me, because I've been blessed with a good understanding, and I can read books and turn them into simple words, which no man will bother to do for them!'

To emphasise this point Annie thrust her hand into the cloth pocket pinned at the waist of her skirt, and pulled out a small, stained red-bound volume and a sheaf of newspaper cuttings folded small. 'I keep one with me all the time, so I can feel it while I'm working, so I don't forget … no matter how tired I am, how cold, that thought keeps me warm. I find a way somehow, every night, last thing, even if I have to read by the embers …'

Embarrassed now, she veered away from the stranger and paced hard, but she heard his steps keeping up with hers. Suddenly, he caught her arm.

'Don't … don't run away … I'd like to see you. To talk. Will you meet me?'

After they parted by the muddy tramway Siôn's mood was elated. Once past the prickliness of her first reaction, the girl had relaxed a little. They had chatted about their work and he had told her that he was new to the town. Then she had agreed to meet him.

His mood wavered as he remembered Bethan. Was it wrong to make a new friend? Surely not. She had left him, he reminded himself, abandoned him and Huw and Mair and in so doing had wrecked his family. He must forget her, and yet, even as he convinced himself, the memory of her light hair and the faraway green of her eyes brought a pang to his heart.

How different they were; Bethan and Annie! Fair and dark, the one untutored and lonely, the other at her happiest reading and talking and seeking knowledge.

And yet Bethan had thirsted for the knowledge denied her. She should have had Annie's chances. He would never see her again, he knew.

And so Siôn and Annie began to meet, first walking home together, he accompanying her to the edge of her district before turning back to his lodgings; then they arranged to meet on a Sunday. He attended the chapel where Elishah preached, and then walked with her afterwards to the hill above the town. Nan watched this with mixed feelngs, glad that Annie had attracted the attention of a young man who seemed upright and honest enough, even if he wasn't the craftsman or even clerk that she had hoped Annie might aspire to before she ruined her chances. Elishah cautiously welcomed the development and eagerly engaged in debate with this earnest young Chartist who so desperately wanted to read and learn.

Siôn was full of the rumours which circulated in the beerhouses and passed from man to man at the mine and ironworks. There was to be a rising, it would be soon – Henry Vincent would be sprung from jail, all the workers would rise up in the mines and foundries and manufactories, all over Britain. The army would come out on the side of the workers, for weren't they just poor boys themselves? Then the rich men could be flung down the pits to dig the coal, and see how they liked it – and the Parliament and the Queen and all the nobs would surrender! Then there'd be a new government, with the Six Points, and every man a vote, and every woman a queen in her own home …

Elishah listened patiently, waiting until Siôn's torrent of words began to falter in the face of his impassivity. Then, gravely, he would put the case for moral force. They had right on their side – any Christian man could see that. How could it be right for a handful of wealthy men to make all the decisions for millions of other men, who toiled to fill the pockets of the rich but had no say in how things were to be ordered? The Bible was quite clear: it was harder for a wealthy man to enter heaven than it was for a camel to pass through the eye of a needle. What was needed was for that moral view, that indisputable argument, to be placed before the public, to be asserted again and again in every way possible, while peaceful tactics like boycotting shops owned by anti-Chartists, and strikes, were carried on. That was the way – not to use force, and not to seek an insurrection, which could only lead to disaster, and murder, and hangings.

While the men talked, Annie observed. Elishah did not seem to notice, now that Siôn was there, that she was not joining in the debate with him as she was wont to do. Somehow it seemed right to the two men that she should be quiet while they talked – it was a mark of her privileged position that she was at the table with them, rather than sitting to one side like Nan, who was stitching silently at some plain work given to her by Miss Falk. Nan darted glances at Annie from time to time, indicating that she should be doing the same, Sunday or no Sunday, as she had brought this disgrace upon them.

Annie fingered the newspaper cutting folded up small in her pocket. She wondered what the men's response would be if she smoothed it out on the table and read its contents. It was a clipping from an old copy of the *Northern Star* which she had begged from Mrs Price. It was a letter from 'A Real Democrat', who described herself as 'a plain working woman – a weaver of Glasgow'. There was one sentence which had leapt out of the page at Annie: 'It is the right of every woman to have a vote in the legislation of her country'. At first the idea had seemed alien and pre-posterous, but as she listened to the men talk she real-ised that there was nothing they said that she could not grasp; she knew that she could read and write better than a good many of the men now signed up with Chartists' cards.

What Annie didn't know was that others around the country had also entertained this outrageous idea; and when the London Working Men's Association cir-culated its People's Charter to radical groups for comments, some put forward proposals for women's suffrage. The Association failed to take this up. They had no argument against this reasonable idea, except that they feared that men's prejudices were such that it would never be entertained, and would thus hold up the movement towards freedom.

And so Annie was left riveted by the thought she could not express, lest her existing privileges be taken from her.

Chapter Sixteen

NOVEMBER 1839

Breathing hard, Siôn pounded up the cobbled lane, his feet slithering on the slimy stones as he turned the corner. Now his clogs struck the paving of the main street as he ran towards the Vulcan public house, dodging passers-by and ignoring their remonstrations as he crashed into shoulders and knocked a basket flying. The light from the inn fell into the damp twilight, illuminating a crowd of men round the door-way, still wearing the sweat- and grime-stained clothes of the day. Without hesitation Siôn plunged into their midst, forcing a way through into the meeting room.

Men were standing on chairs and tables at the back of the room, jamming the passageway between the occupied seats and surrounding the speakers at the front. The heat and moisture in the room were over-powering, fuelled by the oil lamps hanging on chains from the ceiling, and the smell of tobacco smoke mingled with the stink of work clothes imbued with soot, mud and sulphur.

'Whoa, lad!' Firm hands grabbed Siôn's shoulders and stayed his headlong course. Snatching his arms away he stood panting, staring ahead of him at the leader of the lodge, Daniel Martin, who stood with his hand outstretched as if to silence his listeners.

'No, brothers! It would be pure folly! To go now when we know the lodges in the manufactory towns – the hordes of Manchester, Birmingham, Nottingham –

when we know that they are not ready! You might as well go to the military and offer to shoot yourself, or go to the hangman and offer to put your head in the noose – and that's what it would mean, believe me!' He stared fiercely round the room, seeking out the men whose restless gestures and angry faces expressed their opposition. 'We can't do this to our wives and children! Starvation, penury ... what will become of them if we fail? No, my friends, we must wait, wait until the time is right ...'

A murmur ran around the room, suddenly erupting into scuffles as men tried to reach the front of the crowd.

'Now! Now! Now!' the chant began, and was taken up by voices here and there in the room. 'What! Are we cowards, boys? Will it be said that Merthyr men were too fearful to seize the moment when it came?' But the response came from only a few throats, as the other men shifted from foot to foot, looked downwards or spoke to their neighbours in an undertone.

'Let me speak!' Siôn's voice rang out above the uproar. The men turned towards him as he moved forward and pushed his way to the front. He was trembling with emotion, the sweat and moisture on his skin streaking his face with the unwashed dirt from his day's work. They saw that he was young, earnest, his eyes large and a clear blue against his darkened skin. He twisted his cap in his hands as he started to speak.

'I walked here. I *walked* here, all the way from the west, from Pembrokeshire. Why did I come here? To eat. That is all. That is the sum of my living ... to make the opportunity to eat. Out there, in the country – ay you know, and you, and you' – he pointed to individuals within the room – 'they scarcely have that. Their living is but a bare existence – they are balancing

178

on the brink of death. One push, one little shove, and down they tumble, into the abyss. And there are plenty there waiting to give them that shove – the landlord, the bailiff, the toll-gate keeper.

'But I came here for the right to eat. Look at me!' His voice was raised, it began to crack, to tremble. 'Am I a man – or an animal?' He was shouting. 'Am I a pack horse, or a mule, that I must pull carts all day long in the bowels of the earth? And then say, at the end of the day, feed me, feed me, so I may haul again tomorrow?

'No! I have a heart, and an understanding, a good mind and a good body – I want to use the gifts God and nature have given me. I am not prepared to wait any longer. We've made our preparations. We've got our weapons. If every Chartist in the valleys marches on Newport tomorrow night, what price a few soldiers and special constables? I say we go, we take every man in this town with us, and damn every ironmaster and magistrate to hell!'

A few voices greeted Siôn's speech with loud approval and applause, but the majority sat with downcast eyes, while Daniel Martin had his head in his hands.

'Look, son,' he said gently. 'What you want, we all want. But it's not going to work. The word from England is that they're not ready, and John Frost …'

'Damn John Frost!' shouted Siôn, his face twisted with anger. 'If he won't march at our head he'll feel a pike up his backside!' He started to push his way towards the door through the throng of men. 'I will be leaving this town at first light tomorrow. I will meet any man who calls himself a man at the weapons store at that time and we will march to Dowlais. Bring food and say goodbye to your loved ones. And as for the rest of you – sleep well!'

The room was in uproar as Siôn forced his way out into the street. A few men followed him out and surrounded him, patting him on the back and shouting their agreement. They embraced each other briefly, then huddled together as whispered plans for the morrow were made in more detail.

* * * * *

Annie's eyes opened with a start. She must have dozed off, but it was still night. She stared at the low ceiling, illuminated by the glow reflected from the ironworks. This was madness. If she were caught she would surely be put in the bedlam. But she had made up her mind. She was working out on the hillside in all weathers, labouring like a man. Her complexion had roughened, her hands were calloused and her fingernails rimmed with grime. Her body had become thinner, harder: she was wiry like a boy. All day her mind was working, working, way beyond her body; thinking over what she had read, what Siôn and her father had talked about. She would give up being womanly for a while. She would join in.

A few minutes later the latch of the heavy old door leading into the yard was lifted gingerly, and a slight figure slipped into the shadows. The figure flitted along the walls of the cottages before disappearing into a lean-to at the far end of the row. A few minutes more elapsed, then a slim but sturdy youth emerged and swaggered down the lane, hands in pockets.

* * * * *

It was dark at the back of the blacksmith's workshop. A small group of men huddled round the small opening to the storeroom cut into the hillside. The air emanating from the store was dank and smelt of earth and mould. A candle-end was stuck on a ledge inside and large shadows flickered over the stony walls. The murmur of voices was punctuated by the clash of iron. Scraping sounds were heard, as of metal being dragged over the rough floor.

The men waiting for their weapons shifted from foot to foot. Heads down and hands in pockets against the damp dawn of the first day of November, their mood combined edgy nervousness with grim humour. There was an eagerness, almost careless now, to get going, and if the rest of the Merthyr men wanted to miss out on the moment of glory, well so be it.

Siôn emerged from the darkness of the cave holding a sheaf of pikes and staves in his arms like a harvester. Behind him came Joshua Thomas, grinning broadly, holding six long-barrelled guns, some of very ancient vintage. The pikes were tried for size as men lifted them, tested their weight, and measured their length against their own height. The guns were passed reverently from hand to hand, but it had already been agreed that these should go to the men who knew how to handle them. Billy Williams had been a soldier in his youth, and was the leader of the little battalion. Two of the men had gained their experience as poachers, while two more had practised under Billy's eye, way up on the mountain wilderness on Sunday afternoons.

The last gun was for Siôn. Lifting it to his eye, he looked along the muzzle towards the blue strip of light which indicated the doorway at the far end of the smithy.

As he did so a boy appeared, hesitant, framed in the opening. He wore a large cap pulled down well over his brow and his neck was swathed in a muffler. His jacket, too, was over-large, the sleeves well down over

181

his knuckles, and his trousers rolled up at the ankle. A poor lad, in hand-me-downs; but one whose mother loved him, to judge by that muffler.

He crept into the smithy, peering into the darkness.

'Halt! One move and I'll blast you to kingdom come!' roared Siôn, waving the gun wildly in the youth's direction. At this the boy gasped, stumbled, slid and skittered on the stony floor as he turned tail and ran. The men's laughter hit the back wall of the cave and bounced back in a metallic shout.

'It's all right, lad,' yelled Siôn. 'God knows we need all the men we can get, even if they are wearing their Da's breeches.'

When the youth did not reappear Siôn walked to the entrance, leaving the men to complete their preparations. The air was fresh after the warmth of the smithy embers. The street outside was still silent, the sky a dull blue-grey with a glimmer of pearly light just visible in the east.

There was no one there. Curious, Siôn walked to the corner of the building and turned into an alley-way. He started violently as he all but collided with the frightened boy.

'Duw, mun, what are you doing, creeping about by here?' The boy stepped back two paces, his face seemingly bearing an expression of guilt and embarrassment. Siôn hesitated. For a moment he was seized by fear. The boy was a spy. Gripping the barrel of the gun in one hand, he caught the boy's collar with the other, and pinned him to the wall, pressing the end of the long muzzle under the tip of his chin. It was a remarkably delicate chin.

The boy began to wriggle and whimper. His cap started to slip forward over his eyes. 'Let's see who you are, you little brat!' said Siôn, hooking the cap on the tip of the bayonet and flicking it into the mud.

182

Seeing the dark curls released from the cap, the pins and flattened plait awry, the large green eyes a mixture of embarrassment and defiance, Siôn leapt back like a dog from a snake.

'Jesus, Mary and Joseph!' His voice accidentally boomed into the silence. He lowered it to a hiss. 'What in hell's name are you playing at, girl? Have you taken leave of your senses?'

Annie was trembling now, but with deliberate slowness she defied his anger and stooped to pick up the cap. Fixing her eyes on his, she twisted her hair up with one hand and placed the cap on the back of her head, scooping the hair into it as she pulled it firmly forward. Then she wiped her hands on the damp mossy wall and smeared her cheeks with dirt. Seeing his incredulous stare she risked the beginning of a smile.

'I'm no madder than you were when you put on skirts and followed Rebecca,' she said quietly. He gave a snort of derision.

'That was play-acting. That was toy soldiers. This is the real war – what do you think this is?' She pulled her head back as he waved the gun under her nose.

He stood away from her, uncertain. One part of him wanted to slap her saucy face and kick her back up the hill to her father. The other part was amused, admiring even. Wasn't she the bravest, most bare-faced, most bold lass in town, when it came to the Charter, and the Six Points? He was proud of her. He seized her hand.

'All right. You've got your own way. Now listen. You're my brother Ianto. You've just come up from back home, you don't speak much English, and you're a bit twp to boot. Keep your mouth shut, and stick by me. It's going to be hard. It's a long march and there'll be trouble on the way. At the end of it there'll be a battle. Maybe even death. But this way, if we die, please God we'll die together!' With this he kissed her on the mouth.

* * * * *

A purposeful silence settled on the marchers as they continued their long route down the Ebbw Vale. Dark clouds massed above in the evening gloom, and flurries of chilly rain buffeted their faces like handfuls of gravel.

The small band from Merthyr had joined with a few stragglers from Dowlais, then moved along the heads of the valleys through Tredegar and Sirhowy. At last their faith had been repaid, as they found themselves swept along in a huge crowd from Dukestown. At Twyn-y-star groups of men formed orderly bands in the driving rain, as leaders moved among them checking off the names of the captains present. At last, at eight o'clock, the order had been given to march. But even now there was uncertainty. Where were the large groups expected from the lodges of Merthyr and Dowlais? What exactly was John Frost planning? No one seemed to know for sure, but the mustering of hundreds of men armed with pikes and muskets, and blatantly plotting an uprising, now gathered its own momentum. It was happening, at last.

All along the route more men joined them. Some came gladly, eager to play their part. Others left their cottages reluctantly, wives and children clinging to their arms, beseeching. Sometimes screams and shouts could be heard coming from a house, wild shadows would rear up in the candlelit rooms as men rampaged through, chasing a reluctant recruit. Some stole out of rear windows and ran onto the hillsides, while their wives argued at the front door with those who demanded entry.

A mass of people awaited them at Pen-y-cae, greeting their arrival with gunfire and cheers. The Chartist leader Zephaniah Williams had left there only hours before, satisfied that the blast furnaces of the Victoria ironworks had been shut down. But he left no news behind him as to the plans for the march, nor even its exact purpose – whether to coincide with other risings in Abergavenny and Cardiff, in Yorkshire and Lancashire; whether the bridges over the Usk were to be blown up, and the Bristol Channel blocked by sinking ships. Only John Frost could tell them, and they needed to march with all speed to the Welsh Oak a few miles to the north-west of Newport to hear him.

Hour after hour the men trudged the rough track, drenched now by icy rain. The smart order in which they had left Dukestown disintegrated in the darkness, and small bands straggled along in the mist, some stopping at inns and farmhouses, demanding beer, food and tobacco, with a show of pikes, staves and muskets where a reluctance was shown by the landlord.

And so at some time before dawn on the second of November, Siôn and Annie arrived at the Welsh Oak to find themselves in the midst of a great crowd. Now the marchers' spirits rose as the long anxiety of the night seemed to dispel. Men with guns were called forward and the order given to check their weapons. As the crackling shots tore the early morning air, and the smell of gunpowder singed the nostrils, the approaching battle at last seemed real. When the crowd arrived in Tredegar Park, captains on horseback wielding swords and spears ranked them six abreast with a gun at the end of each line. The time had come.

* * * * *

As the procession wound its way down Stow Hill into Newport the long gun rested against Siôn's shoulder. He was at the end of the line, conscious of Annie beside him, her face white and pinched beneath her cap, but determined in its expression as she scanned the scene ahead and around for signals of danger or alerts to action.

'There's something wrong here,' she hissed sideways at Siôn. 'Where are the men from Pontypool? Why have we come the long way round through the Park instead of meeting up with the others at Cefn? And why did we march past the workhouse, stuffed as it is with redcoats? If you ask me John Frost doesn't know his backside from ...'

'Shut it,' came Siôn's rejoinder. He was nervous too. He had a sense they were walking into a trap. The soldiers of the 45th Regiment were known to be in the town, and local Chartist messengers had told of the five hundred special constables rapidly sworn in by the mayor. To cap it all their own leaders didn't seem able to explain for certain the whys and the wherefores of what they were ordering their men to do. But it was happening, now, and all they could do was join in the shouting and exhortations to the faces at the windows and the figures staring anxiously from doorways.

Suddenly three loud cheers were heard from the mass ahead, who had by now reached the front of the Westgate Hotel. As Siôn and Annie turned the corner to the hotel all was tumult as the leading contingent doubled back from its attempt to enter the courtyard on the far side of the building. The crowd was now charging the main entrance with a fearful yelling, demanding the release of the prisoners taken during the night. Siôn plunged forward into the fray, the gun under his arm now, at the ready. If there was to be a chance to express his rage, then he would seize it, even if he were to draw his last breath as he did so.

The air was split by the sound of a gunshot. There was a moment's pause, as of disbelief, a joint drawing-in of breath; then a great roar rose up, filled with the crackling racket of shots as the Chartists attacked. Special constables bolted from the side and rear entrances of the hotel faster than frightened rabbits, accompanied by the whistle of shot as deadly as any poacher's. Now the raiders, their pent-up fury surfacing in the liberation of the moment, tore into the fabric of the building which held their enemies, beating on the shutters and smashing the windows with their pikes and mandrels. The smoke of shot filled the air, and its acrid smell invaded the nostrils and lungs of the enraged makeshift army, and sparked the terror of the redcoats trapped inside.

Siôn fought his way to the front. He had already warned Annie that he intended to be in the thick of the fight, and that he would go forward without her. All around him was a mass of humanity, jostling and surging forward, carried on an intoxicating wave of power which overrode all fear. At last they would show what they could do. In a sideways glance Siôn caught for an instant a familiar face – it was his uncle, Gwyn Hughes, and in that glimpse Siôn saw that he was transformed. No sorrow now in those tired features, Gwyn's face was almost joyous as he poured all his strength and anger into the moment of struggle.

Another instant, and Gwyn was lost to view. There was no chance to pause now, and when the insurgents swept into the hallway Siôn was among them. He heard the order to fire, as the young Irish soldiers of the 45th filed past the windows and assailed the crowd massed at the front of the hotel with round after round of lead. Siôn could hear the screams and groans behind him and craned to see through the smoke-filled doorway to catch a glimpse of the multitude, now fleeing. No time to think of Annie's safety. They must seize their only possible chance. Crouching, Siôn pressed himself against a wall in the shelter of a heavy table. He raised his gun to his eye.

In a blinding flash of light and explosion of sound the inner doorway ahead of Siôn was flung open and blasting guns raked the hall. A man ahead of him was blown from his feet and slammed against the passage wall, as blood and brains splattered against the panelling. Other men screamed and writhed amid the splitting fragments of light and darkness, their nostrils choked with smoke and blood, their ears with stabbing noise and dreadful aeons of silence.

Chapter Seventeen

On the Christmas Eve of 1839 the battlements of Carmarthen Castle rang with wild shouts, the sky illuminated by bursts of fiery light. The streets seethed with running figures, suddenly bright in the flames of the balls of fire they tossed and kicked along the market-place. Drunkenly they lurched in and out of the public houses, screaming slatternly girls and coarse-faced youths. Decent folk remained behind shuttered windows, aghast that the annual madness had taken hold again and praying for a drop in the wind, lest a stray gobbet of fire should start the biggest bonfire of all. With little thought of Christian sensibilities the young pagans chased the winter darkness up and down Market Street and in and out of the narrow lanes.

A young girl waited at the entrance to a darkened courtyard until the revellers had passed. Then she slipped along the street, a shadow weaving through the dark places seemingly made darker after the blinding lights of the wild ones had passed by. Last year she had joined the throng in her fine crimson dress. With hair awry and shawl adrift, her throat had shone white in the blaze of fire. The light in her hazel eyes had been matched by the glitter of the coloured glass earrings Ben Finney had given her. She had been the queen of them all – the Fire Queen, Ben had said. One look at her and all the ghosts of winter would have flown.

Now it was as if all colour had drained away. All that existed was this – thing, that had taken hold of her body and swelled her puny stomach within her scarcely-formed hips. Clemmie leant against the wall, shivering. She could feel the strange bubbling sensation again in her belly. Why wouldn't it go away when she didn't want it? Bethan had taken her to Anne Evans. They had tried gin, and pennyroyal, and finally Anne had inserted a metal knitting needle into her womb. The sweat sprang on Clemmie's brow as she remembered, and the tears began to course down her cheeks in the darkness. She had clung to Bethan, who held her shoulders tight and gave her a folded rag to bite on. But still her lips had been bleeding when she took the rag away.

Anne too had been white with anxiety. A kindly woman, she dreaded harming the girl's tender body. But in her kindliness she knew that a painfully-induced miscarriage would lead to less suffering in the long run. After all, the girl's protector had left her, discarded her like a piece of rubbish when he knew that she was pregnant. Clara, the girl's sick mother, had died, so at least Clemmie no longer had to strive for the wherewithal to feed and comfort her. But a baby and no money coming in would mean the workhouse for sure, or worse, life in a brothel while the child existed as best it could. No, thought Anne, this must be done.

But it would not be done. The abortion failed, and Anne dared not try again. One thrust too deep or wide of the mark and she would have the death of the young mother on her hands. This had happened before, when desperate women had come to her and had been assailed by fever, and she knew that this time she might not get away with it. When Clemmie had returned, her thin little face filled Anne with a despairing pity. She took the girl in her arms and stroked her narrow back as the sobs shook her.

Bethan had tried to make it all seem all right. She said that they would manage between them somehow. Clemmie wasn't the first girl to have a baby before she was wed – the town was full of them, didn't they both know that?

Bethan had tried to make her laugh – they would say they found the baby under a bush and didn't know how it had come there. But it hadn't worked. There was no laughter left in her without Ben.

Clemmie felt a coldness seeping into her. It was like cold, dark water. If she let it come over her it would obliterate this pain. Out here in the dark she was invisible, a shadow against the wall. A passer-by went along the street without giving her a glance. It was as if she were not there, as it would be in years to come when people passed this spot in the night without catching a glimpse of the suffering girl who long before had huddled there.

She began to move again through the shadows at the side of the street, flitting noiselessly down the damp cobble-stones, and disappearing into a narrow alley-way, then plunging down a stone staircase whose walls exuded a smell of moss and mould. Her hand brushed its clammy surface to guide her descent into the blackness beneath. Then she wove a pathway behind the warehouses and taverns of the quayside; she was momentarily visible as she darted into pools of light, but lost again into the darkness of the little lanes where she had kissed and laughed before her youth had been extinguished.

Now she came onto the quay, where several ships rose and fell softly on the ebbing tide. The water flickered dully in the reflected light of a half-moon, smothered in the dark clouds that surged across the sky. Clemmie saw only the gloomy outline of the great bridge as its arches spanned the Towy. Clothed in her invisibility she pressed on towards her goal. She did not see the dark figure lying on the deck of a vessel, whose eye caught the pale fluttering form as it darted by.

As Clemmie came to rest in the centre of the bridge she caught a whiff of the salt sea on the wind. She thought of her father, setting sail for Spain and the bright ladies. She glimpsed momentarily the gorgeous lands set out beneath the sun, far, far, away. But he had never come back to his own Clementina.

Below her the ships bobbed, abandoned by their sailors as they joined the revels. The sky behind the castle glowed with fire, but here, all was still and cool. She clambered onto the parapet and swung her feet over. She looked down for a split second, seeing the swirling current and aware of its sinister, infinite watery sound and motion. Then she plunged. A moment of suspension, then a chaos of noise, an icy penetrating darkness that assailed her ears, her nostrils, her mouth, her lungs. Then the dragging, dragging of her skirts.

* * * * *

The men staggered along the quayside to their ships. The wind had picked up, and the moon had seemed to sail from behind the clouds as nifty as a little schooner. Suddenly a shout went up.

'Get away from her, you black bastard!' The first man home was swaying on the side of the quay. As the others joined him, they gasped, and some crossed themselves.

Black Sam was crouched over the figure of a young woman who lay sprawled in the mud. Her clothing was disturbed at the throat and he had a hand on her chest. Her eyes were closed and her lips slightly parted. Tendrils of hair clung to her white cheeks and spread over her shoulders. In the moonlight she looked as if she were made of wax.

* * * * *

Bethan was startled from her sleep by a tapping on the window frame. She sat up in the makeshift bed she usually shared with Clemmie in their new lodgings and stared fearfully at the dim square of light against which a shadow bobbed. She knew it was Patrick. After nearly a month he was back. Where did he go? The plausible reasons of business he gave somehow didn't ring true when he came back stinking of alcohol, his clothes sometimes drenched with sweat and the stench of horses as if he had ridden hard and fast. From what, or towards what, he rode was a mystery. Now the knocking became more urgent, more reckless.

'Open up ye wee bitch, I know ye're in there.' The refinement was gone from his voice and she knew he was drunk.

The door began to rattle and then suddenly it was assailed with crashing blows as he took the heel of his boot to it, crash after crash until the ancient bolt parted company with the jamb and the door flew open. As the freezing air flooded the room Patrick stood swaying on the sill.

'Light, ye bitch!' His breath plumed in front of him as Bethan scrambled from beneath her covers, seizing a spill from the narrow mantel and poking it beneath an ember in the grate. On her knees, she blew against the spark, willing it to catch, conscious all the time of the heavy-breathing figure behind her. As the pin-point of light grew, with trembling fingers she guided the spill towards a stump of candle in a broken saucer next to the bed. The room was suffused with a gentle light.

She turned her face towards him. His attention had wandered from her as he ponderously strove to maintain his balance, staggering slightly from one foot to the other. His fair hair had escaped the black ribbon that held it at the nape of his neck. His face was livid as he stared dully from under his lowering brows. His dark cloak was smeared with foul-smelling mud and as he unfastened it and slung it to the floor she could see that all his clothes were filthy. With uneven steps Patrick moved over to the room's one chair and slumped heavily in the seat.

At first he leaned forward, head in hands. A groan escaped his lips, then he began to shudder. Bethan realised he was weeping. Huge sobs began to rack his frame, but no pity entered her heart, only watchfulness.

His tears stopped as suddenly as they had begun. Dropping his hands, he slowly raised his eyes to Bethan's face. She felt the full beam of his consciousness turned on her, unwavering now. As he stood she moved backwards. Now he stepped towards her and stood close against her as she felt for the latch of the door into the passageway behind. He uttered nothing, yet his face was a mask of threat.

She opened the door and hastened past the doorways of the rooms where whole families slept, as he kept pace behind her. Now she reached the door to the back yard and again he was over her, his face pressed insultingly close. It was cat and mouse, a game he had played before, and there was almost a smile on his lips. Now she was in the yard, and had scarcely turned towards him when the first blow struck. It rang through her skull with a shuddering echo like a pistol shot in an empty hallway. Then the blows came thick and fast, to the right of her head, to the left, to the right again, as her being was suspended in the fearful echoing silence.

Once it was ended she fell to the ground in the wet cold of the yard. Patrick stood for a moment, his breathing thick, then he turned and walked unsteadily back into the house.

* * * * *

Bethan crept into the scullery and leant against the cold slate shelf where the washtubs stood. She began to cry like a child, in deep silent sobs. Leaning back against the wall she became again the lost girl longing for her mother, weeping in the dark places of other people's houses. She knew now that she was pregnant. She reflected that Patrick's blows might kill the child that he had started.

Exhausted, she began reluctantly to move back to her room. Patrick was in the bed now, his boots and top clothes thrown all around. The door hung awry on its hinges, and cold air whistled through the gaps. Bethan dragged the heavy door back into position, then looked at the comatose figure, whose odour and noisy breathing filled the room. There was nothing for it, unless she was to freeze to death. Carefully she got into the bed behind Patrick and pulled the covers to her shoulders. She just hoped that Clemmie stayed out all night – otherwise there would be more trouble.

* * * * *

When the workhouse master opened the door at half-past midnight he thought he had been brought a corpse. Once the girl had been laid on a bed he called for the female superintendent and dismissed the sailors who thronged in the hallway. It was easy to see what sort of woman she was. Her bodice was torn to the waist and her pale, blue-veined breasts shone preternaturally bright. Williams half-averted his gaze for a moment lest Mrs Jones should think his interest was unseemly. But in a moment his eyes were back on her. The drenched cloth of her skirts clung tightly to her form and moulded the shape of her thighs. Her stomach protruded in a little mound and there was no wedding ring on her finger. She gave off a powerful stench, something dank, evil – that was it, evil.

Attempted suicide, was it? Williams's gaze grew thoughtful. A foul crime indeed. An overweening arrogance for such a flibbertigibbet to take upon herself the awful decision that only the Lord could make: to decide upon the moment when one's being in this world should cease, and life ever after should begin. It was right that she should be punished.

'Filthy slut.' The words startled him as they burst from his lips. Mrs Jones was holding a bottle of sal volatile under Clemmie's nose, and started to rub the girl's icy hands. She darted a glance at Williams, and compressed her lips. She often annoyed him in this way. He could tell that she was thinking.

'Maybe so. But you don't know that.' The last words were muttered as she hobbled out of the room to fetch one of the rough calico gowns kept for the female inmates. This was another of her tricks, reflected Williams. Insolence, but so carefully timed you couldn't quite catch her at it.

Clemmie began to moan. Her hand went to her brow, then she rolled over and was sick, violently, noisily sick, and began to cry. Williams gazed down on her in satisfied disgust. This is how women were when left to their natural devices, without the firm guiding hand of a God-fearing husband or father.

They were as weak in their minds as they were in their bodies, and without the lodestone of a good man were wont to pursue a random course, attracted to every vice put in their way.

'What is your name, young woman? Answer me at once. It will do you no good to hold your tongue. I shall get the truth from you, never fear.'

Clemmie opened her eyes to see a small man dressed in a long flannel night-shirt, with a blanket round his shoulders. His face was pushed towards her, chin jutting, the corners of his mouth pulled down in right-eous disdain. His gaze was intense under fierce eye-brows with bristles which swept up into ginger points. He wore a white nightcap with a long tail which trailed onto his shoulder.

'Who do you think you're talking to, you old hobgob-lin, you?' Clemmie struggled up on her elbows. 'And where am I? I'll kick your bollocks through your arse if you so much as lay a finger on me!' She put her legs to the floor but pitched headlong and Williams found her in his arms, still not fully conscious, her breasts half out of her dress and sliding down his torso. At this moment Mrs Jones returned, and putting her burly arms round Clemmie's body she heaved her away, giving Mr Williams as she did so one of her dryest looks.

It was to be a long night for Williams. Once he had told Clemmie that he would fetch the constable in the morning the girl had gone berserk. She had thrown his jug of tea on the floor and kicked over the tables and chairs. He had had to summon the male superinten-dent too and between the three of them they had managed to thrust her into the women's dormitory and left her tied at the wrists with thick twine which was in turn attached to a metal bar at the window. The other women stirred and complained in their sleep, but mad outbursts were nothing new in here.

As soon as the door was closed and locked again with the great iron key the whispering started.

'Who are ye, darlin'? Don't be afeard, there's no one here'll hurt ye. We like a gel what fights back, don't we now?' The voice was husky, the tones the strongest Irish. Clemmie had heard it before.

She heard rustling movements, and as her eyes became accustomed to the dark she began to pick out the shapes of the women as they clustered round her. Dimly she perceived the pale blur of each face, the tumbled, unkempt hair and the ragged gowns they wore. The odour of their bodies, their sweat, their rancid menstrual blood, mingled with the stench from the piss-pot in the corner. In the half-light they seemed like a throng of curious animals who had crowded round her the way the cows did when she had walked in the meadows with Bethan.

Busy hands now began to work at her bonds, fiddling to and fro with the knots, until suddenly she was free. Rubbing her painful wrists she thanked her liberator. It was the husky voice again.

'To be sure an' we'll tie y'up again in the mornin'. Yon old Bible-basher won't know any different. An' be sure ye weep plenty, now, and throw yourself at his feet. That's something he can't resist, from a comely wee girl like yourself.'

The woman took the thin blanket from her cot and threw it round Clemmie's shoulders. 'Now tell us your tale. I'm Limping Sal, the queen of the turnpike, and if you can tell me a story I've never heard before, it'll be a miracle, and I'll go to mass tomorrow and confess all me sins!'

Clemmie seized the woman by the hand. 'Sal! It's you then! You've got to help me get out of here. I've … I've done a bad thing … they're getting the constable … It could be the scaffold for me.' She gripped Sal's fingers so tight the other woman had to ease her hand away. She felt the wetness of Clemmie's hair, and placed her hands on the girl's belly.

Now she spoke softly, the rough humour gone from her voice.

'Whatever you've done, darlin', worse's been done to you. Now … let's think for a moment …'

A few hours later, the key scraped in the lock and Williams entered the dormitory with both Mrs Jones and Bartle, the male superintendent. He glanced with satisfaction at the prostrate figure of Clemmie, hanging limply from the wrists. The twine was cutting into her thin flesh and her hands appeared blue.

'Women, do not be alarmed. But I have to warn you that there has been a great evil in your midst. This … creature … you see before you is a dreadful warning to all women. This is what happens when vanity and lust set their roots into a wanton heart …'

Williams was interrupted by a groaning. He paused with a momentary menacing glance at the women who now stood staring dully at him. 'This is …' he repeated, but a new groan was heard, then suddenly there was a flurry of limbs at the back of the group and the women all jumped aside, pointing at a flailing figure on the ground.

'She's fittin', sir! For God's sake help us, sir, it's the evil thing you brought in last night has possessed her!' Williams and his assistants rushed to the back of the room to witness this phenomenon, the women closing round them. Surely, the woman was possessed. Her teeth were bared in a fiendish grin and she growled like a dog. Williams put out his hand to hush the bystanders, and drew a Bible from his inner pocket. He placed one hand on the woman's shoulder, and, raising the other to the heavens, clutching the Bible, began to call on the Lord to free this suffering soul.

It was some time before he realised that Clemmie was gone.

* * * * *

The letter came about a week after Clemmie had vanished. It was pushed under the door, but when Bethan lifted the latch and ran into the street there was no one there.

Someone else had written it, that much was certain. Clemmie could neither read nor write. The heavy scrawl looked like impenetrable hieroglyphics. But something told Bethan that she shouldn't seek help with the strange writing. Clemmie was in trouble and she must decipher this herself.

So, late after her work at the Lamb and Flag, Bethan sat down with a candle-end and pored over the scrap of paper.

'Bethan, my Dear Companion and Truest Friend,' it began. 'I beg thee do not tell a soul but I am gone with Spanish Jem and Dublin Dandy who promised Limping Sal to see me right. Do not be Afeared for me my True Friend as I know thou art. If we do not meet again in this world why surely we shall in the Next,

I am,

your own Friend,

Clementina, her mark X.

Limping Sal says that the Swansea boys told her that Jack Morgan has taken the Shilling and gone to be a sojer.'

Bethan stared at the paper. She smoothed it down and retraced every letter of the last sentence with her finger. Then she raised it to her lips and kissed it.

Chapter Eighteen

Bethan opened the heavy old door with difficulty. Since Patrick had kicked it open it had to be lifted over the uneven brick floor to gain access to the room. Once in, she heaved it back in place and jammed a heavy log against it, braced under the cross-piece of the door at one end and lodged in a gap in the brick flooring at the other. That should keep him out.

At last, she was alone. It was past twelve, and a bitter night, but instead of falling straight into bed in her clothes as she might have done any other night, Bethan knelt at the grate, and taking a tinder box and flint from her pocket, began to strike a light. She struck and struck, blowing with concentrated ardour until at last the blessed flame came forth. The tiny, reluctant fire was coaxed with small dry twigs, and finally it was offered a small log and two pieces of coal, courtesy of the Lamb and Flag. This was reckless extravagance, but she didn't care. She must think.

A little water was set to boil in her one cooking utensil, an iron pot with a crooked handle, and a twist of tea was put ready to throw into the pot as it boiled.

Bethan pulled a ragged quilt from the bed and wrapped it round her shoulders. Curled on the floor, she rested an arm on the battered wooden chair and lay her head in the crook of it. Staring into the fire, she was able to feel that long-ago warmth, that scarce-remembered comfort re-kindled in the crackling of the flames as they sizzled round the log. Tiny insects appeared from its cracks and scurried hither and thither, whilst a lumbering woodlouse rolled itself into a ball and fell to the ashes beneath. She and Jack had sat like this together. The heat on her cheeks brought back the memory with a surge. Surely, as children, they had sat like this, late at night, in their night-shirts, and someone who loved them had been with them. It must have been Mam, she thought. Now she had learned how to comfort herself. Someone, once, had shown her comfort and nurturing; and somehow she had reached within herself and found it.

A fierce sizzling snatched her attention. The pot was boiling. Deftly Bethan emptied the ounce of tea into the water, and holding the iron handle with the hem of her skirt, moved the pot to the embers at the edge of the fire to brew.

Her fair skin was reddened by the heat. The contours of her face were smooth and unspoilt, but her eyes under their half-closed lids concealed the greatest trouble. There was a sadness, a loss apparent in these unguarded moments which would be hidden again on the morrow.

As she sat down again she gave a gasp, and tentatively lay her hand on her belly. She had felt a fluttering, the tiniest bubbling motion. A new thought began to grow in her mind, as faint and hesitant as these movements inside her. Perhaps this would make a difference. Although she was without Jack, she would not be alone.

She tried to work out how long it was since she had seen her brother. Eight, perhaps ten years ago; it was hard to be sure. There had been little to distinguish one year from another, until this one, that is.

So much had happened within the space of six months. First Siôn, and Mair and the boys. She visualised them at this moment, amid the night-time rustlings and breathings of the tiny cottage full of sleepers. The fire would still be glowing, and the acrid smoke of furze would enwrap them all. Siôn would be warm amongst his brothers, she thought; or maybe by now he had married Marged. She had faced this thought many times before, but still it sat sadly in her heart, like Mair herself. Absent-mindedly she fingered her temple and brow. The bruises were still there. Would Siôn have beaten her like that? It seemed hard to believe.

Reaching inside her bodice Bethan brought out the crumpled slip of paper bearing news of her brother. She smoothed it against her knee, then held it up to catch the light. 'The Swansea boys.' So he must have gone to Swansea then. And to be a soldier! The thought sent a shudder through her. The country was in a turmoil. The uprising last November! The working men had risen up, as Siôn had promised they would, and so many were dead and wounded. The Lamb and Flag was brimming with intrigue – how could Lovell, Frost and Williams, and the other martyrs of the New-port Rising be rescued? Meetings were being held, funds raised for the defence of the men and the sustenance of their families. People were coming and going at all hours. And Jack a soldier!

Bethan poured the strong tea into a cracked china cup she had rescued from the scullery of the Flag. She cradled it in her palms and inhaled its bitterness, then began to sip the scalding fluid. Without cream or sugar to mellow its flavour the drink sent a shudder through her body, but the stimulants and warmth soon began to soothe and enliven her.

Clemmie had always loved a cup of tea, she reflec-ted. Without her the room was so silent, so empty. She was like a sister found, then lost. Bethan looked down at the tea-leaves wreathing the sides of the cup.

Perhaps she should ask Grandmother Thomas next-door-but-one if she could read in them Clemmie's fortune. But somehow she thought it were better not to.

The rumours had gone round the town on Christmas Day as quickly as the wild fire of Christmas Eve. Clemmie had jumped from the bridge, some said; others that she was drunk, and had fallen. Some said she'd been on the ship with Black Sam and he'd thrown her overboard, having ravished her like the devil he was. Her baby will be as dark as Auld Nick, you'll see, they warned. Black Sam had been arrested by the constable as an accessory to attempted suicide, but after a week they had to let him go. It was obvious that Clemmie was still alive and kicking.

A smile came to Bethan's lips. The tale of Clemmie's daring escape had been regaled a thousand times by now, she'd be bound. The girl's feats were reaching mythical proportions. She had cast a spell, some said, and caused a poor woman to go down into a fit; she had leapt through the window like one possessed, or bounded over Mr Williams's head like a Chinese acrobat.

But what was certain was that Clemmie was gone with the tramping folk, the cadgers; and that they would see her right, as she had claimed. Bethan thought of Clemmie as she had last seen her, on the day after the failed abortion. Listless and frightened, she had seemed to shrink back into childhood, lost without her mother and the glow of Ben Finney's attention. But Clemmie had not given up. When the time came to show her mettle she had done so. Would Clemmie have taken this, she wondered, as her fingers wandered again to her bruises? I think not, was her reply to herself. And neither shall I.

* * * * *

Patrick usually sat with the crowd of radical men who frequented the Lamb and Flag. Bethan was conscious of him as she pushed through the crowds of drinkers, carrying mugs of ale and running hither and thither at the beck and call of every customer.

Tonight the Chartists' excitement was infectious, and soon a crowd had gathered round to hear their discussion. The news had come through only that morning from Newport: the three leaders of the uprising were to be executed! The jury's recommendation for mercy was unlikely to be successful. The judge had warned John Frost, Zephaniah Williams and William Jones to prepare themselves for the cruel death of all traitors. What could be done? The agitation in the manufacturing towns and great cities the length and breadth of England and Wales was such that an execution must spark further confrontation. Already the prosecution witnesses had received threats for their part in the leaders' indictment.

The drinkers fell quiet as Dai Richards's voice was heard above the hubbub of the bar. He spoke forcefully, his head back, characteristically declaiming his words as if addressing a larger crowd. 'If this goes ahead, and those three men are murdered in cold blood, by the so-called agents of law and order, what clearer emblem can we have? They can murder, they can use physical force: and why? Because they have God on their side, is it? No, it's because they have the army, they have the weapons, they have all the power that comes with owning and controlling the very livelihoods of the people. Only when the people who do the work have some control over their ability to put food in their own mouths – that's when that power will end!'

This was dangerous stuff, and some of the country folk grinned nervously amid the roars of agreement.

Even the established Chartists were inclined to be nervous. There had been much talk of Government agents stirring up trouble, or infiltrating Chartist lodges to gather information.

Many were relieved and murmured approval when the elegant Dublin tones of John Healey were heard. 'Surely, brother, it's time to give up such talk? The movement is crushed. It's wild talk indeed to encourage these good people –' he indicated the crowd of listeners in the dull gold light of the lanterns and fire '– to think of risking their lives when everything is in shreds around us. Better surely to retreat and lie low ...'

A groundswell of opposition began to make itself heard. Patrick O'Bryan made to speak, but was cut short with a motion from Bryn Taylor, who in his more measured way recounted what he had heard about Frost's part in the uprising, and a lively discussion ensued on what had gone wrong. Was it Frost's fault for losing his nerve at the last moment? What had happened to the men from Pontypool? Different versions of the story had filtered through to Carmarthen as a trickle of wounded men had fled back to their rural homes to escape arrest.

'Twenty-two of ours dead, boys,' said Bryn. 'Murdered – young and old, working men like ourselves. And what for? For the crime of asking for some dignity; of asking for the right to participate in the rule of the country that treats us like slaves. For that crime, some of those men were left writhing in their own blood for hours without assistance.'

'Yes, indeed they were, my friend!' rejoined Healey. 'And do you want to see more good men mown down in their prime, and hundreds more hounded like dogs, while our leaders listen to the carpenters building their own scaffold! Now is the time to withdraw, wait, and regroup – then plan a new campaign through which the force of moral justice can triumph!'

'Away with your moral force!' Patrick's voice cut through the barrage of murmurs and jeers which greeted Healey's sally. His smooth, deep voice embraced every listener with its assurance. 'Morals never won a war! Whoever heard of a trampled peasant begging a soldier, "Oh sir, I do not think you should kill me, for 'twould be immoral, indeed it would!" And the soldier says, "Be Jaysus, my friend, you're right" and helps the fellow to his feet and dusts him down!' Roars of laughter greeted this flight of fancy and Patrick pressed his advantage.

'No, my friends, morals never impressed murderers, nor kings – nor queens – nor Prime Ministers. Only action impresses.

'What must we do to help the leaders who now face the scaffold? We must make it clear that to take that step would be the gravest folly the government could commit – we must stir the feelings of the people, hold meetings and rallies, and take the people's views up to Parliament itself! And if that doesn't work we must plan, and work, and plan and work – for years if need be – until we are ready to rise up again. Only this time we'll do the job properly, and that'll mean you my friend –' he pointed into the crowd – 'and you, and you – it'll mean all of us!'

Patrick raised his mug. 'To the Six Points! Remember the Newport martyrs!'

A roar of agreement went up as the men drank deeply and gathered around Patrick in congratulation. Healey smiled and quietly pulled a long draught of ale.

By now the business of the bar was at a standstill as the crowd of market-day drinkers thronged around the hub of the discussion. Farmers and labourers stood against the walls, sucking their long-stemmed clay pipes, their stolid faces giving little away. Livelier denizens of the town leant on each other's shoulders, interjecting an agreement, an aye or nay, and applauded loudly when the call for a collection of funds went up, to be accounted for by Landlord Jones on behalf of the Lodge.

Even Bethan was free to pause in her work. With a handful of pewter pots ready to go back to the scullery she stood among the listeners. At last she was beginning to understand what this all meant. The bitterness and anger expressed by the men, their disappointment in the failure of the uprising, symbolised not an ending, but a beginning. The shambles of Newport had done one thing above all others – it had expressed a possibility. Now that had been done, things would never be quite the same again. Working people had seen a vision, far-off and small, of what could be done. And the government too, they had seen it, only to them it looked like hell.

Later that evening she felt a slight pressure on her waist. It was Patrick. Leaning against the wall he pulled her against him. His smile was rueful, his eyes flattering as he gently traced the bruises down her brow and cheek with his elegant hand.

'Let me see you later?' he whispered, his smile ingratiating as he pushed a coin into her hand. She pulled away and moved back into the crowd. The smile died on his lips. He caught the eye of Henry Jones, who stood at the back of the room, his arms folded. There was something in that look which made Patrick turn quickly away.

* * * * *

Patrick stood against the wall outside the pub. The debate was still going on inside, but he needed to feel the cool air. He let his head roll back against the rough stone. The street was dim, with only the light from the windows of the Lamb and Flag for illumination. He could see a few wavering stars up above.

He was feeling increasingly nervous. The way Henry Jones had looked at him. Did he suspect? It could only be a matter of time now before someone started to put two and two together. Then he would have to clear out for good. Once had been enough. He'd asked one too many questions in the days after the Newport rising. He thought his method had been foolproof. He'd joined a lodge in Blaina, attended once a month or so, then after the rising he'd moved lodge on pretence of a change of employment. He'd bumped into this man and that man: How did you get on, lad? Who went, then? Where were the wounded, and so on. But he'd asked one too many. The cry had gone up that there was a Government agent in the vicinity, and he'd been dragged, kicked and punched and thrown into a filthy culvert. He was lucky to have escaped with his life.

If it wasn't for the payment he'd been promised, Patrick told himself, he would have packed it in long ago. But without it he couldn't pay off his debts. And if he couldn't pay off his debts this time, and his father got to hear of it, he'd be disinherited. The damned agent in Dublin had picked his man with unerring skill, he had to give him that.

Something else was eating him, too. The girl. He hadn't meant to hit her, goddammit. It's just she was there when he had been filled with rage and humiliation. There was something filthy about the work, he knew that even if he didn't voice it to himself. He twisted suddenly in an impatient movement. He had the gifts to dazzle: he had addressed meetings, befriended these most sincere of men, and meant every word he said at the time he said it. And yet it was all simultaneously an artifice. He could mimic comradeship, but never really experience it.

It was the same with love. He had charmed women from the most refined drawing-rooms, and enchanted them with his protestations of love. He had seduced servant girls and even made this poorest of waifs feel like a princess. None of it had been insincere – and none of it true, either.

But his sense of discomfort grew as he thought of what he had done to Bethan. She wasn't a rough creature and her eyes had shone with admiration of him. He wouldn't have beaten a dog the way he'd hit her. And he needed to feel her warmth against him and her head nestled in his breast. That had made him feel real.

* * * * *

It was well after midnight when Bethan slipped out of the scullery-door of the public house. Henry's wife Betty had given her a dish of leftovers to take home with her, a little cold beef, some cheese and the end of a loaf. Clutching this under her shawl she began to move swiftly along the pitch-dark street, her footsteps ringing against the flagstones in the iron chill of the January night.

She started as a figure moved from the shadows of a doorway and fell into step beside her. She knew at once it was Patrick. They strode together in a fierce silence while Bethan's nerves tensed with the effort of reading every sign that emanated from him. His breathing – light or hard? Was he looking at her? Was he beginning to walk faster, or was she? Was he going to grab her at any moment?

Instead of the sudden gesture she dreaded, she felt a gentle movement as his hand sought hers. She allowed

210

his long warm fingers to enfold her hand, which lay small and unresponsive in his. She felt him relax, and almost expected a joke or a soft laugh just as it used to be. But he was chastened by what he had done. Her resolve stiffened. He thought he could get away with it again.

Once inside the small, cold room, with a candle lit, Bethan placed her precious supper down rather covetously with the cloth still over it. She had no intention of sharing it. Patrick reached out his hand and made to pull her onto his knee, but she pulled away and stood in front of him.

'What do you want?' His eyes widened in surprise at her question and he looked momentarily uncertain.

'Why, you of course, my darling girl. I want to kiss better those bruises on your brow and ...' As he made to rise towards her she said harshly,

'Don't bother, Patrick O'Bryan. That's the last time you do that to me. And you can take back your filthy shilling!' She held out the small silver coin. Her eyes glittered with unspent tears, but the set of her mouth was new to Patrick. Her lips were compressed with bitter anger, her jaw thrust forward. He seemed to be looking at a different woman to the Bethan he had known before.

He had thought her a pliant young girl. After her initial bewilderment she had been delightfully trusting and wide-eyed as she clung to his arm. He had enjoyed seducing her in the knowledge that she was worthless, a little thing flung in his way as it were by fate. Like a thousand other maidservants, she was destined to provide sexual services without question as she provided every other kind of service.

Seeing her stand before him now, her arm outstretched, she had transmuted. There was a power there. He had seen that same power in the rough

n of the valleys, seen them confront the overman
drunken husband on a Saturday night. He had
seen it too close for comfort on the night they had
attacked him. He didn't have to take it, of course. All
he had to do was stand up and belt her across the
mouth. But somehow he knew that tonight it wouldn't
stop there.

'Take it!' she hissed, her voice a cold command. Her
eyes were fixed on his now. Slowly, he lifted his hand
and plucked the coin from her palm. She turned at
once and took the plate of cold food whilst he fumbled
the coin into his waistcoat pocket. When he turned
towards her again she was sitting on the bed, wolfing
the food. She tore strips from the beef and folded them
into her mouth, chewing noisily. She pulled lumps from
the dry bread and pushed them after the beef. She
saved the cheese till last, then bit indelicately into the
yellow slab without regard to Patrick.

Her meal finished, Bethan turned towards Patrick.
'Let's get one thing clear,' she said. 'I'm not your whore.
There are plenty of those around here if you want one.
I'm not your rag doll to be kissed and petted one minute
and kicked around the room the next. If you want me
to be your girl you treat me decently.' Her clear, light
gaze seemed to penetrate his eyes as she continued.
'And if you ever lay a finger on me again I'll kill you.'

It was preposterous. A sarcastic laugh began to rise
up in his throat. How dare she! No woman had ever
spoken to him like that, let alone this little scullion. But
the laugh died before it reached his lips. Her determination had made her somehow larger in his estimation.

'And by the way, you left this here last time you
came.' She held up a small booklet with a dark blue
cover. It bore the legend 'Working Men's Association.
Blaina Lodge.' Handwritten with a flourish was the

member's name, John Hanrahan, and neatly listed inside were the weekly payments of his twopence. But for some weeks there were gaps, then another week would show a back payment to cover the missing weeks. 'Must belong to a friend of yours?'

Patrick scrutinised the expression on Bethan's lovely face. Was there a hint of irony in those eyes? Really, the girl was cleverer than he thought. Taking the booklet, he muttered something about an old friend who had moved to the valleys and had recently been in town. Then he slipped to his knees in front of Bethan as she sat on the low mattress. Grasping her hand, he placed it to his lips, then held it against his cheek. Then he moved onto the bed and put his arms about her. Lifting her chin he looked into her eyes.

'I may be a rogue,' he said, 'but I swear to God I'll never harm you again.' Gently his mouth touched hers and he crushed her tightly to him. They lay down on the bed, their faces touching.

In her heart she knew he was worthless. But he was there, and his arms were warm.

* * * * *

It was a full twenty hours later before Patrick was awake and ready to rejoin the drinkers at the Lamb and Flag. He intended to ask Mrs Jones to provide him with a good meal to revive his flagging spirits. There was not a scrap of food to be had in Bethan's lodgings, nor could he send her to bring him something from outside as she had long since slipped out to go to work.

After lighting a candle he looked around the pitiful room and saw just how little Bethan had. Her one spare dress hung on a hook on the wall, with a battered straw bonnet she kept for summer hanging over it by a tarnished blue ribbon. There was a small bundle of per-

inen wrapped up in a shawl, and on the sill of
ʒ small window lay a broken-toothed bone comb.
ɪne poor girl hadn't even a hairbrush, he reflected,
thinking of the finery he had seen in other women's
bedrooms. He thought guiltily again of the bruises on
her fair skin. He wasn't sure when he would be back
this way again. He had to go and see his uncle John
Healey to find out whether any instructions had come
through. Perhaps he should leave her some money.

Patrick rummaged in his waistcoat pockets. Surely
he had a guinea in there somewhere. He began pulling
the pockets out, and there was a clatter as a silver coin
fell to the floor. It was the shilling Bethan had returned
to him so scornfully the previous night. Not his whore
indeed! When he had located the guinea, he laid it
carefully on the narrow mantelshelf, then placed the
shilling on top of it.

As he sat on the low mattress to pull on his boots he
began to recall the incidents of the night before more
clearly. An image of Bethan holding up a little blue
book came into his mind ... John Hanrahan! He began
to overturn the mattress, tearing away the ragged
blankets as he searched for the book. He pulled up the
scrap of rag rug which adorned the stone-flagged floor,
tore down the dress and felt through the fabric for any
pockets where the document might be stored. Finally he
tore open the bundle of linen, where he found a piece
of paper, laboriously written with the message from
Clemmie.

'"Gone for a sojer!" He did so, until the life became
too hard for him,' muttered Patrick, stuffing the letter
back roughly into its hiding place.

Angrily he yanked open the rickety door and cast a
look back into the darkened room. He would have to
get the book back from her somehow.

When he entered the Lamb and Flag the room was quieter than it had been the previous evening, but still it exuded a warmth and comfort far removed from the chill of Bethan's lodging. The smell of tobacco and ale and the warm firelight promised the pleasures of male companionship and Patrick instinctively relaxed. He seated himself on the tall wooden settle next to the fireplace, where no doubt Mrs Jones would attend to him.

Looking over to the doorway leading to the kitchen and domestic apartments Patrick was just in time to catch Mrs Jones's white face before it darted back into the shadows. Puzzled, he called for service, conscious of the few other drinkers watching him over their mugs of ale.

Suddenly the rear door opened and Henry Jones stood behind the table which acted as the bar. Jones was a small but stocky man, his face round and rendered intelligent by its large clear eyes. His look was hostile, but Patrick did not notice, as he began to greet Jones in jovial fashion.

'Good evening, landlord. Can I trouble you for a jug of your finest ale and whatever victuals your good lady can find for me at this hour? To find oneself famished at the table of plenty is indeed good fortune, is it not?' he continued pleasantly.

Jones's expression shifted as he came forward into the room. Now he seemed friendly, hospitable, the most civilised of landlords.

'Perhaps, Mr O'Bryan, you would care to enter our private apartments to discuss with Mrs Jones what would best suit your appetite?' There might have been a trace of irony in his tone but Patrick was unaware as he accepted the invitation and stepped into the darkened passage.

'Go forward, Mr O'Bryan, a welcome awaits you

n,' urged Jones, as Patrick fumbled with the door
. A shove in the small of his back propelled him
into the candlelit parlour where he found himself
confronted by six grim-faced men, seated to face the
doorway. Foremost among them were Dai Richards and
Bryn Taylor.

Patrick turned on his heel as soon as he had entered
the room, but found his exit blocked by Jones's sturdy
form. Turning slowly back, Patrick spoke in his most
assured voice.

'Come now, friends. What is this play-acting? I'm a
hard-working man and I've come here for some sustenance' – he risked a smile – 'both physical and spiritual.
And what's this I'm faced with?'

'Indeed, you are a hard worker, and that's a fact.' It
was Dai Richards who spoke, a dangerous smile on his
lips. 'Show him, Iron-Hand.'

Bryn Thomas slipped his thick scarred hand inside
his jacket and pulled out the small blue book. The men
scanned Patrick's face for some sign of recognition or
fear but found none. His composure was absolute as he
half-turned to Jones.

'For God's sake, man, I come here for sustenance and
I end up with a dumb show. Tell them to spit it out,
whatever it is, then I can go about my business.'

Richards made to move towards Patrick but Bryn
Taylor placed a cautionary hand on the his forearm.

'It's your business that we'd like to talk to you about,'
began Taylor in his calm neutral tones. 'Just what
exactly is the nature of your business?'

Patrick's response seemed joking, accompanied by a
smile, as if to maintain the illusion that these men, his
drinking companions of the night before, were his
friends. 'I'll be damn'd if I'll talk to you ruffians about
my business!'

216

'I would if I were you,' interjected Jones drily.

Patrick looked around the room at the faces that confronted him in the dim light. There was Richards, his mouth a hard line of scarcely restrained anger; Taylor, his glance more enigmatic, but his brawny arms crossed over his chest; and of the other four, three stared impassively while one, head bowed, cracked his knuckles repeatedly in the momentary silence.

'Wh … What am I charged with? I demand to know, if I am to be required to tell you my business.' Patrick's voice faltered almost imperceptibly, but the darting movements of his eyes betrayed his fear at last.

Richards could not be restrained any longer. He leapt to his feet, pulling a paper from his pocket and waving it under Patrick's nose.

'This is what you're charged with, you filthy traitor! You're a Government agent, don't try to deny it – we've got your description here, circulated to every lodge in South Wales.' He snatched the blue book from Taylor's hand. 'And this book is the proof! You're calling yourself John Hanrahan in Blaina, and Liam Brady in Tredegar, and for all I know the Queen of bloody Sheba somewhere else.'

'I don't know what you're talking about.' Patrick's voice seemed forceful now, but contained the slightest tremble against Richards's roar. 'You men know me. My uncle is John Healey, the printer. I'm here to assist him in improving his printing works. I have to go up to London to look at other presses and order new machinery.'

'Sure, and I know ye.' The man with bowed head looked up as he spoke. His eyes were forget-me-not blue, dark-lashed in a hungry Irish face. 'And aren't ye John Hanrahan as sure as I'm sitting here? Don't ye remember how ye gave me your tuppence every week,

hen a sixpence when ye'd missed a few weeks?
'e surely were sorry when ye went away, and
...out so much as a word to anyone.'

Patrick's gaze focused uncertainly on the blue-eyed man, who smiled and resumed cracking his knuckles. With a jerk Patrick threw himself at Jones in an attempt to reach the doorway. He found himself encased in Jones's strong embrace, then thrown backwards to Richards who gripped him by the coat collar and spun him around to back him against the wall.

'I think we'll go outside. We don't want to mess up Mrs Jones's parlour, now, do we lads?'

As Patrick was bundled through the back scullery out into the courtyard Jones caught sight of his wife peering through from the bar.

'And don't forget what he did to that poor lass!' she called in a loud whisper, knowing that Bethan was out of the way serving in the front bar.

'We won't,' said Jones grimly. 'And neither will he, after we've finished with him.'

Chapter Nineteen

It had taken Annie three days after the battle at the Westgate Hotel to find Siôn. She had been taken into a safe house in Newport where she stayed for the first night in the attic room with several wounded men. Weak from shock and lack of food, she had lain on the rough board floor listening to the sounds of special constables patrolling the streets and enquiring at the doors whether any strangers had been seen.

The Chartists who had taken her in had fed her and implored her to stay longer. They were well-off people, the husband a lawyer who sympathised with the people's cause. She could be their maid, they said – they could pass her off as a distant relation from the country. But Annie was frantic for news of Siôn. Rumours abounded as to who had been killed and how many. Some men had lain for hours dying in the street in front of the hotel. Others had crawled away, nursing their wounds, only to die in strangers' arms or in alley-ways and fields.

The following evening as dusk fell, Annie crept into the back yard of the house which had given her refuge. Over her man's breeches she now wore an old skirt belonging to the mistress of the house, and she carried a bundle containing bread, cheese and a bottle of wine and water, all given to her by her well-wishers and wrapped in a shawl. Which way to go? After all, he could be anywhere. If he was alive, and able to move, he wasn't going to be walking along the highway. He would have taken to the paths which criss-crossed the fields and wooded hills north of Newport, and then, reaching the wild terrain of the valleys, would have found his way across the tops of the mountains by joining up with the local lads who knew every crag and gulley. She couldn't do that. But, as a woman, she could walk the road. For once, curiously, she had more freedom than a man.

* * * * *

By the afternoon of the second day of her journey Annie scarcely knew where she was. Somehow she had missed the road to return the way she had come with the marchers. She was just having to gauge from the silhouettes of the hills that she was going due north. She must find somewhere to shelter by nightfall.

Ahead of her she saw a tumbledown cottage by the side of the road. No light escaped from the small shuttered window, but a thin spire of smoke rose from the hole in the roof which served instead of a chimney. With an eye on the rain-clouds massed above her, Annie decided to take the risk, and raised her hand to tap on the rickety door.

Furtive noises sounded within, scuffling and whispering. Then the door was drawn back a few inches.

'Who are you,' growled a man's voice, 'and what is your business?' Annie could see dark eyes glinting suspiciously through the crack.

'I beg your pardon, friend,' she began. Her voice faltered a little at the man's tone. But she had started and had better continue. 'I am a travelling woman in search of lodgings for the night …'

With a startling abruptness the door was slammed to and more furious whispering could be heard behind it. It scraped open again, and a withered old woman stood in front of Annie. She appraised the younger woman.

With her man's cap, and the old shawl wrapped over the over-large jacket, Annie looked like a cadger.

'We've no lodgings for the likes of you,' said the old woman, beginning to close the door. Anger surged inside Annie and she stepped forward suddenly and jammed her foot against the planks.

'What do you mean *the likes of me*?' she demanded. Exhaustion and hunger made her reckless.

Alarm sprang into the old woman's face and she thrust hard against the door to shut it. Annie threw her shoulder to it and forced it back again.

'Whore!' croaked the woman.

'Get you gone!' shouted her husband.

Annie continued to resist, using her body weight to jam the door open. She wheedled now, desperate for information on where she could get shelter.

'Please help me friends. Where can I lay my head this rainy night?' Then, risking all, she added, 'Have you seen any of the Chartist brethren returning this way?'

There was a slight release in the pressure behind the door, and a pause as her antagonists consulted each other urgently.

'Who wants to know?'

'Why, I do, of course, you silly old she-goat. My husband's a lodge-man,' she lied wildly, 'of the Vulcan in Merthyr. He marched to Newport with Zephaniah's men, but hasn't been seen since, and I'm out of my mind with worry, and me with three little ones ...'

Slowly the door opened and both old people stood in front of her. The hovel behind them was lit only by the glimmer of a smoky furze fire.

'You can't come in here,' said the man. 'The soldiers have been here already.' He pointed up the road towards the north. 'That way,' he said. 'That's the way to go. Four, five miles up there, you'll find a barn by the roadside. Look there. Some of them have been there. That's all we can do for you.'

* * * * *

The road was rough and unmetalled. The heavy rains had taken their toll and great potholes and furrows churned its surface. Night was falling now and the leaden skies held only a faint light in the west. The road became darker, its irregularities merely patches of deeper black against its murky surface, and Annie herself was scarcely distinguishable amidst the tones of grey and black which gathered around her. As she trudged painstakingly onwards her thoughts were racing ahead. What would become of them both? There was a hunt going on, she did not doubt, the length and breadth of the valleys to find the culprits.

How could she explain to her parents that she had been away with Siôn? In fact, it was scarcely worth returning there at all. But where else was she to go? At least she knew that if Siôn were still alive he would get word to her there somehow. She felt a tightening in her chest at the thought of him. She longed for him. His strong body, his good humour, the courage and mad bravery he had shown in their last moments together: was she never to see him again? No one else could so fill her mind with thoughts and ideas that satisfied her craving to see, to understand, to know.

Suddenly a tiny noise caught her attention, a scraping sound breaking through the buffeting of the wind. Raising her eyes from their scrutiny of the road surface, she gasped as a figure leapt the dry-stone wall and landed in the road just ahead of her.

'Good evening, sweetheart.' The voice was slurred. The man stood four-square in front of her, blocking her way.

'Let me pass, if you please,' responded Annie tersely, making to dodge the stocky figure. He moved sideways as she did so and caught hold of her arm. His breath filled her nostrils in a warm alcoholic blast. 'Let go of me!' she screamed and pulled away, running as best she could over the muddy stones of the roadway. She felt a huge blow between her shoulders as the man's full weight hit them and his arms clamped tight around her. She kicked and struggled as he heaved her through a gateway into a barn that stood by the roadside.

A candle-end guttered perilously on a cross-beam. Someone had set up camp there. The man flung Annie down into the hay and snatched the cloth bag out of her arms, greedily searching for food. Finding the stale end of a loaf he tossed it aside, then uncorked the bottle with his teeth. Sniffing its contents he grinned at Annie, then began to swig, fixing his eye on her. He was a swarthy man, unshaven, and with the walnut complexion of the vagrant. Throwing the bottle down, he stood over Annie.

'I only wanted yer grub or yer money. But as you're a fighting sort of a gal, how about a kiss and a cuddle?' With this he dropped to his knees beside her, and as Annie began to rise up and struggle he pushed her down into the hay.

Annie turned away her face as the man's mouth sought hers. She was repulsed by his fumblings but a terror froze her body so that her limbs seemed leaden and unable to force him off her as she wanted to do.

Dimly she sensed a movement behind him, then there was a rush of air and a cracking sound as a heavy boot met the side of her attacker's head and lifted him to crash against the wall of the barn. She saw the vagrant's eyes nearly bursting from his skull, his teeth bared in a grimace of fear as a wild-haired man held the muzzle of a long gun beneath his chin.

'Get out of here, you filthy piece of shite!' Siôn released his victim who grabbed his few belongings, and darting a look at his assailant and at Annie, scrambled out of the low doorway.

Siôn stood panting, holding his left arm at the shoulder. Slowly he raised his eyes to look at her.

'Is it really you?' he said softly. She rose up from the hay, wisps clinging to her hair and clothes. Gently she laid a trembling hand against his cheek, then stroking his long tangled hair she lifted her mouth to his and kissed him. Siôn closed his eyes, and a deep sigh escaped his lips. Suddenly she felt him waver against her, and as his full weight met her shoulder she staggered backwards, and helped him to the ground before he fell.

There was a little of the wine and water left in the bottle, and when she had revived him with drink and bread he began to talk. He had managed to escape during the confusion in the immediate aftermath of the shooting. He could find neither Gwyn nor Annie and so he had left to make his way over the fields and rough pathways during the hours of darkness. Sometimes he was alone, sometimes with others, once or twice calling at the back doors of cottages and public houses where sympathisers were known to live. They had given him bread, and an old woman had bathed and dressed the wound on his arm. It was only skin deep, but it hurt and drained his energy.

Lying together in the hay, they fell into a warm drowsiness. It was the first time each had felt the other's body in such unrestrained closeness. Soon the fears and darkness outside their fragrant cocoon melted away into nothing, and all that existed was the other's presence.

Siôn's caresses, tentative at first, soon became impatient of the thick, unwieldy garments Annie wore. With trembling fingers he struggled to open the buttons of the thick shirt, and pulling it down from her shoulder he began to kiss her ears and neck while she lay as if adrift in a sea of sensations, new and strange but not to be resisted. He wrenched the shirt from her waistband and lifted it to find and kiss her white breasts. He pulled up the bedraggled, damp skirt and undid the incongruous breeches, laughing a little as he did so, while Annie lay still and alert, compliant to his touch. He kissed her white belly and she moaned, a low sound which enchanted his ears as he undressed her. With an impatient movement he unlaced and pulled off one of her heavy boots, then the other, and then removed the trousers. Now he could see her pale thighs above the thick woollen stockings.

In a moment he had entered her body. After her first indrawn breath she had relaxed, and as he moved back and forth he could feel the stirrings of response in her. 'Cariad, cariad,' he murmured. 'My wife, my only one.'

* * * * *

Annie's face as she looked up at Siôn was different somehow than he had ever seen it before. There was a pallor there which it never used to have, but that was only to be expected after the pain and troubles of the last few months. There was something more, however. The fine, speckled green eyes had lost their optimism. Instead she looked up at him with a vulnerability and unmistakable, child-like appeal.

'What is it, cariad?' he whispered, touching her cheek with his hand. He stood in the doorway of the dirty little room she was sharing with another girl from the ironworks. She had not been welcomed home when she returned, muddied and dishevelled, after her seven-day absence in November. Elishah had been willing to listen, but not Nan. She had physically chased the girl out of the house.

The tears welled in Annie's eyes. For answer she took his hand and guided it to her belly. He didn't catch her meaning at first. Her body seemed as spare as ever beneath the rough apron and thick skirts.

'I've fallen for a baby, what do you think?' She snatched her hand away from his in an instant of irritation. 'That's it then, isn't it? They'll never have me back now.' Now her tears began to flow and as she stood with one hand on the wall and leant her forehead against it, sobs shook through her body. Siôn stood uncertain, staring at the slender back in its dull brown workaday dress, the dark curly hair twisted into a braided rope at the nape of her neck. He was to blame for this. She was alone, away from her family. Her fearlessness had evaporated, her boyish bravado. She, and only she, would have to pay the price for this. He could walk away, but no matter how far she walked, she would still carry this burden.

'Come here, girl.' He turned her round to him so that her head lay against his shoulder. She was reluctant, tight-lipped, her eyes closed and her body rigid and unyielding. It was as if she had closed off her senses to him, trying to gather strength against this assault on the order of her physical world.

'We only did it the once,' she said bitterly. 'When I think of some girls I know … If there was any justice …'

Siôn snorted. 'Well, there isn't, that's one thing you can be sure of. Besides, the girls who go with anyone know what they're doing. It's the good lasses, like you, that get caught. Now then.' He held her away from him. 'Wipe your tears. You'd better make yourself presentable, if we're going to see your parents.'

226

She pulled away, her swollen face full of suspicion. 'I'm never going back there! Not after what she did to me. And now this – are you mad? She'll kick me down the street! The neighbours'll love that.'

Siôn was moving round the room, pouring water into a basin and finding a clean cloth to use as a towel. He pushed her towards the bowl on the rickety table in front of the fireplace.

'Wash yourself, now, or do you want me to do it for you?' He dipped the corner of the cloth into the cold water. Annie snatched the rag from him and began to bathe her face while he found her one good shawl and the bonnet which had suffered a battering since she had left Miss Falk's employ.

When she was ready and turned towards him, her face had steadied into her old expression. She was defiant, not to be pushed around.

'You'd better tell me what you're planning this time,' she said. 'I've been on one too many mystery marches with you.' She sat down on the bed, as if an explanation were due and she was going to be comfortable to hear it.

He smiled at this return of her customary awkwardness.

'This one should be a lot easier … or perhaps not,' – catching her glance – 'depending on your point of view. We're going to march straight up to their door, straight inside, then I'm going to ask Elishah to marry us at the chapel.'

Annie's head snapped towards him. 'Oh, are you now? And what makes you think I want to marry you?' Her tone was sarcastic now. 'Poor little ruined woman, is it, has to be rescued? Let me remind you it was you who did this to me!'

'I don't recall you saying no!' Siôn's eyes were blazing and he turned angrily away. Here he was trying to do the right thing, and this was the response he got. He could walk out of here now and leave her to it. Then she'd be just another girl who'd managed to get a baby but not a man. He glanced at her sideways on. She sat stiffly on the bed, her chin tilted and her lips clamped. She looked small and vulnerable but it was quite clear that she didn't see herself as shop-soiled goods, to be taken at a bargain price because they weren't quite what you wanted.

He pulled the rough chair in front of the bed, and sat down, legs astride. He leant forward and took her hands.

'Annie Taylor. Ever since the moment I first saw you, speaking at the Vulcan, I knew you were the bravest, finest girl in this town. If we were married, why ...' His voice seemed to tremble and deepen, and Annie turned her gaze towards him in surprise. 'If we were married, it would surely be a marriage of true friends – a marriage fitted for two people who have risked all for liberty!'

Her face, at first solemn, broke into a gentle, gratified smile. Siôn drew her onto his knees and they kissed, shyly at first, then with a lingering tenderness, until it was hard to prevent their love-making going further. Siôn pulled away and buried his face in Annie's soft hair as it escaped from its braid.

'Enough,' he said. 'There's work to be done. And there'll be plenty of time for that, later,' he added with a smile, stroking her still-flat belly.

Chapter Twenty

Clemmie's baby had been born dead. She didn't care, she said. It was the best thing that could have happened to the little bastard. What did she want being lumbered with a baby at her time of life? In any case it would have got in the way of business.

When she had pitched up at Merthyr with Dublin Dandy and the others she had been in a sorry state for sure. They had kept their word to Sal, shown her the tricks of the road and seen her right. Dandy had brought her straight to Pontystorehouse, the area known as China, and led her through a maze of lanes to a yard of ramshackle cottages.

The Dandy was a sprightly man of indeterminate ancientness, his eyes a bright blue in a wizened, weather-worn face. Around his neck he wore a red and white spotted handkerchief, the last remnant of the past sartorial splendour from which he got his name.

'Now you bide here, like the good wee girl ye are, and I'll get you a place, never fear.' She stood in the corner of the yard, conscious of her swollen belly, and watched the Dandy as he knocked with his fist on the door of one of the cottages. It was opened by a grim-looking woman, with a broad, square face deliberately void of all expression, and a solid, misshapen body. As the Dandy swayed and gesticulated in front of her in a parody of elegant conversation, the woman's deep-set eyes swivelled towards Clemmie, instantly appraising her situation.

In a swift gesture a coin passed between the woman and the vagrant, who returned to Clemmie smiling his most blissful smile.

'And what did I tell you? Here's Mam Wylde, once Empress of China, and only too pleased to welcome you to her home.' He pushed Clemmie forwards, and when she glanced back a moment later, he had gone.

When the cottage door had closed behind her Clemmie found herself in a small neat parlour, with a warm fire roaring in the grate and a kettle on the hob. There was a brown velour cloth on the table and a teapot waiting to be filled. She stared around her at the comforts of the tiny room, before her eyes met the acute gaze of Mam Wylde.

Mam moved her swollen, bloated body uncomfortably and with a wheeze in her breathing. Yet in her appraisal of Clemmie there was no mistaking her authority.

'Too far gone to get rid of it, by the looks of you,' she said bluntly. 'Still, it won't show in the dark, will it, love? she added. 'Sit down, girl,' she ordered, pointing at the hard chair by the fireplace while she sank into the armchair. 'These are my terms. You can have a bed in the house next door with the other girls. No fighting, or you're out straight away. I get two shillings a night from you. And if you get your own bully then out you go and find your own place.'

Clemmie gave the impression of being a hard little piece. Her pinched face was sulky as she listened to the older woman's instructions, and her eyes roamed the walls and ceiling of the small room while the woman spoke. She might have been drunk, or hazy with laudanum, for all that Mam Wylde knew or cared. So many girls had been, and none the worse whores for it.

'And when it's born, I know a woman who takes babies, who'll have it for you for a few shillings a week, all found, and you can visit it on Sundays. But if you take my advice, you'll leave it on the workhouse step, knock the door and run away. Let those good Christian folk look after the little bastard.'

Clemmie hadn't thought that far ahead. Despite the stirrings of the infant in her womb, and the fierce tightenings of the muscles that made her belly feel like an overblown football, she did not think the birth was ever going to happen.

Later Clemmie found herself in the cramped back bedroom of the cottage next door, where three mattresses took up nearly all the floor space. A few rough garments were hanging on hooks on the wall – some grey-looking underskirts, a corset where the stitching had come asunder to reveal the whalebone stays like a discarded ribcage. Here and there a piece of feminine frippery suggested a desire for beauty or a quest for love. There was a battered blue velvet bonnet with a feather, and a smattering of rouge powder on the wash-stand. The room smelt of stale bedclothes.

It was here that her waters had broken, a week after her arrival. Seven days and nights of turning tricks in and around the pubs, gin shops and alley-ways brought about what Anne Evans's ministrations had failed to achieve. In a short but ferocious labour she had been delivered of a bloody doll, a stiff, blue little manikin. Its eyes were tightly closed and its little hand clutched at the cord around its neck.

The woman who came to see to her wrapped it in a piece of old sacking and took it away under her arm. As Clemmie lay in the blood-soaked bed the little creature's image would not leave her mind. Its clutching haunted her. It had suffocated, surely that was it, and she remembered the dreadful roar of the water round her ears and the blood within her head and she buried her face in the pillow.

* * * * *

She was bending over to lace up a fine leather boot which showed off the shape of her ankle, grunting slightly with the effort. Then she stood up and, holding her skirt to her knees, leant forward again to look down and admire the effect of the shiny black boots against the black silk stockings with the red clocks up the calves. She was momentarily conscious of the twinge in her lower belly, but dismissed it as a natural consequence of the birth. After all, the old woman who attended her had seen to everything. And John Wylde had paid her handsomely.

Clemmie considered John Wylde as she brushed out the long brown waves of her hair, glancing sidelong at herself in the foggy surface of the old hand mirror which had lost its silvering. Wylde by name, and wild by nature, she thought with some satisfaction. She had done well for herself, to get herself set up with the best-known bully in China, and when she was so far gone.

She wasn't going to make the same mistakes again, though. She wasn't going to cling to him and be his little sweetheart, the way she'd been with Ben Finney. She knew her value. With the fine clothes he'd bought her to get set up, her skin freshly bathed, and her hair clean and well-brushed, she could now bring to bear all her experience with men. She was going to be queen of this place.

The door of the mean little room opened abruptly and Wylde stood with his hand on the latch, grinning broadly. He was a well-built man of twenty-two. He wore a tall black hat tilted at an angle and only slightly battered, pulled down over a swarthy brow and dark eyes. His features were coarse, the mouth wide over irregular teeth. He looked at Clemmie with self-congratulatory lust. She should make him a good profit.

'Well! And what a fine sight you are!' He moved

towards Clemmie and caught her hand as she extended it in a parody of fine manners. She twirled around, raising her skirt to show her red garters and a flash of white thigh. 'No mug is going to stand a chance once you set your sights on him.' He pulled her mouth to his, holding one hand behind her head while the other roved roughly over her body. The moist motions of his lips and tongue were faintly repulsive to her, but she appeared to smile when he moved his face back to look at her.

'Now then, let's get down to business. This is my offer. You do the tricks every night, or most nights except when we want a night off.' He caressed her breast through the blue velvet bodice and paused, as if preoccupied at the thought of what lay beneath. 'When you get the chance you pull a pocket watch or someone's Saturday night wages. I follow you, and make sure nothing goes wrong. If some fellow argues with you, I'll say you're my wife and punch him. If the peeler gets you, I go for him. If the magistrate gets you, I get the witnesses. You can't go wrong with me.'

Clemmie smiled, a clear-eyed warm smile of admiration, or so it seemed to Wylde. Reaching up, she twisted a lock of his long dark hair in her fingers. 'And in return?'

'In return, my love, you come home with me to Storehouse Yard. And you share your takings, and your findings, straight down the middle, half and half.'

'Half and half!' Clemmie's calm slipped momentarily and her voice acquired a sharper edge. 'It's me who's got to bare me backside!'

Wylde turned, a slight smile twisting his lips. 'Ay, and a very cold backside it'll be if you don't throw in your lot with me. There's dozens of girls in China who'd step into your place at a wink from me. You won't regret it. I'm the best-respected bully in this part of town. If we partner up properly we can make a mint of money and you'll never want for anything. And we'll have a bloody good time while we're at it. Come on, girl, what do you say?'

Clemmie hesitated momentarily, sulkily picking at the hem of the dress he had bought.

'All right. But nothing less than half, mind.'

She stood up and smoothed her skirts. The twinge was still there in her lower belly but she couldn't mention that to him. He wouldn't be interested in that sort of woman's business. In any case it was surely only to be expected.

* * * * *

The young couple first caught Clemmie's attention when she followed them through the narrow alley on her way back from the market. She thought she knew most of the bullies and their girls round here after several months working and drinking with Wylde in every beerhouse in China. In any case, they didn't look as though they were in business. The woman, with a mass of dark curls, was pregnant and very near her time, while the man, to judge from his boots caked in mud and his coarse garments, was some kind of labourer.

The man's arm lay along the girl's shoulders and his hand gently gripped her upper arm. As they walked slowly along, their steps matched, and she looked up into his eyes with a faint smile. He kissed her, and she laid her head into the crook of his neck.

Irritated, Clemmie increased her pace and pushed past them, barging the girl's shoulder as she did so.

'I'm so sorry,' she said sarcastically. 'Some of us have work to go to.'

'And we can all guess what sort of work that is,' muttered Siôn.

'What did you say?' Clemmie had whirled round and stood four-square in front of Siôn. Her eyes glittered dangerously and she gave off the perfumed odour of gin.

'I said I wonder what sort of work that is,' replied Siôn with deceptive mildness.

'Don't get too clever, friend.' Clemmie's voice seemed to make her delicate frame resonate with threat like a fine steel blade. 'If you cross me you'll regret it, and so will your milk-and-water mare'. A bolt of anger flashed through Siôn and he made to move towards the brightly-coloured figure standing just out of arm's reach, but Annie's hand snatched his wrist and held it firmly.

'I'm sure we didn't mean any harm, my friend. And if you know of any work I can do, even' – she indicated her swollen belly – 'in my condition, why, I'm sure we'd be very grateful.' Her voice was firm and disingenuous, and her green eyes friendly.

Clemmie was momentarily disconcerted. 'Where … where do you live?'

'In Storehouse Yard … we have a cellar there. I can do sewing, or I could mind babies …'

Clemmie's expression shut like a trap. 'Ask Mam Wylde, corner house. She might be able to help you.' With that she turned and hurried on.

There was something about them that troubled her. It was the man, the way he spoke. English wasn't completely comfortable for him, but that wasn't unusual round here. No, it was his accent, the particular way it swooped and rose. It reminded her of Bethan.

* * * * *

The sailor was a thickset man, his eyes screwed into a narrow gaze as if countering the hard light reflected from a sunlit sea. His teeth were crooked and yellow-brown from chewing the coarse tobacco which tainted his breath along with the overpowering smell of beer and spirits. In the candlelit shadows of the room Clemmie had scarcely noticed his face. As she lay back on the rough blankets of the bed she scrutinised every item of clothing removed by the staggering figure, breathing heavily in his infantile deliberation. She listened for the chink of coins, and looked for the tell-tale bulge of his six months' wages stuffed into an inside pocket.

But he was too canny to fall into that trap. No doubt he had visited whorehouses in every port from Swansea to Bombay and regarded the ladies of Merthyr as strictly amateur.

Clemmie's role in the embraces which followed was strictly passive, which was something to be thankful for. At least he didn't seem to be interested in anything special. All that was required was for her to lie beneath his humping weight as it pressed into her rib-cage. Her face as she stared into the candle-light over the man's shoulder was a mask of disgust and pain, her lips compressed, her eyes flickering closed, then half-opening again at each thrust. She must go and see the midwife. This pain could surely not be right.

After the man had finished he fell into a deep, snoring sleep. Carefully she squeezed out from under him, rolling onto the floor to avoid waking him. She began to search through his clothes systematically, checking the pockets, then feeling the seams and linings. Nothing. The only money he had brought seemed to be the florin he had placed on the floor by the bed, saying that it should be hers if she did as she was bid.

The waistcoat, however, was of good quality. She lifted the doorlatch gingerly, never taking her eyes from the sleeper's face. She held the garment out into the passageway and in a moment a hand had snatched it from her. Then she turned, and with a boisterous tone began to exhort her customer.

'Come on now, my dear! There's more work to be done this night, and sleeping here's not part of the bargain, unless you want to pay five shillings rent!' She pushed the groaning man into a sitting position, then began to thrust his shirt over his head and his arms into his dark blue jacket. Next he struggled obediently into his breeches, his hand on her shoulder as she knelt in front of him like a mother dressing a child. As she picked up the florin his gaze became momentarily more acute, but he grinned stupidly as she bit the coin and slipped it into her bodice.

'Come again, my darling, when next you're back from your travels.' With this she hustled the sailor towards the doorway and out.

Once the door was closed Clemmie went quickly to the corner of the room and poured some water into a tin basin. Already the man's semen was coursing down her thighs. Her mouth screwed with distaste as she crouched over the basin, washing herself in the cold water with a rag. The other women had shown her ways of preventing pregnancy, but there was nothing to be done to prevent disease. She must be quick or Wylde would be at the door, shouting that she was a lazy slut and had a living to earn.

Soon she was back on the chill streets, sauntering easily, with the face of a pale, bright little doll.

It was not too long after that she was on her way back to the room, arm in arm with a collier who'd had a few, 'But not too many that I won't be able to see to you, lass.' This one was promising; he'd had a few bets and seemed to have some money on him. There was a silver watch chain, too, visible across the belly of his waistcoat.

He was the type who wanted a bit of romance with it. He had his arm round her shoulders, and she hers around his waist, as if they were a man and his girl on the spree. Every so often he would sway against her, and stop, pulling her face to his for wet and beery kisses.

As she guided him into the dark courtyard, lit only by the candles and lamps flickering in the windows of the houses advertising the services offered, he paused for an embrace.

Suddenly there was a shout. 'That's her! That's the thieving bitch!' The collier staggered back in confusion, then backed off with his mouth open as a constable stepped forward and gripped Clemmie firmly by the shoulder. 'Right, Missy. It's the magistrate's court for you.' As Clemmie made a dash for it the constable gripped her clothing and yanked her back into a bear-hug as his arms wrapped around her. Now the girl set up a furious screaming, kicking and writhing, so that it was all the man could do to keep his grip on her.

Windows began to bang open, doors threw shafts of light into the dim yard and cries went up. 'It's the peelers! Get Wylde!' There was a scuffling of boots and clogs on the cobbles and rough paving and within moments the constable was aware that he was sur-rounded.

'Let her go, ye filthy peeler! Harm a hair on her head and you're a dead man!'

The constable maintained his grip on the girl, who had now gone limp, dragging down with all her weight so that he felt himself tilting forward. His tall hat was knocked sideways and he could feel the sweat breaking out on his lip. He scanned the crowd, recognising a face here, a face there, mean pinched faces for the most part. There were painted girls with whitened faces and red lips, reeking with cheap scent; fat old brothel-keepers with wobbling chins, shaking their fists and screaming obscenities; cocky young 'rodnies' with spotted handkerchiefs at their neck. Every one of them a criminal.

He shouted in vain for the sailor. 'Get help! Fetch reinforcements!' But his ally was nowhere to be seen.

Suddenly the crowd parted and a stockily-built youth thrust his way forward to stand four-square in front of the constable with his now alert burden clamped to his chest. The young man seemed to be trembling with anger, the energy rippling through him and evinced in the glitter of his eye and short inhalations. He adopted the posture of the fist-fighter, his white knuckles gleaming a few feet from the older man's chin.

'Give her to me,' he uttered between clenched teeth.

'I am arresting this woman in the name of the law, on the grounds that she did rob one Samuel Walker, a sailor of this town, of his waistcoat.'

'Like buggery you are! One move with her and I'll kick your guts out!'

With this Wylde leapt forward and struck the constable a fearsome punch on the right ear, knocking his hat flying and causing him to let go of Clemmie. Wylde seized her wrist and they flew into the crowd, which opened and closed around them before the officer had picked himself up. He stood up, dusting down his hat and staring nervously about him, as the crowd pressed its advantage, moving ever closer. Trying to muster some dignity he moved off, glancing back over his shoulder as the crowd followed, shouting and laughing with a tremendous cacophony.

'What's up? Lost the little bit of skirt you were after? What would your wife say? Get out before we give you some more of the same medicine!'

As the crowd were giving every sign of following him to the main street, keeping up this humiliating barrage, he decided to make a break for it.

Chapter Twenty-One

Siôn had hesitated anxiously at the doorway in the dawn light of the fine late August day. Annie had laughed at his nerves, chafed him for a soft-hearted father already, and no baby born yet! But now, as she stood half-bent holding on to the back of a chair, she wished he had stayed. Her limbs were shaking uncontrollably and her skirts were damp where her waters had broken.

The contractions had started now, a relentless, unforgiving process, the relief felt as one receded soon replaced by a terror at the inevitability of another wave. Annie's mother, Nan, had steadfastly refused to take her daughter back into her affections; and without her mother's support in this ordeal, she was as helpless as a child against the onslaught her own body was bringing to bear.

Every renewed surge of contractions possessed her like a bodily madness, drawing her away from consciousness into a clenched, gripping agony. Every cell of her brain, every layer of muscle, even the molecules of air suspended in her lungs seemed immobilised into an eternity of pain.

Then the madness would recede and she would return, temporarily, to awareness. She would be left cold, sweating and terrified, wondering at the illusion and frantic to escape its next assault.

Slowly Annie moved towards the door. Once she had opened it she scanned the courtyard for a child who might knock a neighbour's door, but for once, there was none to be seen. There was nothing for it – she would have to go herself.

She lifted the iron knocker on the dingy door opposite and slumped against the door-frame. The sun was over the roof-tops now and beginning to penetrate the dank yard, drying the slops on its rough cobbles and filling the air with foul odours. Dogs nosed eagerly amid the rubble and human and animal waste which lay strewn on the pathway, accompanied by a following of flies.

Clemmie opened the door a crack. She recognised the young woman from the house opposite who had asked her for work. Mam Wylde had given her some sewing to do and she made and sold babies' clothes. She was too much of a good thing for Clemmie's taste. It made her sick to see the other woman parading up and down with her big belly, holding on to her husband's arm like lady this and lord that! And what was so special about her, that she couldn't earn her living the same way as the other women round here?

'The midwife ... get me the midwife. You said you knew one ... who wouldn't be more than half-a-crown ...'

'You can't stay here.' Clemmie had the door half closed.

'Please ...' Annie's voice trailed as the contractions caught her. She rolled her head back against the door post. A livid flush spread over the glistening pallor of her cheeks as her eyes closed and she seemed to hold her breath.

When it had passed she raised her hand slowly and laid it on Clemmie's fingers as they clutched the edge of the door, ready to slam it at the first sign of intrusion.

'Please, friend ... I would do the same for you.'

Clemmie's resolve faltered. No woman had called

242

her friend since she had last seen Bethan. Unwillingly she remembered the moment when Bethan and Anne Evans had cradled her, eased her through her pain.

She grudgingly opened the door. 'Hold on, you'll be all right. Megan!' She yelled back into the darkened passageway. 'Run down and get old Betty, straight off now. Tell her there's one on its way, number two, Storehouse Yard. And hurry!'

* * * * *

Siôn held his head in his hands. This had been going on for hours now. He himself had been here four hours, since the boy had run up to the works to fetch him. The sweat poured off him as he sat in the room above the cellar, watching the boiling pot, and replenishing the water when it seemed in danger of boiling dry.

His anxiety rose right into his throat and threatened to choke him as he realised that he could hear no sound from below. The intermittent yells and animal cries, gasps for air and inarticulate murmurings had ceased. He leapt to his feet and rushed to the staircase as his chair crashed to the floor.

'Let me in! Let me in, you old hag!'

Betty had pushed Siôn out when he had arrived home from work, as was the custom, scolding and cursing him and eventually tying the latch. Now he burst through the door and pushed the woman aside.

'Annie – Annie! Speak to me!' He clasped her hands and chafed them, his eyes fixed on her face as if just by looking he could draw life and strength into her. Her eyelids flickered, but she scarcely knew his voice. He turned to the woman in anger.

Betty was slumped into a chair, her haggard face red and sweating. The case had defeated her. Her bulging, watery eyes stared in a kind of terror towards Siôn, as if she expected him to butcher her on the spot. One trembling hand began to slither down beside the wall towards a stone jug. As she began to lift it towards her lips Siôn leapt forward.

'So that's it, you drunken old crone! Get out of here, and bring me a bucket of boiling water from upstairs.'

He pulled back the bedcovers and examined Annie's body. Weakened by her fruitless labour, she seemed unable to respond to the contractions any longer. When they came her body shuddered and shook like a rag doll, and she bared her clenched teeth as if on the verge of madness.

Siôn removed his filthy waistcoat and shirt and washed his hands, arms and chest. He had delivered enough lambs, he reasoned, gently inserting his hand between Annie's thighs. Probing deeper he felt the smooth globe of the baby's buttock, and the hard lump of its heel. A breech birth. He steeled himself. He was going to have to hurt her to get this child out. He pressed his fingers in further, forcing the vagina to open, to stretch and finally, to split. Annie moaned as he brought forth a boy child, his limbs still clenched into the position that had so pained his mother, and dead, dead, dead.

Weeping, Siôn put the child aside and yelled at the old woman to swaddle it, for decency's sake. Then, frantically, he sought to revive Annie with warm cloths to her face, and brandy and milk to her lips.

* * * * *

As evening fell, the room took on the blue tones of the summer night sky. In the yard outside no sound could be heard except the screeching swoop of the martins as they pursued each other around the roof-tops. Even the children had been quietened by neighbours from their summer evening wildness.

Siôn stood at the side of the bed, staring at Annie's motionless form. This was the bed where they had enjoyed the first passion of their relationship, free for a few blessed months of the physical hardships that would surely follow. Here each had gazed in love and admiration at the other's face and body, free at last to look, touch and kiss. In the light of a single candle they had made precious the hours of darkness when they were free of all demands, no matter the cost in tiredness on the morrow; and the slender, pale light, as it flickered over the walls of the dingy room, had somehow made it beautiful.

Annie's expression was remote, ethereal, her eyelashes lying as lightly as moths' wings on the white skin. But on her brow was the faintest etched line of pain, a furrow which had not been there before. Her first childbirth had made this, the first mark on her shining youth, like the mark of a woodcutter's axe on the pristine bark of a tree. Looking down he knew his responsibility for the deeper lines which their physical union would have etched in years to come.

A woman was a prisoner of both life and death. Every childbirth was a journey where the traveller was a woman, alone and naked, and with no resources but her mind and her body. Behind her closed eyes was a voyager braving the elements in a universe of chaos. On and on went the journey, to the very rim of life itself.

Annie had not come back.

* * * * *

Bethan lay back weakly in the bed, conscious of Anne Evans moving briskly to and fro as she set everything to rights in the overheated room. Although it was August, a fire roared in the grate whilst the great iron pot full of water simmered on the hob. The window was wide open, with the curtains drawn to keep out the strong evening sunlight. Every so often a light breeze would waft through, causing the curtains to billow, and the screeching sound of the martins as they sped round the eaves grew shriller, as if they would burst into the room in their excitement.

She thought of Patrick. He would come and go like the martins, she reflected. Dashing, unpredictably, hither and yon, disappearing who knew where, only to return when you least expected him. But somehow she knew he would not return this time.

Now the pains began to return, and all thoughts fled as she strove to follow Anne's instructions.

'Breathe through it, my dear, breathe. It'll pass, it'll pass.' And Anne held her hand, and mopped her brow with cool water until the spasm had gone. 'There is no need to fear. You're a fine, strong girl, and I'll see you come to no harm.'

As her condition became apparent, Bethan had begun to visit Anne daily, helping with the sewing work in exchange for Anne's advice and company. Now the time had come and she felt safe here. Anne was indeed an expert midwife and nurse, taught by her own mother and the exigencies of childbirth in poverty repeated over and over in this crowded part of the town.

Bethan's labour was arduous, but Anne never left her side. Women from neighbouring rooms brought meals and tea and hovered at the door with a mixture of anxiety and curiosity to hear how Bethan was progressing. Another woman's childbed was a mirror to their own experience: every new life borne by a healthy mother a message of hope for their next delivery. Everyone had some advice, from the best way to ensure a speedy delivery to how to swaddle the baby in order to ensure that it should grow up with straight limbs.

Anne smiled rather absent-mindedly at the constant stream of whispered comment which could be heard every time the door opened and her chosen assistant, Tabitha Wilson, came in and out. Tabitha was a clean, tidy woman, intelligent enough to do Anne's bidding in a crisis without getting into a panic. Like Anne, Tabitha was swathed in a clean apron and her hair was tied back in a scarf.

Anne felt confident that her method was the correct one. Gently, deftly she inserted her hand into the girl's body at the peak of a contraction, while Tabitha held her shoulders and soothed her. The opening to the womb was well dilated now, and Anne could feel the baby's downy head. 'Push, my lovely, push! Nearly there, nearly there!'

Bethan did not seem able at first to comprehend the words that were being spoken to her. Tabitha was behind her, propping her up, but her head lolled stupidly and the words seemed opaque, as if in a foreign tongue. But then came the sensation, a deep driving need to bear down with all the strength of her abdominal muscles. It seemed to be her, and yet not her who gathered all the power into a tight mass and then forced it downwards.

'One more, one more!'

Bethan looked down and saw the crown of the baby's head appearing between her thighs. She felt the opening stretching, stretching, as if the lips of her mouth should be pulled apart wider, ever wider, by the grip of a giant, so wide, that they must split apart ... but no! Suddenly the child's head appeared and Bethan cried out in astonishment.

Anne seized him as he slid forth and raised him by the heels to make him cry. As his thin, tremulous cry penetrated the evening air it seemed to her a strange, animal sound, like that made by the little kid goats she had sometimes heard on the mountain.

Anne came towards her with the boy swaddled tightly in the special wrappings she loaned to new mothers and laundered to spotless whiteness.

'Here, let him suckle.'

Bethan looked into the child's face and saw its pearl-like perfection. He looked back at her with eyes of the darkest blue, a gaze at once pure and intent, like that of a sleeper roused from the deepest of sleeps.

She bared her nipple and held the child against it. She felt his mouth, soft and tentative, brush her lightly, as if uncertain. But soon he began to suck and her breasts were hard with the nourishment he craved.

'And what will you call him, cariad? Patrick after his daddy is it – or Jack after his uncle?'

It was hard to account for it afterwards, but she knew at once what it should be.

'No, he shan't be Patrick, nor Jack. He shall be Siôn.'

Thus it was that a lonely, unloved girl returned from her voyage and turned her eyes towards the future; while a beloved woman and her child passed away.

* * * * *

Clemmie watched as the cheap wooden coffin emerged from the doorway opposite, manhandled precariously through the narrow opening into the yard outside where the neighbours had gathered to join the funeral procession. Rough and ragged they mostly were, in harsh cloth jackets and dark shawls brought out despite the heat. Faces seamed and marked, they turned

248

towards the mourners in the bright sunlight, a mass of grey and shoddy clothing. Only the light of a blue eye or the sweep of a girl's nut-brown hair distinguished the young from the old as they stood in their silence. Death was ever there among the yards and cobbled lanes, within the foul walls and the tainted water.

As Clemmie swayed in the heat, a cold dew formed on her lip and she reached out to steady herself on the doorpost. She seemed to see into the coffin, to see the young woman, her dark hair spread like a cape, her arms crossed on her breast, enclosing within them the doll-like child. As they carried Annie away, so with her went Clemmie, the girl who might have been. Not for her the father, the mother, the sisters, nor the loving husband, nor the child.

PART THREE

Chapter Twenty-Two

JUNE 1843

The warm June day was drawing to its close. As Siôn tramped westwards the shell-pink of the sky began to deepen in reflection of the sun's bloody hue. Sombre tints suffused the lower sky and the rich foliage of the summer trees was still and black as iron filigree against the dying light.

Siôn tramped with resignation, a brisk marching gait that surrendered nothing to surroundings. His eyes seemed unseeing to those who passed him on the road, and his demeanour unfriendly, as of one who had seen rough service and had no time for chat. He might have been a soldier home from war, his body hard and used to privations, his weather-beaten face tight and expressionless, a lifetime's experience crammed into a few short years which could never be released by words.

As he walked he thought of the man he had been when first he walked east four years before. He was at once amused and saddened as he thought of his young self, mourning his lost love and still wearing a shirt his mother had made him. Mourning! How deep the pains of youth had felt, how shallow they now seemed as the loss of Annie's vibrant spirit shuddered through him again, as it still could do, unexpectedly, at any time.

It was nearly three years since she had died. In that time he had devoted himself to the cause of the working man, first in the underground regrouping of Chartists following the Newport trial, and latterly through the growing system of combinations. He had poured his energy, his anger, his love and his loss into this work and it had helped him survive.

He had exhausted himself and fallen into a fever. He had reached the brink of death in the cold damp cellar, dreaming of gunfire and the screams of the dying. He dreamt he lay amongst the bloody corpses outside the Westgate Hotel, and turning his face saw his wife and child stiff and cold beside him. But as he lay with his face bathed in tears his dream turned, and he found himself standing on the Preseli hillside, the wind driving the cool rain into his face, a soothing balm to the heat of his fever.

When he awoke he knew that he must go back there, back to the pure air and clear light free from the sulphurous smoke and stench of the town of iron.

Then the strangest thing had happened. As he was making his preparations to leave, looking around the bare room where Annie had fought and lost her last battle, the door latch lifted and the girl Clementina from over the yard had stood on the step. Her customary insolence of manner was gone and Siôn saw the unhealthy tone in her skin against the bright greens and yellows of her dress.

He turned towards her with a look of surprise and enquiry, expecting perhaps a demand for more rent for Mam Wylde or even an offer of sex – at a price. But Clemmie stared nervously for a moment and then said directly: 'Are you Jack Morgan?'

For a moment Siôn stood in confusion. Where had he heard that name before? Then suddenly it came to him and he grabbed the girl's arm and pulled her into the room, scarcely observing the fact that she flinched at his action as if expecting a blow.

'What do you know of Jack Morgan?' he demanded.

'Nothing ... nothing ...' Clemmie's glance slid from his face, searching the corners of the room as if for something to steal. Her temporary innocence now fled, she seemed once again a hard-bitten slut.

'Then why do you ask, if you know nothing?' Siôn shook her by the elbow, exasperated yet excited by her, both by her questions and the musty mixture of sweat and stale lavender water that emanated from her garments. 'Why do you ask me that?' he screamed, his voice breaking with rage and frustration. Clemmie's eyes widened as she saw that he was nearly weeping.

'I. ... I knew his sister once ... and she helped me. When I heard the way you talk I thought ... and I thought if you were him I could pay her back.'

There was no artifice now in Clemmie's expression. For a moment Siôn saw the eighteen-year-old that she was, a child without love beneath the harsh glamour.

And thus Siôn had learnt of Bethan's life after she had left him. He knew that he must find her, seek her out, and if she were still free he would make his life with her.

As he stooped to pick up his bundle and lift it to his shoulder he looked into Clemmie's face, pale in the shadowy cellar room. Stepping towards her he placed the palm of his hand against her cheek and saw her eyes close sadly at the gentleness of his touch. He lifted her chin and softly kissed her lips.

'Thank you, sister,' he said, then he turned and walked through the door.

Clemmie stood alone, her eyes closed, her lips pressed close.

* * * * *

As he entered the town from the north Siôn sensed the old excitement tingling through his veins. All around him groups of men were joining the roadway, women and children behind them, walking down from the hill farms and villages surrounding Carmarthen to the north. As he had moved westward on his journey he had begun to pick up rumours from fellow-travellers on the road and labourers in the wayside taverns supping ale after their day's work and exchanging news of the latest activities of 'Rebecca' and her children.

Siôn had grinned to hear of the dance that the old crone, whoever 'she' might be, was leading the magistrates in a wide area in the vicinity of Carmarthen and further west in Pembrokeshire. Never had one woman managed to be in so many places at once, he observed wryly, wondering that the movement had spread and become so powerful that gate after gate had been destroyed, some of them several times over. Huge crowds of men were gathering, guns were fired into the air, tollhouses dismantled or burnt to the ground and special constables threatened with terrifying letters. 'Rebecca' promised to call upon them and use long knives like those used by Hengist to kill their forefathers. The place was becoming ungovernable, and the authorities were terrified.

Siôn was glad. The rage had never left him since Newport. The deaths of so many whose crime had been to ask for dignity and an acknowledgement of the working man, shot like animals and left to die in their own blood – how could he forget? Now the country folk were refusing to accept their lot and that was right, no matter how rough they had to be.

Once he had heard about the big demonstration planned in Carmarthen he had determined to be there. The confidence of the rebels had grown, as time after time they had outfaced the magistrates and the special constables. They were angry at being fleeced at toll-gates by turnpike trusts, and now the poorest were resisting the Poor Law and the hated workhouses. Today they were to march through Carmarthen and present the magistrates with petitions setting out their grievances.

The demonstrators had been persuaded to leave their firearms at a house on the edge of town by two magistrates who feared the worst. As the procession set off from the Plough and Harrow the band at its head puffed and blared its way through favourite hymns and patriotic tunes, followed by a contingent of men on horseback and hundreds of others marching behind. A rag-taggle crowd of women and children brought up the rear, enjoying the holiday in the bright sunshine.

* * * * *

Hearing the band, the people of the quayside slums had poured out of their cramped and squalid homes, and jostled through the alleyways and narrow lanes as the children raced like whippets between them to get the best vantage points.

Holding her little boy's hand Bethan joined the throng, first urging him along and then sweeping him up and running as the excitement of the children caught her. The crowd assembled on the quay comprised the fisherfolk and assorted riff-raff who had washed up on this shore which, though ramshackle, was at least hospitable, in that it turned no one away, no matter what his story. Misshapen matrons knitted constantly on steel wires, their work pinned to their aprons, while gaudily-dressed trollops from the Half-moon and the dozens of other alehouses in the vicinity

254

stood with linked arms and yelled at groups of sailors. The old fishermen stood with hands in pockets, smoking their pipes, weather-beaten faces stolid in the uproar, but the younger men were restless, calling back over their shoulders into the darkness of the taverns to the stragglers reluctant to put down their jugs.

There were few families here that hadn't felt the threat of the workhouse, or experienced hard labour there when fishing hauls had failed. They had known the meaning of their poverty when husband had been split from wife, child from parent, boy child from girl child. Even love was denied.

The labour of the workhouse was the most demeaning labour. The poor were shiftless, feckless and degenerate, and they must work to atone for their sin of poverty before being granted the manna of workhouse porridge. Each man was required to break one and a half tons of stone a day, and even now six men were in Carmarthen jail for refusing. The younger men and women were fired by news of 'Rebecca's' successes in the countryside, which had washed right up to the gates of Carmarthen only a few weeks before. They were hard, wiry men and strong-armed, foul-mouthed lasses whose way of settling a quarrel was the fist. What did they care for constables and magistrates and respectable folk?

The Irish tongue mingled with Welsh and a smattering of English as the band turned the corner and the crowd roared its approval. When the leading marchers approached, applause broke out amongst a few onlookers at the placard borne aloft at the front of the procession, inscribed 'Cyfiawnder a charwyr cyfiawnder ydym ni oll' – but a chorus of voices could be heard asking what was written on the placard or for a translation. 'Justice, and lovers of justice are we all!' came

255

the cry, first in Welsh, then English, and a cheer rose up as the spectators watched line after line of horsemen riding by.

Bethan lifted little Siôn to her shoulder and jigged him in time to the music. A lurid figure among the riders, a grotesque man-woman with a hooked nose and long ringlets under a straw bonnet, waved and winked at the little boy, who burst into tears and hid his face in Bethan's neck. The watchers laughed and cried out 'Rebecca! Rebecca!', but the little boy was inconsolable.

Bethan gazed at the apparition, remembering the first time she had seen 'Rebecca'. In that instant, as the faces in the crowd swept past her, she thought she glimpsed Twm Rees, head and shoulders above the other men: the flash of a grin, thick brows, dark hair. She swiftly bent down to place little Siôn on the ground as her heart pounded. When she stood up the tall figure had vanished in the crowd. It was just her imagination playing tricks.

Now the young fishermen were jostling and thrusting to the front of the march. Others were weaving through the spectators, laughing and calling to their mates up ahead. Once assembled, they linked arms and marched forward, grinning self-consciously at taking the lead in such a public demonstration. The band and the leading riders yelled at the usurpers to get behind, feeling the dignity of their display somewhat undermined, but the response from the front was unequivocal.

As the march wove back up into the town more and more people joined it, pouring out of the slums huddled beneath the grim walls of the castle-prison, half in holiday mood, half serious, but all responsive to the possibilities of this moment when for once, they held the power in their hands, simply by being there in this mass. These were folk who roamed the streets in winter festivals, drunken, anarchic, and chasing balls of fire. Now they were marching with countrymen who for months had confronted authority with pikes, staves, scythes and latterly, guns.

The mood began to change as the energy of the wild young men stirred its response in the marchers behind. The Guildhall and the magistrates' resolution was forgotten as the cry of 'The Workhouse!' went up. The band fell into disarray and the orderly formation dissolved, but a thousand voices picked up the words and the chant 'The Workhouse! The Workhouse!' rippled the length of the mass and back again. A glorious mood of defiance, of pleasure at thronging through the narrow streets in this invincible mass, swept through the men at the head of the march. There was a chance with these numbers to go further than toll-gate-breaking, and they weren't going to miss the opportunity.

* * * * *

Siôn pounded forward, darting hither and thither between mounted men and the spectators at the roadside. He reached the yelling, chanting crowd of demonstrators at the front of the march just as they approached the forbidding walls of the workhouse at the top of Pen-lan Hill.

There was a momentary pause as the tall, bleak building was reached. Then the leading men marched to the front door and beat on it with their fists. Trembling, the Master opened the door, and at the men's insistence passed over the keys. With a roar the crowd raced into the courtyard and began to open the doors.

Some of the paupers rushed out into the yard, some as wild as their rescuers, others alarmed and cringing back into the outhouses. A wild girl led the marchers on, showing them the way into the house. She climbed onto a table in the hallway and lifted her skirts in a triumphal dance as she urged the men up the stairs. Now their work began as they vented their anger. The sounds of splintering wood and smashing glass resonated against the boundary walls that had confined so many. Cheer after cheer rose as bedding and smashed furniture flew from the windows. The children in the schoolroom screamed with terror, their only security, the chilly regime of the workhouse, turned topsy-turvy by their avengers.

Siôn worked in a frenzy, kicking and smashing anything he could lay his hands on as, with the flood of other men who had reached the upper floors, he moved through the grim chambers redolent of unwashed bodies and urine. The hard little cots where children had wept for their mothers filled him with rage. He broke one to sticks and began to lob it through the broken window. As he did so he looked out on the seething crowds still moving up Pen-lan Hill. Suddenly he noticed a disturbance amongst the people at the lower end of the hill.

Screaming could be heard, a change in the noise of the crowd, a pause, then a great thunder of horses' hooves as the mounted demonstrators stampeded up the hill. Then a terrifying vision appeared: a mass of dragoons, charging on horseback towards the workhouse, with sabres flashing in the sunlight and the bugle blaring. The horses surged forward, their muscles glinting, the riders laying about them to right and left. Siôn saw the crowd ripple around them and seemingly buckle upwards as waves of people tried to struggle out of their way.

There was pandemonium inside the workhouse. Siôn flung himself from the room, racing through the corridors and down the stairs yelling a warning. In the yard loose horses reared and whinnied their alarm as rioters ran in every direction trying to escape. One soldier's horse fell dead with exhaustion. The soldiers were half-mad with riding fourteen miles in seventy minutes in the broiling June sun.

Siôn ran back into the house and climbed out again through a broken front window, dashing into the path of one of the squadrons of dragoons as they chased the fugitives up the hill. Head down, he ran straight into the mêlée and once out on the other side he threw himself over a wall and ran up into the countryside.

Chapter Twenty-Three

Long ago, far away:
Things like that don't happen
No more, nowadays, do they?

Bethan trembled as she looked down at the letter. The folded outer sheet bore her name, Mrs Elizabeth Morgan, written with a sweeping flourish, addressed care of The Landlord, The Lamb and Flag, Carmarthen. And it was sealed with red wax imprinted with the initials PB, and had been sent from Dublin.

'Aren't you going to open it, then?' asked Henry Jones gently.

It was more than three years since she had seen Patrick O'Bryan. What could he possibly want from her now? She felt a grip of fear. Perhaps he had heard that he had a son, and wanted to take him away from her. She tore open the seal and smoothed out the thick paper on the rough bar table. The writing spread elegantly across the sheet and she began the unaccustomed task of deciphering it.

'My Dear Bethan,' it began. 'I write to you now to keep a promise I made many years ago, and to show that, contrary to what others may tell you, I am a man who honours my word.

'I promised you once that I would get word for you regarding your brother Jack Morgan, and that I have done. He enlisted for the army in 1836 and served as a private soldier until 1839, when he deserted. My intelligence tells me that he refused to participate in the quelling of a riot in a manufacturing town. His officers knew that he had become infected with Chartism and arrested him, but he escaped his prison cell – no doubt with the aid of sympathisers – and is still at large.

'Fellow soldiers believe that he has emigrated to Pennsylvania where he believed that he could make a new life as a republican.

'And now, my dear Bethan, I feel I have paid my debt to you, and will close my letter, commending you to God for his care. As for your betrayal of me, I absolve you of that, for I firmly believe that you knew not the import of your action.

I remain,

Your friend

Patrick Vincent O'Bryan.'

Bethan pored over the letter, marking each word with her finger and whispering to herself as she went. When she reached the end she began again, just as intently, while Jones sat at her side resisting the urge to take the paper from her.

As she read he mused over O'Bryan's ability to survive and renew his life. They had left him for dead on a piece of waste ground by the quayside. Now here he was again, writing letters on fine paper, sealed with his own seal. But he was a rich man's son, and all his adventures and misdemeanours could be put behind him whenever he chose. There would be a profession for him, and a fine home, and a wife to put in it, no doubt.

Jones looked at Bethan as she earnestly worked at the letter, her fair hair falling from its pins, her hand clutched against her forehead to keep the stray locks out of her face as she read. She looked tired, her bloom damaged by the years of working long and late to make enough to keep herself and her child. She had been determined to keep the infant, and with the help of complicit women was just managing it. There was Anne Evans, who had the child during the evening while Bethan served in the bar; and his own wife Sarah who turned a blind eye when she brought little Siôn into the kitchen now and again; and various neighbours who cared for him during the day. He himself had become fond of the girl and made sure that any spare victuals went her way.

'It's about Jack,' she said at last. She turned her green eyes to Jones and he saw that the light had returned to her face. 'He's alive!' But then her expression changed, as she hardly knew whether the rest was good or bad news. Her mouth quivered a little as she added, 'He's not a soldier any more, thank God. But he's gone to Pennsylvania, and I don't even know rightly where that is.'

The letter had thrown her into confusion. All her pain had turned into the determination that she would keep her child, and had fuelled the labour that made that possible. Siôn Hughes, Patrick O'Bryan, the dreams of love and home that they had opened to her – all this was behind her. All that mattered was her baby, and keeping alive the certainty that she would see her brother again.

She had long since learned of Patrick's double life. She recalled how she had heard of his disappearance, the enigmatic references between the men, the suppressed smiles. Then she had been congratulated on her cunning in turning in the miscreant, when all she had done was pass the blue book to Henry, asking him to give it to Patrick because she had put it in her pocket by mistake.

'Pennsylvania! He might as well be on the moon, or dead, as on the other side of the world.'

Bethan's strength crumbled from her as the significance of the message sank in. Leaning forward onto her elbows she covered her face with her hands, struggling to hold back the violent emotions that shook her. She had to face reality. Finding Jack had been a dream, too. Her hope of regaining her lost family had been a thread running continuously from her childhood to the present day, and now Patrick O'Bryan had snapped it. She was adrift, alone.

Sarah was at her side, called over by a gesture from Henry who could not cope with tears and had gone to tap some fresh barrels. The older woman sat silently for many minutes, then laid her hand gently on the girl's shoulder.

'I wonder, my dear, if you have seen this.' She placed in front of Bethan the closely-printed page of a newspaper. She indicated a point in the display of advertisements which adorned its front page. Beneath a small engraving of a sailing ship was the legend 'Passage to New York'. There followed a list of ships sailing from Carmarthen, picking up at Fishguard, Cardigan, Newquay and Aberaeron, before sailing to Liverpool, whence passage could be obtained in the steerage for the sum of £4.

'But ... how could I go? I would need money for myself, more than £4. Money to get to Liverpool, then to start myself off when I'm there ... and what about little Siôn?' Her eyes filled again, but she bit back the tears and dried her eyes firmly on the back of her sleeve. 'Damn this crying!' Her mouth snapped tight.

'There is a way,' began Sarah. 'Our minister at Bethesda, he knows of good Welsh people in Pennsylvania who would take you in. In fact, they're asking for

Welsh women – widows and the like ...' Bethan
flashed a look, half anger, half scorn, but Sarah persisted. '... Well, who's to know, love, a wedding ring's
easily come by ... Henry and I have talked about this
already, after the minister mentioned it at chapel. We'd
be willing to help you. Come to the service with us this
Sunday, and we'll see what can be arranged.'

* * * * *

Siôn stood at the bottom of the incline and looked up
towards Tŷ Gwyn. He could just make out its pale
shape against the hillside in the gathering twilight. The
windows were dark and its roof seemed awry, as though
part had collapsed. As he stared, the meaning of this
dereliction came clearly to him. To any other passing
stranger this would be just an empty shell, a ruin to
ponder with curiosity in passing. But to Siôn, the dark
windows, void of the faint glow of rushlight, and the
chimney, empty of smoke, shouted their message into
the silence: lost hope, lost people, lost future.

The urge to walk up and look at the ruin evaporated,
and was replaced by a chill fear, a terror, as if to walk
through that black door hole would be to walk through
to his own grave.

He turned fiercely to the east and began to walk
across the heathland towards Rebecca's house. The
night darkened as he strode and stumbled over the
rough stones and tummocks of heather. His boots and
the legs of his woollen breeches were soaked with dew
and the air of the summer night was moist with the
smell of peat and grass. As he crashed forward over the
wilderness he saw the white stars shimmering above in
their masses and refused to remember another starlit
walk five years before. His anger fulminated inside

him, directionless, as he recalled the battles he had fought, when every effort of brain and muscle had been pitched against the enemy, when months and years of work had come to nothing. Children were still dying, women still suffering, men still without dignity.

He felt half-crazed, hungry and exhausted as he was after his weeks on the road. It was only because his feet instinctively knew the way to Rebecca's house that he saw it ahead of him, low and dark-thatched in the star-light, a gentle stream of smoke issuing from its chimney, and a faint light from its window. He broke into a run, and fell against the door amid wild barking from the dogs. Half-crying, half-laughing, he called to them, 'Bouncer! Sal! Shep! Down, now, don't you know me?'

The door sprang open behind him and he stumbled into the house surrounded by leaping dogs, now yelp-ing joyously as he ruffled the fur at their necks.

'Can it really be you?'

Siôn turned to see a tall, sturdy figure rising from her chair by the fireplace. Rebecca's face seemed stern, harsh even, as if she had seen a ghost. Siôn saw now that she was old: her back slightly stooped, her hair iron-grey and her face a map of lines in the walnut-brown skin. But her demeanour was still dignified, and she stepped forward strongly to grip him by the shoulders.

'Mair Hughes's boy! You've come back!' As she embraced him Siôn smelt the characteristic aroma of camphor, peat smoke and lavender he recalled from his childhood. 'Huw! Huw!' she shouted, turning round to look for the boy, but he was already there, watching uncertainly. He was a fine, tall boy of eight years old and his blue eyes bore a look of hesitancy and hope. Siôn paused for a moment before scooping the boy up into his arms and hugging him. Rebecca turned away and busied herself by placing the heavy kettle back on the hearth, where it began at once to sing.

It was not long before she was able to place in front of Siôn a meal of cawl and bread with a cup of precious tea to mark his welcome. As they talked through the night Siôn poured out his tale, and spoke for the first time to anyone of Annie, her death and the loss of their child.

It was late in the morning when Siôn finally woke. He was still lying on the bundle of sacks in front of the fire where Rebecca had made him a bed, and long, warm fingers of sunlight reached into the cottage through the open door. He could smell sun-warmed grass on the breeze which wafted in and mingled with the smoke of furzewood and peat which smouldered alongside him in the hearth. He lay still for a long time, savouring the silence of the moor's edge, broken only by the whisper of the wind and the rustlings and scratchings of the hens near the doorway. He felt comforted at last. He could lay Annie and the baby to rest now.

He rose and walked to the doorway in his bare feet. On the other side of the dirt track the hillside ran away gently from the cottage. Beyond was a broad panorama of woods, tiny fields and nestling farmsteads, bathed in the golden light of a June day, the sky a crowning hemisphere of intense blue. It had stayed the same, through all those years: while his toil and journeys had marked his soul, this landscape had simply moved through the rhythms of its year again and again, four times, and there was no perceptible change. New blades of grass replaced the old, the baby skylarks flew their nests and soared. Annie and the child had died.

When Rebecca and Huw returned from their visit to a neighbouring cottage she found Siôn sitting with his knees drawn up on the rough grass, eating the bread and cheese she had set aside for him under a cloth. In the bright sunlight she could at last examine his appearance as she sat down for a rest on the three-legged stool which the boy brought out for her.

His mid-brown hair was long and ill-kempt and his face, unshaven for many days, was thin and gaunt, the skin weather-beaten. His eyes were still as blue as cornflowers, she noted, the slight downward cast of the outer lids more pronounced now. New lines were etched from his nose to the corners of his ironic mouth, which was less ready to laugh, and seemed more easily to form into the clamped line of cynicism. However, as he turned towards her, he gave a smile of greeting which brought the beauty back into his face. He was still a fine-looking man, and one who should not go to waste, reflected Rebecca.

'You know, Siôn,' she began, 'I sometimes think of that young lass Bethan. Do you think we were a bit hard on her?'

Siôn flashed a look at Rebecca. Was the woman serious? She was looking towards the horizon, without irony, as if musing on the subject. Noticing his gaze, she turned towards him. Her stolid face, framed by the dark crocheted shawl she wore on her shoulders, seemed to contain a slight consciousness of troublesome emotion – shame was it, or perhaps embarrassment?

'Why do you stare at me like that?'

Siôn bit into a long blade of grass he was holding between his fingers and turned away.

'You know why,' he said at last.

Rebecca spoke gently, but measuring her words as though she knew they might cause an explosion if she misjudged his mood.

'We were doing it for you – me, Twm Rees and Ebenezer. You were promised to Marged, it was all set, then along came Bethan Morgan and before we know it she sets herself up right under your mother's nose!'

Siôn seemed to give a rueful laugh as he looked away again to the far horizon. But when he spoke his voice was cold with anger.

'She was a good woman. She saved my mother's life and cared for Huw like a sister. You drove her away and when you did that you took from my mother the new daughter she had found. And now you ask me whether you were too hard!'

Now they sat in silence, both unravelling the consequences of those actions of years before. At last Rebecca stirred. When Siôn looked up he saw her rough brown hand extended towards him. Slowly he took it, and felt its iron grip of encouragement.

'Why don't you go for her then?'

Siôn dropped her hand with a weary smile. 'Ay, but where? I know she was living in Carmarthen four years since, but God knows where she is now.'

'I know,' said Rebecca.

'What?' Siôn was on his knees in front of the old woman and grasped her hand again. 'What ... what do you know?' His voice was harsh and urgent, his expression almost threatening in its intensity.

'Carmarthen. Twm saw her, on the day of the attack on the workhouse. You don't think he'd miss that, do you?'

Her attitude was maddening. 'Where? Where did he see her? For God's sake, Rebecca, why didn't you tell me this before?'

'Down by the quayside. She was watching the procession, staring at the Becca. Laughing, she was, Twm said.'

'What else? Did he say anything else?'

'Yes, he did.' Rebecca looked directly into his eyes

268

now. 'He said she had a child with her, and that she held him in her arms as if he were the most precious thing on God's earth.'

A child! So she was married then. Released from their trap, Siôn's feelings sped away like greyhounds, hither and thither, in search of some quarry. He pondered her life since she had left him, and knew that she must have suffered. Could it be that she had moved into a town and found respectable work after weeks on the road? He doubted it. And could she then have met and married a decent man? It seemed unlikely, and the memory of her friend, Clemmie, a pale and unwholesome whore, reminded Siôn of the most likely origin of the child Twm Rees had seen.

He rose from the ground. He would find her.

* * * * *

Bethan stood on the quayside holding little Sioni by the hand. The little brig *Sally Ann* was nearly ready to sail for Liverpool, her hold packed with the luggage and lifetime possessions of her passengers. The sailors busied themselves on deck preparing the sails, while porters carried the last fresh provisions up the gangway.

All along the quay other craft made ready with their routine cargoes of lime, woollen cloth or fine Welsh cattle. The waterfront swarmed with horse-drawn vehicles unloading their goods, while beasts waited patiently in makeshift pens. Children darted between the humans and animals, eager to earn a penny by holding a gentleman's horse, or to steal an apple that might fall from a porter's basket and roll along the stone paving.

As Bethan watched, the passengers for the *Sally Ann* began to form up on the quayside. Clutching bundles, holding babies beneath their cloaks or heavy toddlers in their arms, young women stood thin and pale-faced in the sharp morning light, while their husbands glanced nervously at the sky to make a judgement about the weather and the strength of the wind they might encounter. Others, travelling alone, stood slightly apart, wondering silently about the step they were about to take, and what the future might hold.

The minister from Bethesda chapel moved among the crowd, greeting the migrants, offering comfort to a mother, chucking a child under the chin, and shaking a man warmly by the hand. As they gathered around him he began to preach to them the last sermon they would hear in their homeland.

'My dear friends – as you venture forth to leave the land of your birth – think not that you are departing into the wilderness. Think rather, that like Moses and the Israelites, you are leaving behind your chains, and going forth to freedom.'

Holding aloft a black Bible, he began to declaim against the background of the bustle and chaos of the quayside.

' "And the Lord said, I have surely seen the affliction of my people which are in Egypt, and have heard their cry by reason of their taskmasters; for I know their sorrows; And I am come down to deliver them out of the hand of the Egyptians, and to bring them up out of that land unto a good land and a large, unto a land flowing with milk and honey ..." '

'Amen,' came the earnest rejoinder from several voices in the crowd. Some watched the minister with hungry eyes, their expressions full of a desperate eagerness to see the Promised Land. Others were lethargic, their eyes downcast as if unwilling to look at the bright sky.

'... Now therefore, behold, the cry of the children of Israel is come unto me: and I have also seen the oppression wherewith the Egyptians oppress them.'

'Brothers and sisters – have not you, like the Israelites, been oppressed?'

'Yes indeed,' came the cry.

'Have you not been enslaved, like those people of old? And have you not turned to the Lord for deliverance?'

'Yea, we have.'

'And now, this vessel makes ready to take you to the land flowing with milk and honey, where you will find people of your faith waiting to greet you ... Good people, Welsh people. So do not mourn your lost home, your lost parents, your lost brothers, sisters and neighbours. Your brothers and sisters in faith will greet you and make you their kin.'

The minister glanced around the dishevelled group, noting the pale faces of the women, many of whom were biting back tears.

'Nor must you fear the power of the sea. Entrust yourselves to God, have faith, for he will deliver you, as he delivered the Israelites.'

'Think of how St Paul, on his great journey, was caught in a terrible tempest, and how he reassured the sailors, telling them how an angel of God had stood by his side, and told him to fear not, for he must be brought before Caesar. Those who do the work of the Lord need have no fear.

'Think of the time when Our Lord was in a ship in the sea, and there arose a great storm of wind, and the waves beat into the ship, so that it was full. Do you recall how the disciples went to Jesus and woke him, and said "Master, carest thou not that we perish?"

'And he arose, and rebuked the wind, and said unto the sea, "Peace, be still". And the wind ceased, and there was a great calm. And He said unto them, "Why are ye so fearful? How is it that ye have no faith?" '

'Therefore, when the tempests rage, have faith.'

'Amen!'

'When the ship is tossed with waves, have faith.'

'Amen!'

'For he who stilled the sea of Galilee to save his followers will also preserve you, so that you can go forth and do his work in the new land you have chosen.

'Now let us pray together.'

Together they bowed their heads and murmured the Lord's prayer, led by the minister's vigorous tones as he raised his hand to still the passers-by, many of whom slowed down and joined the crowd of onlookers and friends come to watch the departure.

As the service ended, Bethan held Sioni's hand tight while passengers and members of the congregation bade farewell. Brothers, sisters, friends clung to each other, whispered their farewells, fearful to look too long in each other's faces. An old man cried silently as his son shepherded his young family towards the gangway, and a widow waved away her eldest boys with a tight smile, while her hands wrung her hand-kerchief. Those who were to leave friendless stooped to pick up their bundles, touched by a double sorrow.

All the while a wind slapped at the rigging, and a stray seagull mewed its cry of the wild sea which awaited the little craft once it left the comforting banks of the Towy.

* * * * *

'Are you Jack Morgan?'

The question stunned Siôn. He was standing in the doorway of the Lamb and Flag, his eyes squinting into the gloom after the bright sunshine outside. His questioner was a small, round-faced man, with large clear eyes, whose wife bobbed behind him, her white cap glinting in the shadowy room.

'Why do you ask me that?' Siôn's voice shook slightly as he bent his head to enter the room beneath the low beam at the door. He looked down on his two questioners.

The room held the familiar musty daytime smell of stale beer. Mugs and tankards gleamed on shelves, and stools and benches were up-ended on the tables while the recently-mopped floor was drying.

His question as to whether anyone knew the whereabouts of Elizabeth Morgan, known as Bethan, had been repeated dozens of times around the quayside alehouses during the last twenty-four hours. He had met with thinly-disguised suspicion, covered by professions of ignorance as to the existence of such a woman in Carmarthen. Bethan was respected on the quayside as a friend of the never-forgotten Clemmie Williams, and the fisherfolk and washed-up sailors and their lady-friends knew better than to squeal to a stranger on one of their own.

So Siôn continued his enquiries, while unknown to him a darting boy had sped that morning from the Half-moon, sent on a quest for Bethan, to warn that a stranger was asking for her.

At last Siôn's question had hit its mark, and the rejoinder had thumped him full in the chest. His heart pounded and he raised his hand to his throbbing temple.

'Sit ye down, friend,' said Henry Jones, pulling down a stool and placing it against the wall. 'Sara, bring ale and bread, for this man is weary.'

Siôn dropped his bundle on the floor and sat heavily in the proffered seat. As he closed his eyes with relief in the cool atmosphere Henry examined his appearance with curiosity. The man was unshaven, his tow-coloured hair long and lank, and streaked with a lighter gold from the sun. His face was tanned as from many weeks of travelling, and his brow was paler from the shade of the dark hat he had thrown onto the table. His boots were worn and dusty and he emanated an odour of sweat. The hand which swept the lank hair from his eyes was scarred with toil, and the nails broken and embedded with grime. When he opened his eyes and turned them towards him, Henry saw that they were a deep, bright blue.

When he had drunk deep from the cool beer which Sara brought to him, Siôn spoke at last. His voice was calm, deliberate, and Henry and Sara recognised the Pembrokeshire accents of Bethan's speech.

'Yes, I am Jack Morgan,' he said.

If that's what it was going to take to get himself in front of Bethan, then so be it.

* * * * *

Bethan turned away sorrowfully as the last of the passengers boarded the *Sally Ann*. The sailors were making ready, pulling up the gangway, receiving the stout ropes which slithered from the bollards, dropped to the river's surface, then snaked up to the deck trailing streams of water.

She pushed through the crowd of friends and relatives who now clustered towards the edge of the quay, straining upwards to see their loved ones who stared nervously over the railing. Some held up children who smiled shyly and waved goodbye.

Little Siôn chattered excitedly as they walked, yanking backwards to see the ship, longing to see it set sail. But Bethan did not want to witness the tearing of

274

the bonds of those who stood at the rail and those who stood below on the quay.

She had thought about Henry and Sara's offer. It was a good chance for her and the boy, she could see that. She could pass herself off as a respectable young widow and begin a new life. And Jack? His memory was best laid to rest, she determined, as surely as if he had died. There was little likelihood of finding him in the vast wilderness of America. So perhaps, in a way, she was a widow, after all – mourning a lost life, the might-have-been that never would be. Yes, she would ask Sara to speak to the minister for her.

It was at this moment that the first messenger found her. As she trudged with Sioni up the narrow stone staircase towards the upper part of the town a breathless boy charged up behind her, his heavy boots scraping each step.

'Misses Beth! Misses Beth! There's a man, and he's come for you! A tall man, he is, and dirty-looking, and me Dad says to watch out for him!'

'What man is it, Mammy, what man?' Sioni's eyes were round with curiosity bounding on fear.

'I don't know, pet,' whispered Bethan, scooping the boy into her arms and holding him against her. A flood of thoughts entered her mind. Patrick? Come to take the boy? She clutched him more tightly. Never. He would have to kill her first.

She sat down on the step with Sioni on her lap, and asked the boy messenger to stay with her on the promise of a penny.

Twm Rees! The memory of the dark head, the flash of a smile, glimpsed through the crowds on that wild day came back into her mind. Had he come for her? Or ...

There was a commotion at the head of the stairs, and

275

Bethan leaped to her feet, clutching Sioni under her arm despite his wriggling. Without looking behind at the panting figure who was descending as fast as his ungainly form would allow, she pushed the messenger ahead of her and started back down.

'Beth! Bethan! Stop, please, it's me, Henry Jones!'

But Bethan did not stop until she had reached the bottom, when she turned towards Henry, but backed away, still holding the squirming boy under one arm and gripping the urchin messenger by the hand.

'What do you want?' She was at bay, backed against the wall. Her fair skin now held a high colour and her lips were drawn back – she looked almost mad, thought Henry, as he came towards her with his hand held out.

'It's only me, love – Henry. I'm not going to harm you. There's someone come for you ...' He paused, seeing her agitation. 'He says he's your brother ... Jack ...'

She gave a great exhalation of breath and fell forward, so that Henry caught both her and the boy and held them upright. Sioni set up a screech of terror and began to wail at his mother's distress.

'What ... What does he look like?' she demanded.

'Tall ... light hair ... blue eyes ... like an artisan or labourer, not a gentleman ...'

Not Patrick then, not even in some cunning disguise. Nor Twm. But Jack? She realised with despair that she could not remember the colour of Jack's eyes.

* * * * *

When Bethan entered the doorway of Sara's best parlour with her child in her arms her heart was pounding with a fearsome rhythm, try as she might to quell both fear and hope.

The tall figure stood with his back to her in the shadowy room made darker by the bright June sun outside. He was stooping slightly to see out of the low casement, but as he heard her enter he turned, slowly, as if to see a vision glimpsed once and lost long before.

'I'm sorry, Beth,' he said.

Bethan bent to place the child gently to the ground, her gaze fixed to Siôn's face. She seemed stunned, puzzled as to how one ghost could replace another. Then she smiled, a sweet, uncertain smile.

'Jack will never come back,' she said. This conjuring trick had proved it once and for all. When his presence was invoked, another man sprung up in his place. Perhaps this man was more of a true brother to her than the long-lost boy of years ago.

Siôn came towards her and held out his hand. She saw the sorrow in his face beneath its familiar outlines, the longing in his eyes as she clasped his fingers in her own. She raised her hand to his cheek, reading in his expression the sufferings of his four-year journey long before he told her of them. Then they moved together, his arms binding her to him and her face against the dusty cloth of his rough shirt. She felt the heat of his body against hers as he pressed his face into her hair and wept.

'Come with me, come with me. Tell me you're not married, Bethan, you're not ...'

She pulled back a little. He saw the light green of her eyes, reflecting the flash of sunshine from the window, before she turned away to pick up the child. She lifted the flaxen-haired boy until he sat in the crook of her arm, and she placed her other hand proudly on his rounded belly as he stared shyly at Siôn from his long-lashed eyes with the velvet blueness of childhood. Before long the boy's thumb was in his mouth and he turned away and hid his face in Bethan's neck.

'His name is Siôn,' she said, as she lay her hand on the child's back and rocked him gently to and fro. The child was her reason for living, and there was no ring on her finger.

'He is a fine boy, and I will love him as my own son. Come with me, we will go to Rebecca and find Huw, who will love him as a brother.'

She moved over to the tall wooden settle near the fireplace, and sat down to nurse the child against her breast.

Siôn sat by her side and marvelled at the beauty of the sleeping infant, the fair lashes lying against the curved, translucent cheek, the sweet abandon of his body as he lay in his mother's lap. This was indeed the child he had loved and lost.

Bethan closed her eyes and leaned her head back against the hard wood of the settle.

'I have paid for a passage to New York. I have the chance of a place as a housekeeper in Pennsylvania, to a minister of the chapel. I couldn't keep Sioni with me, of course. I would have to give him to someone else to look after.' Her voice faltered, but she turned to him with an expression he did not recall, her mouth tight and determined. 'A new start. No one would know me there and I would have a good place. I could be proud of myself.'

Inwardly Siôn cursed his poverty. He had absolutely nothing material to offer. He took her hand in his.

'Bethan, we can be proud together. There is no need for you to be a servant, no need for you to give your child to someone else. We can work together for Sioni and Huw.

'Do you remember how we used to talk, about the Charter and the Six Points, and a world without master and servant, mistress and maid? It's going to come, Bethan, that world, but not without us. It will only happen if we make it happen. You saw what happened here, in Carmarthen.' She turned to him in surprise. 'Yes, I was here, I went into that filthy Bastille and smashed it ... but you saw what happened, how we banded together and did what we wanted. And even though they sent the troops in and crushed the demonstration, the toll-gates are being withdrawn.

'Yes, we've been beaten, time after time we've been beaten ... Merthyr, Newport, Carmarthen ... But we're not going to stop. In towns all over England and Wales there are people who are giving all their hearts, their minds, their labours, so that children like this won't have to cry in the darkness of mines and the sick heat of factories – so that mothers like you won't have to see their little ones go hungry.

'I can't turn my back on that. I don't think you can either. You're a fighter, Bethan. Come with me.'

As Bethan looked at Siôn's face she saw a man who had a great possession, an ideal, a desire that went beyond himself. He had a reason for living beyond the need to get the next day's bread. He had a mind which reached out beyond the limitations bequeathed to him by his station in life. He knew he was worth something, and she, and little Siôn, and so were all the other men and women of the poor and labouring classes. Brotherhood: that was his gift.

In her glance he saw a new wonder and optimism, illuminated by her smile, which had lost its sadness. At last she gave him her answer.

'Yes ... Yes. I will come.'

At dawn they set off. Siôn carried the child in his arms, and Bethan smiled up at him as they walked in the tender morning sunshine.

* * * * *

HISTORICAL NOTE

The Rebecca Riots

The Rebecca Riots were a series of uprisings which took place in west Wales, mostly during the late 1830s and 1840s. The uprisings focused on the toll-gates placed across the roads which were maintained by the turnpike trusts. The toll-gates were attacked by groups of men dressed in women's clothing and with blackened faces.

Travellers had to pay every time they passed a toll-gate, and this placed heavy burdens on country people taking their goods to market or carting lime for fertiliser. The unrest was also an expression of general discontent caused by tithes (taxes paid to the Church), and the effects of the Poor Law Amendment Act (1834). The new workhouses, nick-named 'Bastilles', were particularly unpopular, and were sometimes attacked, as at Carmarthen in 1843.

The Merthyr Rising

In 1831 the people of Merthyr Tydfil took control of the town in a series of riots following wage-cuts, job losses and the use of bailiffs against the poor. Troops fired on the crowd and sixteen people were killed before the uprising was put down. One participant, known as Dic Penderyn, was later executed in a blatant miscarriage of justice.

Chartism was the first large-scale popular movement to try to obtain democratic rights for working-class people.

The People's Charter, or the Six Points, was drawn up by London radicals in 1837, and by the end of 1838 there were Chartists meeting regularly in clubs all over England, Scotland and Wales.

Their six demands included a vote for every man over 21. At this time only men with a certain amount of property could vote, and no women at all. The other demands sought to reform elections and the House of Commons, including payment of MPs so that poor men could stand.

Some Chartists were in favour of votes for women, but others feared that this demand would damage support for the Charter as a whole, so it was not pursued. There were however many women Chartists.

'Physical force' Chartists believed that violence would be necessary to obtain these reforms. They were opposed by the 'moral force' Chartists, who believed in the superior power of persuasion.

In 1839 Welsh Chartists took part in an armed uprising in Newport, wrongly believing that similar uprisings were taking place elsewhere in Britain. Over twenty people were killed when troops opened fire.

The leaders of the rising were sentenced to death, but their sentences were commuted to transportation.

VIVIEN ANNIS BAILEY

Vivien Annis Bailey was born in Kent. She has a degree in English and has worked for many years in further education. She has a long-standing interest in working-class and women's history, particularly of the nineteenth century. She has one daughter and lives in St Albans. *Children of Rebecca* is her first novel.